THE VEIL

Also by Megan Chance

YOUNG ADULT FICTION

THE FIANNA TRILOGY
The Shadows
The Web

ADULT FICTION

Inamorata
Bone River
City of Ash
Prima Donna
The Spiritualist
An Inconvenient Wife
Susannah Morrow

THE VEIL

THE FIANNA TRILOGY
BOOK THREE

MEGAN CHANCE

SKYSCAPE

SKYSCAPE

Published by Skyscape, New York

www.apub.com

Amazon, the Amazon logo, and Skyscape are trademarks of Amazon.com, Inc., or its affiliates.

ISBN-13 (hardcover): 9781503945715
ISBN-10 (hardcover): 1503945715
ISBN-13 (paperback): 9781503945722
ISBN-10 (paperback): 1503945723

Cover illustration by Don Sipley
Cover design by Regina Flath

Printed in the United States of America

For Maggie and Cleo

And down the river's dim expanse—
Like some bold seër in a trance,
Seeing all his own mischance—
With a glassy countenance
Did she look to Camelot.
And at the closing of the day
She loosed the chain, and down she lay;
The broad stream bore her far away,
The Lady of Shalott.

Lying, robed in snowy white
That loosely flew to left and right—
The leaves upon her falling light—
Through the noises of the night
She floated down to Camelot:
And as the boat-head wound along
The willowy hills and fields among,
They heard her singing her last song,
The Lady of Shalott.

"The Lady of Shalott"
—Alfred, Lord Tennyson

❦ Cast of Characters ❦
[AND PRONUNCIATION GUIDE]

──────── THE KNOX FAMILY ────────

Grainne Alys Knox [GRAW-nya]—*Grace*

Aidan Knox—*Grace's brother, and the Fianna's stormcaster*

Maeve Knox—*Grace's mother*

Brigid Knox—*Grace's grandmother*

──────── THE DEVLIN FAMILY ────────

Patrick Devlin

Lucy Devlin—*Patrick's sister*

Sarah Devlin—*Patrick's mother*

──────── THE FIANNA (FINN'S WARRIORS) ────────

Diarmid Ua Duibhne [DEER-mid O'DIV-na]—*Derry O'Shea*

Finn MacCumhail [FINN MacCOOL]—*Finn MacCool,*
the leader of the Fianna

Oscar

Ossian [USH-een]—*Oscar's father*

Keenan

Goll

Conan

Cannel Flannery—*Seer*

——— THE FENIAN BROTHERHOOD [FEE-NIAN] ———

Rory Nolan

Simon MacRonan—*Seer*

Jonathan Olwen

——— THE FOMORI ———

Daire Donn [DAW-re DON]

Lot

Tethra

Bres

Miogach [MYEE-gok]

Balor

——— IN LEGEND ———

Tuatha de Dannan [TOO-a-ha dae DONN-an]—*the old, revered gods of Ireland, the people of the goddess Danu*

Aengus Og [ENGUS OG]—*Irish god of love, Diarmid's foster father*

Manannan [MANanuan]—*Irish god of the sea, Diarmid's former tutor*

The Morrigan—*Irish goddess of war; her three aspects: Macha [MOK-ah], Nemain [NOW-mn], and Badb [BIBE]*

Danu—*Irish mother goddess*

Domnu—*Mother goddess of the Fomori*

Neasa [NESSA]—*the Fianna's Druid priestess*

Cormac—*ancient High King of Ireland*

Grainne [GRAW-nya]—*Cormac's daughter, promised in marriage to Finn, eloped with Diarmid*

King of Lochlann—*Miogach's father*

Glasny [GLASH-neh]—*Neasa's protector*

Tuama [TOO-uhm-ma]—*Archdruid in Neasa's stronghold*

Bile [BEL]—*Irish father of the gods, husband of Danu*

Cliodna [KLEE-uh-na]—*Irish goddess of beauty who was taken from her mortal lover by a great wave sent by Manannan, which brought her back to the Otherworld (Cliodna's Wave)*

Slieve Lougher [Sleeve Lawker]—*a mountain in ancient Ireland where the three sea champions released their vicious hounds to chase Diarmid and Grainne*

——— OTHER PEOPLE ———

Rose Fitzgerald—*Grace's best friend*

Miles—*member of the Dun Rats gang*

Bridget—*woman who sheltered Diarmid and Grace in Brooklyn*

Roddy—*former archdruid, owner of Roddy's Grotto pawnshop*

Stag—*a sailor transformed into a stag*

Cuan [KOO-awn]—*a cheat transformed into a whippet*

Torcan [TURK-awn]—*a thief transformed into a boar*

Leonard—*Patrick's carriage driver*

——— THE SIDHE [SHEE] ———

Battle Annie—*queen of the river pirates*

Sarnat [SAWR-nit]—*member of the river pirates, Grace's guard*

Iobhar [EE-ver]—*archdruid*

Deirdre—*leader of a* sidhe *gang*

Turgen—*Deirdre's lover and member of the river pirates gang*

———— OTHER WORDS ————

a leanbh [ah LON-a]—*oh child*

ball seirce [ball searce]—*the lovespot bestowed on Diarmid*

cainte [KINE-tay]—*one who speaks/sees, Druid poet*

deogbaire—[DEI-baw-ray] *Druid potion maker*

dord fiann [dord FEEN]—*Finn's hunting horn*

éicse [AYK-sha]—*Druid concept meaning "the truth of all things"*

geis [GISE]—*a prohibition or taboo that compels the person to obey*

milis [MILL-ish]—*sweet, an endearment*

mo chroi [muh CREE]—*my heart, an endearment*

morai [MO-ree]—*grandmother*

ogham—*ancient form of Irish writing*

Samhain [SOW-in]—*ancient Celtic festival, October 31*

veleda—*ancient Druid priestess; her three aspects: eubages (Seer), brithem (Judge), and vater (Prophet)*

ONE

New York City
July 28, 1874
Grace

E ven at night, the Buttermilk Channel was alive with steamers and sloops, their lanterns and gas lamps twinkling through the darkness like stars. The water lapped against the hull of Battle Annie's sloop; the sail fluttered in the light wind. Beyond, Manhattan was a web of lights resting upon shadows.

The moonlight glittered on the water; a full, bright moon that reminded me of the girl I'd once been, standing in my backyard, wishing for romance, for adventure.

So much had happened since then, and yet it had been little more than a month since my fiancé, Patrick Devlin, had told me that he and the Fenian Brotherhood had called the legendary Irish warriors, the Fianna, to help them win Ireland's freedom from British rule, and that I was the *veleda* priestess whose destiny was tied to theirs.

But things hadn't worked out as the Brotherhood had planned, and when the Fianna failed to appear, the Brotherhood called the ancient Irish gods of chaos, the Fomori—the enemies of the Fianna. Now the *veleda*—I—had to choose which of them was worthy: the Fianna or the Fomori. I had to die to release my power to my choice. Patrick and the Fomori had promised to find a way to save me. But that was before one of the Fianna, Diarmid Ua Duibhne, had kidnapped me. Before I'd fallen in love with him. Before being with him had proved to be the key to unlocking the power I now felt coursing through my veins.

Everything had changed. The only thing I knew for certain was that I must find the archdruid my grandmother said would help me. I hoped he would know a spell to change my fate. The prophecy that bound me said the ritual must take place on Samhain—only three months from now, October 31, when the veil between worlds thins—and Diarmid must be the one to kill me.

"Fate is ever-changing," Diarmid had said. I hoped he was right.

"You're sure the archdruid is here?" asked Battle Annie as she came up beside me. The river pirate queen glowed silver, as did all the children of the *sidhe*—the fairies—to my eyes. They were dangerous to me, to anyone with Druid blood. Though their touch could siphon my power and leave me a shell, I was not afraid of them tonight. The *sidhe* on this boat would not hurt me. I'd made an alliance with their queen.

I told her, "The ogham stick said he was. 'The rivers guard treasures with no worth.' He's in a pawnshop somewhere near here."

She smiled. It was horrifying—her two front teeth had been filed into points. Her braided hair, decorated with beads and feathers, and the tattoos on her cheek and arms, only added to the gruesome effect. "So you found the key to decipher it."

"Yes. I found the key." *Diarmid.* I hadn't waited for him to return to Governors Island, where we'd been hiding, because I couldn't let my love for him or anyone else influence what I had to do now. The thought of him made me ache.

Battle Annie gazed out at the dark harbor. "Seems odd we haven't felt your Druid if he's here in Corlears Hook."

I stifled a shudder. I couldn't pretend I was glad to be going there. Corlears Hook had been a nasty place even before the depression. It was a haven for thieves and for other river pirates.

It wasn't just the gangs that worried me. There were *sidhe* everywhere now, more every day, drawn by the magic of the Fianna and the Fomori, by me and my older brother, Aidan, who'd discovered he was a stormcaster and joined with the Fianna.

But I didn't have a choice. If the archdruid was in Corlears Hook, it was where I must go.

The sloop rounded the Battery. The East River was crowded with boats and ships. As we approached the pier, my nervousness grew.

Battle Annie whistled a command. "I'm sending a guard with you. This is Sarnat."

A girl appeared at the railing beside us, so quickly that it startled me. She was tall, but very slight, with pale skin like all the *sidhe* and translucent, eerie eyes. Her hair was light and straight and fine. She had a sharp face—high cheekbones, a pointed nose and chin—and she wore a ragged, too-short dress and dusty boots. Her silvery glow made her look even more delicate. *She* was to be my guard? She looked as if I could pass my hand right through her. But I wasn't stupid enough to complain. And at least she could turn anyone who troubled us into a stag or a boar. It was better than nothing, but I wished for one of the boys climbing the rigging.

Battle Annie said, "You'll do well together, I think."

Sarnat's gaze was open and curious. I felt her yearning for my power, though she made no move to touch me.

"You'll accompany the *veleda* to the archdruid," Battle Annie said to her. "And keep her safe until she has no more need."

"Archdruid?" Sarnat's pale brow rose. "Where is there such a thing?"

Battle Annie said, "She knows."

The sloop maneuvered easily through the crowded river, and then we were docking at a falling-down pier poking from a cluster of darkened buildings.

Sidhe sailors jumped onto the pier, which tilted and creaked. Battle Annie said, "Keep Sarnat near, *veleda*."

"I will."

"Don't forget our bargain."

"You have my word." In return for her help, Battle Annie expected me to use my power for telling truth from lies to aid her in ruling her gang. Assuming that the power grew stronger under an archdruid's training, and that I was still alive to use it, which was no small thing and hardly certain. "I've just one more request. The Fianna and the Fomori will come looking for me. Don't tell them where I am."

Battle Annie's sloe eyes sharpened. "Your Diarmid too?"

I wished the sound of his name did not hurt. "Him too."

She nodded. "As you wish, *veleda.*"

I heard the *thunk* of the boarding plank as it hit the pier, and one of the boys called out, "'Tis ready!" and I steadied myself. The pier was empty, the streets beyond dark.

Sarnat jumped onto the pier, making hardly a noise, and I gathered my courage and followed her. The sloop departed, leaving the two of us standing alone.

Loud voices and arguing escaped from the saloon at the end of the pier. Sarnat walked, and I followed again, jumping at a sudden scrabbling that came from beneath the dock.

"What was that?"

Sarnat shrugged. "Rats."

We were almost to the end of the pier when I heard the scrabbling again, but this time a shadow appeared with it, a moving, gray mass that surged from underneath the dock, creeping over the edges, swarming to block our way. Gang boys, dozens of them, forming a gauntlet. Some were chuckling, one or two calling out, "Look at that, boys, somethin' sweet for bedtime" and "Come on over, lass, 'n' give us a kiss!"

I remembered what gang boys had nearly done to me once before. I looked at Sarnat, who looked at me.

"Come on, sweetie! Ah, don't stop! Come on now." One of them made clicking noises, as if he were calling a dog.

Sarnat said, "Well?"

"Well what?" I whispered back.

"Aren't you going to raise a storm?"

"A storm?"

"You're a *veleda*, aren't you? Rain'll send them back into hiding. Go on."

"I can't raise a storm," I said.

Sarnat frowned. "Well, then, what can you do?"

"Are ya comin' to us, or are we goin' to have to come for ya?" The boys sauntered toward us without waiting for an answer.

"I can't do anything," I snapped at Sarnat. I glanced over the edge of the dock, thinking it might be possible to jump and run, but there were boys there, too, cutting off escape. I knew already that screaming would be no help. It had only caused people to turn away last time, and Corlears Hook was an even worse part of town.

Sarnat looked incredulous. "Nothing? What kind of *veleda* are you?" She sighed heavily, as if I were the greatest disappointment to her. "Come on, then."

She began to walk toward the boys. I could only trail after, my heart thudding. The boys' catcalling grew louder and more obscene. As we walked, they drew in, surrounding us, jostling and pushing. Sarnat kept walking, her gaze straight ahead. I did the same.

Then we reached the wall of boys. The others gathered closer, penning us in.

"Well, well," said a snaggletoothed boy, obviously the leader. He stepped in front of Sarnat, forcing her to stop—and me with her. "Lookee what the river brought."

"Let us pass," Sarnat said.

The boy laughed. The others echoed him. "Oh, I don't think so."

People staggered out of the saloon and went about their business as if it were a usual thing to see two girls surrounded by gang boys bent on rape. Probably it was. The arguing from the saloon grew louder.

"I'm askin' you once more, you stupid rabbit. Let us pass, before you regret it," Sarnat said.

"Oh, look at that! Ain't it cute, lads? This mab thinkin' to scare us?" The leader leaned close to Sarnat, his face less than an inch from hers. "We'll be gettin' our hide today, lass. I'll take this one. Who wants the other?"

Sarnat's movement was so quick I didn't see her knife until she'd gutted him with it. The boy's eyes grew wide, his mouth gaped. He looked down at the cut she'd made in his stomach, grabbing at it with both hands before he collapsed, sprawling onto the wharf.

"She's killed 'im!" cried one of the boys.

Sarnat brandished the bloody dagger, her smile thin and humorless. "He won't be the only one either, if you don't let us go. Anyone else care to try?"

Some of them backed away. One called, "Come on, boys, what, you feared of a little flimp? We can take 'em. There's only two!"

"Aye, but one's got a sting," said another.

Sarnat stabbed at the nearest boy, who fell into the others in his rush to avoid her knife. "You going to let us pass, or do I have to skewer another one?" she asked.

I was grabbed from behind so hard that my breath rushed from my lungs.

"I got this one! An' she's got no—"

Sarnat twisted around, her knife at his throat, slashing before he had a chance to release me. Hot blood gushed over my shoulder, spattering my face, and the boy's hold eased; he fell against me and then thudded onto the dock. I stared in speechless horror.

Four of them rushed her. Sarnat turned into a lunging dervish, her pale hair whipping about her face. None of them could hold her. One boy grabbed her around the throat, and she went down on one knee, flipping him. In the same motion, she slammed the heel of her hand into another boy's nose— he howled and fell away. Another collapsed from a kick in the groin. Two others were slashed and bleeding. All around her, boys lay writhing and groaning. Ten of them, I counted, before she crouched, breathless, knife gleaming in the moonlight. "Anyone else?"

They scattered like cockroaches, leaving their dead and bloodied behind, flinging themselves over the edges of the pier. Sarnat straightened, wiping the knife on her skirt and slipping it away. "Well, you're a mess."

I looked down at myself. Felt the sticky, cooling blood on my face and my throat, dripping from my hair.

"Don't tell me you're going to swoon," Sarnat said. "You can't be so useless as that."

"No, I—"

"Let's go, then. Before some others decide to come at us."

My feet were wooden, my legs not quite working. She grabbed my arm, and I felt my power responding to the pull of her magic. I jerked away. "Don't touch me."

"Listen, *veleda*, we can't tarry. Look about you."

People had gathered to watch. I remembered where we were, what I was supposed to do. *The rivers guard treasures with no worth.*

"Where is he?" Sarnat hissed. "I can't feel an archdruid. There's no Druid here but *you*." Spoken with contempt, which I supposed I deserved.

I closed my eyes, using my power to listen to the music of rats gnawing and squeaking, the horrified whispering of the river boys dragging the fallen bodies of their friends from the dock, creaking and water splashing, and stones rolling beneath feet on the riverbank. Arguments and someone laughing, a shot glass slamming on a table, doors opening and closing, and children murmuring as they huddled sleepily in doorways and alcoves.

"Hurry," Sarnat urged.

And then . . . the tinkling of bells, not just one, but many. And beneath those, the archdruid's song—otherworldly and at the same time earthbound, a melody both sad and joyous—the same I'd heard as I listened for him from Governors Island. A dog howling. The *clack* of . . . of hooves on a wooden floor, and through it all, the song winding, the direction—

I opened my eyes. "This way." I dodged a drunk lurching from the saloon. I hardly saw the shadows or the horses or the people we passed; I was dimly aware of Sarnat behind me. I followed the song, which grew louder with every step.

The street was narrow and pitted, broken pipes bubbling sewage into gutters already running thick and slimy with horse piss and emptied chamber pots. The stench was terrible. We stumbled over piles of garbage. Drunks and the homeless curled in the corners. Down one block, turning onto another.

Here.

I stopped short. Sarnat barreled into me. The moonlight illuminated a dark window painted with "Roddy's Grotto, Sell or Trade."

"This is it?" Sarnat asked dubiously.

The door was locked. I rattled it hard, knocking.

"No one'll be answering at this time of night," Sarnat said. "Why don't you just summon him with your *veleda* power?"

I just looked at her.

"You can't do that either? What *can* you do?"

"I can find the archdruid," I said, rattling the handle again, trying to peer through the glass into the darkness inside.

Sarnat said, "Are you sure of that? I hate to tell you this, but I don't feel him. There's no power here, not like yours—"

"Hold on! Hold on, I'm coming!" The voice came from inside, muffled and weary.

The music in my head grew louder. The archdruid at last. The man who could help me. I saw a flash of pale in the darkness beyond the glass, and then the door opened to reveal a man wearing a nightshirt. His white hair was rumpled in all directions, his nose large and hooked.

He looked at me, at the blood, and then at Sarnat, and then he stepped back, his small eyes bright with fear. "No. You must go. Please. I don't know why you've come, but you must go."

I pressed my hand on the door to keep him from closing it. "I know who you are. I know you're the archdruid. I'm the *veleda*, and I've come all this way—"

The old man grabbed my arm. The music crescendoed in my head and then stopped abruptly and completely, and I stared at him in consternation as he said, "Quiet! Quiet, do you hear me? Say nothing more! Go away. 'Tis dangerous for you here. You must go."

I recognized the way this man looked. I recognized his words and his fear. He was like the Druid that Diarmid and I had met on Coney Island. I saw the madness in his eyes.

No. Please, no.

Sarnat said, "My people have been here."

His eyes flicked to hers, and I knew.

The *sidhe* had already got to him. He was the archdruid, but his power was gone.

They had sucked him dry.

That same night
Diarmid

Oscar groaned as Conan laid a slab of raw meat on his swollen, black eye. His white-blond curls were matted with blood, his face lumpy and bruised, a seeping cut on his cheekbone. "By the gods, be gentle! Where's the light touch of a maid when I need it?"

Conan grunted. "Stop your whining, or I'll take the meat back. I'd rather cook it for dinner than waste it on your sorry self."

The others laughed, but Diarmid could barely smile. He leaned against the wall, arms crossed, watching. He'd returned to the squalid basement flat to find Oscar safe and in better condition than he'd expected. He guessed they had Patrick Devlin to thank for keeping the Fomori from doing worse.

Diarmid had never expected to thank Patrick for anything, and now he had two things for which he had to be grateful to Grace's fiancé. Because Patrick had saved his life tonight as well. During their rescue of Oscar from the Tombs, the city's House of Detention, Diarmid had been trapped. It was Patrick—his supposed enemy—who had helped him to escape.

Why?

The question troubled him, as did the words Patrick had whispered in his ear.

"Keep her away."

He'd meant Grace, of course, but it made no sense. Patrick had done everything he could to get Grace back. He'd put up "Wanted" posters and offered rewards. He'd announced his engagement to Grace and taken her mother and grandmother into his house. He had Fomori on the police force and in city government searching for her. After all, the Fomori needed the *veleda* as much as the Fianna did.

So why now had he told Diarmid to keep her away?

"Ouch!" Oscar said, pushing at Conan. "Stop! Get out with that stinking fleece."

Conan tugged at the filthy sheepskin he never took off, no matter how hot it was. "Tend to yourself then, addle-cove."

Oscar's father, Ossian, laughed and shook back his curls—the same color as his son's. His relief over Oscar's rescue made him look younger and more like Oscar than ever. "He's always been a bad-tempered patient."

Oscar settled himself more firmly on the rickety crate that served as a chair. He put his hand to the beef to keep it in place and cracked open his other eye. "Where's Derry? I haven't heard his voice in a while."

"Right here," Diarmid said.

"I heard Balor went after you."

Diarmid winced at the memory of the chase, the poison-eyed god gaining with every step. "Nearly got me, too, but for some gang boys that came between us."

Oscar tilted his head back. "You shouldn't have come, Derry. 'Twas too big a risk."

"He knows that. He's going back in the morning." The command rang in Finn's voice. An oil lamp dangled from a hook above his head, and although it didn't do much to illuminate the basement—which was dank, with seeping brick walls and a dirt floor—it lit Finn's golden-red hair with a fiery glow, haloing him so he looked like a god. Diarmid wondered if Finn had chosen that spot on purpose, just for the effect. *Probably.* Finn knew how to impress. It was one of the reasons he was their leader.

"So the *veleda*'s safe?" Oscar asked.

"Safe and bound," Finn said with satisfaction.

Oscar cracked his eye open again, looking at Diarmid. "You used the *ball seirce*?"

"Aye." Diarmid's hand went involuntarily to the mark on his forehead, the gift from a fairy that made any lass who gazed upon it fall in love with him. He'd hated it for years, kept it hidden behind a shock of dark hair, rarely used it. He glanced at Aidan, Grace's brother, who favored him with a hostile stare, and Diarmid felt guilty and ashamed. Finn had ordered him to use the lovespot on Grace, but Diarmid had been unable to do so. He had hoped Grace would want him for himself. He hungered for her love, but he'd wanted it to be real.

And then she'd seen the lovespot. It had been an accident; he'd been caught off guard. He hated himself for what had happened after, how he hadn't been able to resist her, even knowing her feelings for him were a lie. He'd felt bewitched, fated to love her. And it turned out he was—her power was released when they lay together. One good thing to come of it, he supposed; but still, he wished . . .

What was the point of wishing? The *geis* was still in place. "*'Tis by your hand the veleda must die.*" That was the law laid upon him by his old teacher, Manannan, the god of the sea, a spell that bound him. If Diarmid didn't kill the *veleda*, he and the others would fail and die. He had Grace hidden on Governors Island so he could help in Oscar's rescue, but now that Diarmid was here, he wished he was with Grace, helping her search for the archdruid they both hoped could change fate—hers and his.

Oscar said, "Patrick Devlin told me to keep Grace out of the city."

Diarmid straightened. "He said that? When?"

"During their 'questioning,'" Oscar explained. "None of the others heard it. 'Twas a surprise. I thought he was in league with the Fomori."

"He said the same to me," Diarmid said. "In the Bummers' Cell, when I was trying to escape. I would have thought it the last thing he wanted."

"He said exactly that? Keep her away? You're certain?" Aidan asked sharply.

A little too sharply, Diarmid thought.

Finn's eyes gleamed. "Do you know something of this, stormcaster?"

"How would I? I find it as strange as you do. Patrick loves her, and he knows about the *geis*. I can't think he'd want her anywhere near Diarmid. Especially because of the lovespot."

That guilt again.

"'Tis curious," Finn said. "But for now, let's take Devlin at his word. Diarmid, you'll keep her on Governors Island until I say otherwise."

Diarmid couldn't hide his dismay. "At least let me take her to Brooklyn. How can I find an archdruid from Governors Island?"

"You were nearly captured in Brooklyn," Finn said. "'Wanted' posters are everywhere. Keep her where she is, and let us worry about finding the archdruid."

"Are you even looking for him?" Diarmid asked.

Ossian's green eyes narrowed. "Do you doubt us?"

"No," Diarmid said. "No. But . . . I think the Fomori have us running so there's no time to think. We can't forget that we need the archdruid. Grace doesn't know the incantation."

"None of us have forgotten that," Finn said. "Leave the search to us. You'll go back at dawn."

The discussion was over. Finn went to talk to Cannel, their Druid Seer, who was alternately laying out tarot cards and running his hands nervously through his reddish hair, pulling it into little spikes. Dark-headed Keenan watched him carefully. Goll sat on a pallet of rags beside them, jerking his newsboy's cap to cover his eyes as he shifted his bony limbs to find a comfortable position.

Diarmid thought of Grace on Governors Island, no doubt asleep by now, perhaps dreaming of him. It only raised a desire he had no right to feel. He forced it away and went to Oscar.

"I feel like I've been trampled by horses," Oscar grumbled. "How do I look?"

"I wouldn't be asking a lass for a kiss anytime soon."

"That bad?"

"That meat on your eye looks better."

Oscar cursed and motioned for Diarmid to come closer, saying quietly, "You *did* use the lovespot?"

"I told you I would."

"Aye, but . . . you're still in love with her?"

"Did you expect it to go away?"

"It usually does—sooner or later."

Which had been true in the past, Diarmid had to admit. But this was . . . different. He'd never felt anything like he felt for Grace. "'Tisn't the same."

Oscar sighed. "There's still the *geis*, Derry, don't forget."

"Believe me, I haven't."

"You haven't told Finn why you really want to find this archdruid, have you? You haven't told him you're hoping there's a spell to save her."

"He'd only doubt me," Diarmid said. "And I've got enough of that from you."

"I don't doubt you—"

"Aye, you do. But I understand. Just . . . I've got to go back, but I'm not likely to find any archdruid there. If you discover where he is first . . ."

"I'll ask him if he knows of such a spell," Oscar agreed, but it was clear what he thought the answer would be.

Diarmid didn't press it, not wanting to make Oscar's doubts worse, nor reveal his own. "I'm glad you're back. But you should lie down, brother. You look a little green."

"I'd welcome a bed," Oscar said. Diarmid helped him to his feet, leading him over to one of the two stinking, thin, and stained mattresses against the wall. The other beds were only pallets of straw or heaps of blankets.

After that, Diarmid felt restless and uneasy. Ossian and Finn and Cannel were debating some plan or another. Conan and Keenan played cards as they drank the last of a keg of ale. Goll was finally still and sleeping. Only Aidan was separate, as he usually was, staring into space as if there was something to see beyond crumbling brick and mortar or the shallow puddle of water in a corner.

Then Aidan rose and went up the stairs.

Finn said over his shoulder, "Go after him, Diarmid."

Diarmid was annoyed, but did as he was told, following Aidan into the kitchen above, which was packed with people, all of them asleep, and then out the open back door. At the edge of the cesspool, Aidan stopped.

Diarmid hung back. He had no wish to talk to Aidan, who was obviously angry about what had happened between his sister and Diarmid. But Finn had given the order, and Diarmid was already on shaky ground with his captain, and so reluctantly, he went over.

Aidan didn't even turn as Diarmid approached and said, "Finn sent me after you."

"He's worried I might run off to a saloon."

"Is that where you were headed?"

"No. I think I'm done with that. To be honest, I'd like to, but there's too much else to think about. Being addled doesn't help." He flung a thread of purple lightning into the cesspool, where it reflected crazily before it sizzled and turned to smoke.

Diarmid glanced over his shoulder at the people sleeping on the roof. "You don't want to be showing that off too often."

"I know." Aidan curled his finger back into his palm. "If I asked you to tell me the truth about something, would you?"

The words echoed; Grace had said nearly the same thing to Diarmid only a few days ago, when she'd asked him what it felt like to die. "About what?"

"About your intentions toward my sister."

Diarmid stiffened.

"Don't misunderstand me. I don't like what you did, but I know her power required the two of you to—" Aidan swallowed, obviously uncomfortable. "You even probably felt . . . I don't know . . . compelled . . . yourself."

It was exactly how he'd felt. Compelled, out of his head in love, helpless. "How do you know this?"

Aidan stared off. "It's hard to explain. Mostly I feel connected to Grace and . . . and to you too. Which is strange, because I don't like you."

Diarmid was startled, though not surprised. He'd never liked Aidan much either. Whatever powers Grace's brother had now, in the past he'd been a wastrel and a drunk. He'd caused Grace endless worry. He'd destroyed his own family.

Aidan's smile was grim. "Grace was an innocent. She'd had a few kisses, I think, but that was all. And now you've ruined her. What do you intend to do about it?"

Diarmid was taken aback. "D'you mean—Are you asking if I'll marry her?"

Aidan laughed. "Marry her? Do you take me for a fool?"

"It seems to be what everyone in this world expects—"

"But she's not just an ordinary girl, is she? She's the *veleda*, and there's the ritual. The *geis*. Things like marriage . . . how can they matter?"

Exactly what Diarmid thought too. "Then I don't understand what you want of me."

"I want to know what you feel for her, you idiot. Do you care for her at all? Or is it only that you're following Finn's orders? I know you used the lovespot—"

"That was an accident. I didn't mean for her to see it."

"Just like the story, was it? Of you and the first Grainne. It was an accident then too?"

Uncertainly, Diarmid admitted, "Aye. That was an accident too."

"But you ran off with Grainne. The legend says you loved her."

"'Twas . . . more complicated than that."

"Was it?" Aidan's gaze was searching. "Is it complicated with my sister too? I thought the question simple enough. What do you feel for her?"

Diarmid hesitated. But there was no point in hiding it from Aidan, who probably sensed it anyway. "I love her."

"Enough to save her life?"

"If I could change everything, I would. I'd thought—I'd *hoped*—the archdruid might have some answers. Another spell, something . . ."

"So it's not just the incantation you care about?"

"No. Oscar knows that, but not Finn or the others. If there's a way to avoid her death, they'll take it. No one likes blood sacrifice. But . . . this kind of magic . . ." He let the words trail off, unable to say what was probably true. That there were no other spells, that the sacrifice was necessary.

Aidan frowned.

"What is it?" Diarmid demanded.

"Nothing." Aidan shook his head. "Nothing. Listen, those words on the ogham stick you and Grace found—d'you remember them?"

The ogham stick that Grace had insisted was a clue to find the archdruid. The words on it had been those her grandmother had said before the old woman lapsed into a coma. "I'm not likely to forget them."

"Word for word? Do you remember it that well?"

"I looked at it enough, trying to figure out what it meant. 'The sea is the knife. Great stones crack and split. Storms will tell and the world is changed. The rivers guard treasures with no worth. To harm and to protect become as one, and all things will only be known in pieces.'"

Aidan repeated the words.

Diarmid said, "Does it mean something to you?"

"Not to me, not yet. But Grace understands some of it."

"No, she doesn't. She—"

"She knows how to find the archdruid," Aidan corrected. "But the rest of it . . . I know everything my grandmother knew, but her madness keeps getting in the way. It's all confused and . . . I know those words are important, but that's all. I need some time to figure it out. But I can tell something's not right. You should go back to Governors Island quickly."

"At dawn. You heard Finn."

"That might not be soon enough."

"Gods save me from cryptic Druids! What does that mean? What do you know?"

"God save me from obtuse, arrogant warriors! Don't be slow, Derry, that's all. There's something happening; I don't know what. But nothing's as it should be. Grace is . . . not as she should be. It's just what I feel. I can't explain."

There was something in Aidan's expression that disturbed Diarmid, a distraction, a shuttering, as if Aidan knew more than he was telling. Diarmid followed Grace's brother back to the basement flat. He should have gone straight to the dock after escaping Balor, instead of returning here. He should have hired a boat. He should be stepping ashore on Governors Island right now.

But there would have been no boats to hire in the dead of night. Dawn would come soon enough, and he'd be gone. It would be all right.

He went to one of the straw pallets and had just fallen into a troubled sleep when a scream jerked him awake. Aidan had bolted upright in the corner, stark terror on his white face. "Grace, no! It's too late! It's too late!"

THREE

Later that night
Grace

The old man tried to shut the door. I stopped it with my foot. Everything had come to this, and I was too late. The archdruid's power was already gone, and with it, all my hopes. "Please. Please, let me just talk with you."

"Go away. There's nothing for you here."

Sarnat said, "I don't suppose you'd like to be a boar. Let us in."

The man's gaze flicked to her. He swallowed nervously.

"I only want to ask a few questions," I said.

"I've lost it all, missy," the old man whined. "Please, you must go *now*. I'm trying to *save* you. You must go before—"

There was a sound behind him, a tinkling of many bells—I'd heard them before, in his music. He sagged, closing his eyes, whispering, "I told you to go."

Sarnat went very still.

The door opened wide, though the old man hadn't touched it. A dog—a long, thin whippet—wove around his legs. It looked up at me and Sarnat with an unsettling, almost human gaze before it slinked back into the darkness. The old man sighed and stepped back.

"Please, won't you come in?" he asked politely, as if he hadn't been ordering us to go only moments before.

You should go. You should run. But I wanted answers, so I stepped into that darkness, shadows within darker shadows and the smell of dust and old things and a faint and alluring perfume.

Sarnat took a great, deep breath. She turned back to the door. "We must leave."

Her tone was so urgent and fierce that I turned too. But before we went a single step, the door slammed shut in our faces, as if some invisible hand had shoved it. The old man stood there like a puppet with cut strings, his head bowed, his nightshirt limp around his bony shins.

Sarnat grabbed the door handle, trying to wrench it open. "Let us go!" She kicked at the door. "Unlock the door!"

The old man spread his hands helplessly. "I told you."

"You can't keep us prisoner. You can't—"

"He's not keeping you," said a voice from the darkness. "He's just an old, helpless man."

Sarnat twisted away from the door, her eyes wide.

I turned to face the unknown speaker. "We mean you no harm. Let us go."

Something—an animal—brushed me. Fur, stiff and short. Something hard as bone, textured. I held my breath, more afraid than I could ever remember feeling. Then it moved away, hooves clacking on the wooden floor.

"Please," I said. "We only came looking for the archdruid. He's been drained, so we'll leave. We'll—"

"I thought you wanted answers, *veleda*," said the otherworldly voice.

I went cold. "I'll find them somewhere else. If you'll just open the door . . ."

"Show them to their rooms, Roddy. And draw her a bath. She stinks of blood."

"Our rooms? We're not staying. Please, let us go. Let us go, or I'll call for the police!"

The only answer I received was the fading tinkle of bells. The old man took Sarnat's arm and mine in a surprisingly firm grip. "This way, milady."

I struggled against him. "Let us go. You can't keep us!"

"'Twas a mistake to come," said Roddy mildly. "But now you're here, and there will be no leaving."

I couldn't see Sarnat's expression, but I felt her fear. My own was a metallic taste in my mouth. Roddy drew us through mounds of shadow, into a heavy, cloying darkness.

"Here are stairs," he directed, taking us up a very narrow stairwell. It seemed to go on forever, walls pressing close. At the top, it was still so dark, I couldn't tell if there was a floor or if one step might send us tumbling to our deaths. The smell of the blood on my dress and face and in my hair filled my nose, along with that perfume, which seemed to permeate everything. What was it? It was so familiar and yet so . . . strange.

The store hadn't seemed this big from the outside, just another single-story ramshackle building, but we went up at least two flights of stairs, and three smaller sets of steps that twisted and turned through corridors and mazes. I struggled more than once in Roddy's grasp, and each time, his hold only tightened, his wiry fingers bruising my arm. How could we ever escape this darkness? I wished Diarmid was with me. I wished I hadn't been so stupid as to set out on my own. I'd only put myself in greater danger, as he'd predicted. The arch-druid had been drained, and I was in the grasp of some . . . *something*, and no one knew where I was, and I'd made Battle Annie vow not to tell. *Stupid, stupid, stupid*—

Roddy paused at a barrier before us, a wall. He kicked at it, and a door creaked open, something I heard rather than saw, because it opened to no light. "Here we are, milady." He gave me a little push. I went stumbling. The door closed behind me. I heard Sarnat protesting:

"No! Leave me with her. Leave me—"

Her voice just ended. There weren't even footsteps leading away, just an abrupt silence.

I took a deep breath, trying not to panic.

"Hello?" I ventured cautiously. "Is anyone there?"

There was a *whoosh*, a flash, and light filled the room so suddenly, it blinded me. I staggered back and saw that the light was gaslight, from two bronze sconces on the wall, and I was in a small room, with a bed in the corner laid with red silk coverlets edged in gold. The carpet beneath my feet was thick and richly colored. There was no window, but lush tapestries.

A gilded trunk stood against one wall, along with a dressing screen embroidered with flowers.

It was a moment before I saw that the tapestries told a story. In each were a man and a woman. The first showed the man petting two dogs as a star blazed from his forehead, while the woman watched. The second was the two of them on horseback, with an army following behind. The third was a battle between the man and leaping, vicious dogs with teeth like knives and eerie red eyes. The fourth was the two of them in a cave, his head in her lap and her hand upon his brow; and in the last, they were standing in a wood while he offered her a handful of red berries.

The story of Diarmid and Grainne.

Except the Grainne in this story wasn't blond, as she always was, as the tales told her to be. This girl had dark hair, like mine, and dark eyes.

The Grainne in the tapestries was me.

This was a spell. I felt its power pulsing gently about me, like water in a bath. I felt the glamour as I'd felt it in the riverfront warehouse where Diarmid and I had sought out the *sidhe* to ask questions about the archdruid. There were fairies in this place. Very powerful ones. So powerful that even Sarnat had been afraid. I should never have come here.

There's no going back. There's only going forward.

Diarmid's voice was in my head as if he stood beside me. He was right; I could not change the choices I'd made. I couldn't surrender to despair. I had to go forward, which meant I had to somehow harness my fear and think. There was no one to help me here—even Sarnat had been useless.

You have to be clever. You have to be smart. Listen.

I closed my eyes, casting out the web. I could no longer feel my brother; the connection had snapped. The hovering, watching *other* was not there either. But I heard the bells, and the archdruid's music, faint but clear, and that was puzzling, because when I'd touched Roddy, the music had vanished instead of growing stronger. Now, when I listened more closely, I heard what I hadn't before. The music was cloaked in other strains, foreign chords that screamed danger.

I opened my eyes. There *was* power here, and I felt my peril. Whoever had spoken in the darkness had glamoured this room especially for me, which meant he already knew too much about who I was and what I wanted.

But I was the *veleda*. I could not let some *sidhe* or demon take choice away from me. Whatever this place was, I had to fight it. I had to keep fighting.

Exhaustion overwhelmed me. It had to be near dawn. The last time I'd slept seemed forever ago, and there hadn't been much of it, thanks to Diarmid—well, it hadn't been only his fault, I had to admit. Thinking of it brought a rush of heat, but it gave me courage too. Diarmid would expect me to do what I must to survive.

And for now, that meant sleep. I curled up on the bed and stared at the tapestry before me, the one with Diarmid's head on Grainne's lap. It was the part of the story where she'd sung him to sleep with the "Wandering Song," and I closed my eyes

now and let the poetry play in my head . . . *sleep here soundly,*
soundly, Diarmid, to whom I have given my love . . .

Tonight, I would let myself dream of him.

Tomorrow, I would fight.

Patrick Devlin stared out the window of the meeting room in the Fenian Brotherhood clubhouse. The traffic on Broadway was at a standstill thanks to a collision between a carriage and a delivery wagon. Bright green peppers and cabbages rolled in the street, and passersby were trying to right the carriage while the drivers screamed obscenities at each other.

Not much different from what was happening in the room behind him. The Fomori were arguing over the Fianna's rescue of Oscar, which had been a disaster—though not for Patrick, who struggled to hide his relief. It had gone as he'd hoped. Oscar had escaped with Patrick's message for Aidan. All Patrick hoped was that Aidan understood it.

"You should have killed Diarmid." Bres, the leader of the Fomori, said to Balor. "All you had to do was lift that eye patch and strike him down. Now, two of their best warriors are returned to them."

Bres was so blond and handsome that it was hard to believe he could be as ruthless as he sounded right now. But Patrick knew the deadliness in his tone was no illusion. Patrick glanced over his shoulder as the giant Balor crossed his massive arms over his equally massive chest and gave his leader a steely, one-eyed stare.

"'Tis only Diarmid who knows where the *veleda* is." Daire Donn, the former self-proclaimed King of the World, tried to placate Bres. "If Balor killed him, we would never find her."

"You think the rest of the Fianna don't know her whereabouts?" Bres snapped. "Don't be a fool."

"In any case, it was badly done all around," said Simon MacRonan, the Fenian Brotherhood's Druid Seer, who sat at the table, rearranging rune sticks.

"'Twas clear they were ready for us," Bres said, pacing. "I grow tired of spies. Who among us is the traitor?"

"You're too suspicious, my love."

The beautiful blond Lot entered, followed closely by Patrick's closest friend in the Fenian Brotherhood, Jonathan Olwen, and Miogach, whose gray eyes were always sharp and assessing. Patrick had not spoken to him since the gang riot a few days ago, when Miogach had sent an assassin after Aidan.

Bres stopped his pacing and sighed, but his chiseled face was hard. "Aye, perhaps 'tis so. But the Fianna are stronger with Oscar, and when you add Diarmid's return . . ."

"Without the *veleda*," Simon noted. He shoved the rune sticks on the table, pushing one and then another. "Which is very interesting, wouldn't you say? Why not bring her with him?"

"Indeed. Why not? Especially now that the lovespot is working its magic." Balor scowled. "He has her well in his control."

"Please," Jonathan protested. "Consider Patrick when you speak of her. She is his fiancée."

Patrick couldn't face the compassion in his friend's gaze. He turned back to the window. The overturned carriage was righted; traffic was starting to move. Peppers had rolled up against the piles of garbage at the curb, bright green spots of color that stood out among the refuse like the emeralds in the necklace he'd planned to give Grace on their wedding day. So many times, he'd imagined putting them around her neck, the way she would kiss him as she had in his parlor, tangling her fingers in his hair, pressing against him. To think of her kissing Diarmid instead, wanting *him* . . .

Patrick wanted her back desperately. But more than that, he wanted her safe. He suspected that the Fomori weren't looking for the archdruid at all, despite their promises, and the attempt on Aidan's life bothered him greatly. And there was also the fact that Aidan had told him the Fianna believed Grace had the threefold power of a goddess, the kind of power that, once released, could remake the world. If the Fomori discovered it . . . Patrick didn't quite trust them to resist it. No, it was best if Diarmid kept her away from the city, at least until Patrick understood what he was dealing with.

Miogach came up beside him. "A fine mess."

Patrick wasn't certain whether he spoke of the accident in the street or of Oscar's escape.

"I owe you an apology for what happened with the stormcaster."

Patrick's stomach tightened. "Bres said you were only trying to protect me."

"Aye, but I took it too far. I won't lie to you—I hate the Fianna. They stole everything from me. Seeing them again . . . I forgot myself. I shouldn't have sent that boy after the stormcaster. 'Twas foolish. There were other ways to manage it. 'Tis Ireland I should be thinking of, not my own petty revenge. It won't happen again, I vow."

Miogach looked sincere, and Patrick was relieved. "That's good to hear."

Miogach leaned close. "But a word of warning, Devlin: old friendships can get in the way. I know from experience that Bres is quick to see disloyalty where there may be none."

Patrick tried to hide his guilt. The Fomori didn't know of his alliance with Aidan to save Grace's life, and he wanted to keep it that way. It looked like betrayal, though it wasn't. It was just . . . caution. "He thinks I'm disloyal?"

"Not yet, though your actions troubled him. I've reminded him that the stormcaster was your friend and is the *veleda*'s brother."

"I understand," Patrick said quietly.

Miogach smiled. As always, it softened the sharpness of his features and made Patrick want to smile back. "I like you, Devlin, and I'm glad you called us. We'll protect the stormcaster if we can. But 'tis war, you must remember. You cannot be on both sides."

"I'm not on both sides," Patrick insisted. "But I am worried that there's no progress in finding the archdruid."

"Aye. We're looking, believe me. No one wants to see Miss Knox die. When I think of what we can win together, of a free Ireland . . . 'tis what we want above all. We shall have it, I promise you."

Patrick was reminded of what was important. The Fomori were the only ones who could help him win Ireland's freedom. He needed them, and when it came to Ireland, he trusted them.

Lot came up to them, saying, "I'm going to your house, my darling, if you'd like a ride. Your fiancée's mother asked for my opinion on your wedding supper."

It was a relief to know that, whatever else changed, the plans for his future with Grace continued on. Patrick felt a hope he sorely needed. "I think I would. If you—"

"What could this be?" Simon's voice cut through the talk.

Patrick turned to see him frowning over the rune sticks.

Bres demanded, "What is it? What do you see?"

"Something has changed."

"Things are always changing." Daire Donn raked his long hair from his face as he looked over Simon's shoulder. "'Tis the nature of divination, is it not?"

Simon tapped the rune sticks. "But this is to do with the *veleda*. This shows . . . three."

"'She sees, she weighs, she chooses,'" Daire Donn quoted the prophecy. "She is the *eubages, brithem*, and *vater* combined."

Patrick tensed. *Eubages, brithem*, and *vater*. The Seer, the Judge, and the Prophet. The *veleda* played all these roles. *Let them read it only as that. Don't let them see the goddess that the Fianna do.* Why would they save her life, if her death would release such staggering power?

Then Simon said, "It's not that. The runes seem to indicate a greater power."

"A greater power?" asked Lot.

Here it is, then.

"The power of a goddess," Simon said.

"That can't be," Patrick protested. "I know Grace. She doesn't have that kind of strength."

"She was very unformed when you saw her last." Bres's voice vibrated with excitement. He strode to the table and contemplated the rune sticks. "If this is true—such power could win us this city. It could win us Ireland. With her, we could have it all easily. It could give us the world!"

"But we don't need the world," Patrick said. "We need only Ireland's freedom. I thought we were agreed that we would try to save Grace's life."

Lot's water lily perfume filled his nose as she squeezed his arm. "Yes, of course, my darling. Gaining her power without her death is what we still hope for."

"Aye," Bres said shortly, though he did not meet Patrick's eyes. "We'll find another spell."

"But if there's not another spell, we may not have a choice," Simon added. "Think of what's at stake, Patrick."

"Think of the *cost*, Simon," Patrick countered. "We aren't murderers."

"This was all your idea. *Yours*," Simon reminded him. "Have you changed your mind now that things have got a little dirty?"

"Not just a *little* dirty," Patrick snapped. "You're speaking of the death of the girl I love."

"You loved Ireland too. Once, you were willing to do anything for her. You made the vow, as did we all. Do you mean to take it back?"

Patrick knew Simon was asking only what they all wondered. Just where did his loyalty lie? He looked at Jonathan, who looked away. "No. But I'm begging you all—find another spell."

Lot pressed into his side soothingly. "We will. Your wedding will go on as planned, darling, and you'll spend the rest of your life with your love."

"But first we must find her," Bres said.

"Which may be another problem," Simon muttered, consulting the runes again. "There's something else that keeps coming up."

"Another obstacle?" Daire Donn laughed. "Have there not been enough?"

"Otherworld," Simon told them. "It keeps reappearing."

"Does it predict her death?" Bres asked.

"This isn't a prediction. It's what's happening now."

"You mean she's already dead?" Daire Donn asked in alarm. "But what about the prophecy?"

Patrick's heart seized. "She's not dead. I would know."

"You would know? How?" Bres's eyes were hard.

"Because I love her," Patrick said, though that was only half the truth. He didn't tell them about his dreams of stone walls and oracle fires, which felt more and more real, so that sometimes he wasn't certain when he was awake and when he was dreaming. In them, he was racing to protect the *veleda*—Grace. She was in danger, but she was alive, and he *knew* it the way he knew the sky was blue. It was her presence he felt in those dreams, though it sounded mad to say it.

Though which was more insane? Feeling the girl he loved was alive or being afraid to admit it to gods and men who'd burst to life from *stories*?

Once again, Simon pushed at the runes. "*Otherworld* can mean uncertainty or change or danger. But I think here it means another *place*. Time that passes differently."

"The *sidhe*. Time passes differently inside a glamour. She must be in the hands of the river pirates." Bres commanded Balor, "Double efforts to find them. If the *veleda* is with the *sidhe*, we have no time to lose."

Simon picked up the sticks, tossing them in a small leather bag so they clattered together, then spilled them again onto the table. The smell of hemp smoke filled Patrick's nose. Oracle smoke, like that in his dream. It stung his eyes and choked him as if he were standing in a cloud of it. He felt lightheaded. *The veleda is in danger.* The air around him shivered.

The hallucinations were happening more and more often too, but this . . . this was so real, as was his panic. He should tell the others. Patrick clutched the windowsill. The Fomori might know why it was happening and what it meant. They were in this together, after all.

But he turned away to watch the bright green peppers roll about the street. And he said nothing.

FIVE

That same day
Diarmid

It was late morning when Diarmid reached the brambly clay scarps on Governors Island where he'd left Grace. He climbed quickly to the vacant storehouse, impatient to see her. A vine snagged his boot, nearly tripping him as he shoved his way inside, calling, "Grace!"

The storehouse was empty. No Grace. No sign of Miles, the boy he'd left her with. Miles was a member of the Dun Rats, the gang from Brooklyn that Diarmid and Grace had stayed with for a time. Diarmid had trained the lad himself. He knew Miles would not fail in his vow to guard her.

Don't panic. They'd probably just gone in search of food. Grace had promised to wait for him, and he knew she would. The lovespell had been soft in her dark-brown eyes. Where were they?

He heard a sound coming from outside and stepped against the wall, waiting. A footstep, a low curse—Miles. They were back, thank the gods! Diarmid stepped out just as Miles came through the door.

The boy stopped short. "Derry!" A look of alarm crossed his face.

And Diarmid knew.

"No. No. Don't say she's gone. Don't tell me that."

"I don't know what happened!" Miles cried. "I been looking for her half the night and all morning. She was here. Then she just disappeared! 'Twasn't my fault."

"How isn't it? You were to guard her."

"I did! She was right here with me! We played some cards, and then she went to sleep. I promise, Derry, she was here! When I woke up in the night, she was gone. I didn't hear nothin'! I've looked all over. Even went up to Fort Jay this morning. 'Twas like a spirit swept her away or somethin'. There weren't a sound! She just . . . disappeared. Like into thin air."

She'd promised to stay. The lovespot would have guaranteed it. She wouldn't have left of her own volition. Which meant either that she had to be on the island somewhere, doing something innocent like looking for food or water, or she'd been taken.

"Like a spirit swept her away."

He remembered Aidan's fear in the night. The *sidhe* could have taken her. Or the Fomori. But last night, Balor had asked him where the *veleda* was. Patrick Devlin had told him to keep her out of the city. The Fomori didn't have her. But the *sidhe* . . . the *sidhe* had known she was here. Battle Annie knew.

Diarmid should never have trusted the river pirate. He told himself he was wrong. It wasn't Battle Annie. Grace must still be on the island. She'd ventured out—*aye, that was like her*—and got lost. She was picking berries or talking to soldiers or drowned in some little eddy because her boots were made for city walks and not climbing and she was always tripping—

Stop. Diarmid took a deep breath, trying not to think of Aidan and his *"Grace, no! Too late!"* When he had some measure of control, Diarmid said to Miles, "We'll search every stone on this island."

It took all day. The sun was dipping below the skyline before Diarmid had to admit defeat. Grace wasn't there. Back at the storehouse, he found the ogham stick, but other than that, there was nothing to show she had even been here.

He picked it up, feeling her in it, though that was impossible. It was his imagination, wanting her to be where he'd left her, wanting to see her, to touch her. *How can she be gone?* What a fool he'd been to leave her. He should have known . . . *By the gods, where is she?*

"She's probably gone back to the city," Miles tried. "This ain't no place for a girl like her. She was bored once you left."

She is gone. Diarmid loved her, and he'd failed to protect her. What would happen to her, the dangers . . .

He couldn't bear to think of it. He refused to imagine. What was there to do now, beyond going back to the others and telling Finn—*sweet Danu, telling Finn.* Diarmid would be lucky if he survived the hour.

But there was no help for it. He and Miles hailed a couple of boys out fishing who took them to Manhattan. It was dark when they arrived. Miles took the ferry back to Brooklyn, and Diarmid trolled the waterfront, looking for Battle Annie's sloop, or any of the *sidhe.* He saw only "Wanted" posters bearing his face, and homeless and drunks and thieves. The night began to turn ugly, and he knew he could delay no longer. He made his way back to the tenement, sick with dread and worry.

Grace, where are you?

Diarmid was halfway down the dark, narrow steps to the basement flat when Aidan bounded up to meet him. Grace's brother stopped, his gaze leaping beyond Diarmid, to nothing.

"You were right," Diarmid said hoarsely. "It was too late. She was gone."

"Gone?" Aidan echoed, as if the word were foreign. "What do you mean, gone?"

"I mean she wasn't there." They reached the bottom of the steps. "The guard I ordered to stay with her said she'd disappeared in the night."

"Disappeared?"

The others gathered around. Oscar raised a brow, but Diarmid turned away from his friend, to Finn. "We searched the whole island. There was no sign of her. She'd promised to stay. She was bound to me. She wouldn't have gone on her own. Someone must have taken her."

"Someone got past the guard you left?" Finn asked, his expression settling into a chill that Diarmid knew to be wary of. "He didn't wake? He heard nothing?"

"Yes."

"This was the guard you said you trusted?"

Diarmid answered uncomfortably, "Aye. Miles can be trusted. I've trained him, but . . . 'twas only a few days, and he's just a gang boy."

"Not a good enough guard then," Finn said.

Diarmid felt the noose, and he was so miserable and afraid for her, he didn't care about walking into it. There was nothing but the truth. "Aye. I shouldn't have left her."

"The *ball seirce* worked? You're certain?"

"She's in love with me. There's no doubt."

"The Fomori must have her," Ossian said, crossing his arms and looking murderous. "Who else?"

Aidan said, "I don't think so. Remember what Patrick told Derry? What he told Oscar? Why would he tell us to keep her out of the city if they had her?"

"I'd thought maybe the *sidhe*," Diarmid said. "I told you she made a bargain with the river pirate queen."

"And you think they may have spirited her away?" Finn asked.

"Maybe. I didn't trust them, but Grace did."

Finn rubbed his chin. "We've little time. We'll spread out across the city—all of you go now but Oscar, who's in no condition, and Diarmid. Look for the *sidhe*. Find out what they know. Especially where this Battle Annie and her gang are."

"I know what Battle Annie looks like," Diarmid protested. "I should——"

"You should stay here and follow orders for a change," Finn barked. "We've some things to settle, you and I."

Diarmid's heart sank, but he stood back to let the others pass. He glanced at Aidan, who was intently weaving threads of purple lightning through his fingers. Oscar clapped Diarmid's shoulder, leaning close to whisper, "Finn's watching you. Don't look so love struck." And Diarmid realized he'd been so worried, he'd made no attempt to hide his feelings for Grace.

Oscar went back to the mattress. Finn motioned for Diarmid to follow him to the far end of the room, where barrels served as stools near an old coal bin. Finn leaned against the metal bin.

"I'm sorry," Diarmid said. "I thought I was helping——"

Finn waved off his excuse. "You've lost the *veleda*, possibly to the *sidhe*. Have you thought about what will happen if they destroy her?"

Diarmid hadn't thought past his fear for her, but Finn's words reminded him how disastrous it would be if they didn't find her and the ritual wasn't performed on Samhain. The Fianna would fade, never to return to any world. The Irish would be left to the Fomori—to chaos and terror and enslavement.

"Do you realize what you've done?"

Diarmid let out his breath. "Aye. She's the *veleda* and—"

"She's much more than just a *veleda*." Finn glanced at Cannel, who was spreading his tarot cards. "There have been troubling elements to her, things we haven't seen in a *veleda* before."

"Something's not right," Aidan had said. *"Grace is not as she should be."*

"Cannel's seen the triune in her," Finn went on. His full lips curved in a smile that was a bit too satisfied. "She has the power of the goddess."

Diarmid stared at his captain. *"Grace?"*

"You released her power. Did you not feel the strength of it?"

Diarmid struggled to think. He'd felt power in Grace, but *that* kind . . . "I never felt anything like that. Are you sure?"

"The cards say it. And I'm thinking you aren't the most reliable judge of whether or not 'tis there. You didn't see such power in her brother either."

That was true. He hadn't seen the stormcaster in Aidan, as obvious as it was. Diarmid didn't know why.

Finn leaned closer, his bright hair coming forward to narrow his face and frame the pale fury in his gaze. "It's also clear you've fallen in love with the lass."

Diarmid's chest tightened so he couldn't breathe.

"How often must you make this mistake?" Finn asked, low and lethal. "Why is it that every time I turn around I'm questioning your loyalty because of love? Did Aengus Og addle you so when you were a boy that no common sense remains?"

"This isn't the same as before—"

"No, last time, 'twas only me you offended. This time, you put all of us at risk. I've grown weary of being at odds with you, Diarmid. I want to know I can trust you. So perhaps you can tell me: Are you one of us? Or do you care more for the *veleda*?"

"I'm one of you," Diarmid insisted. "I won't fail you."

Finn paused, measuring, deciding. After everything that had happened between them, Diarmid did not think he could bear losing Finn's trust again, and so he was relieved—more than relieved—when he saw his leader's face soften. Finn had chosen to believe him.

Finn said, "Good. Then you'll have no complaint of the task I assign you."

"None," Diarmid said, though his every muscle tensed.

"You'll find her, and you'll bring her back here. And then you will leave her to me."

This was what Oscar had warned him of. The thought of what Finn would do, what he could do— *"He'd seduce her himself and make sure 'twas well done."*

Diarmid opened his mouth to protest, but then realized this was a test. He'd longed to be one of the Fianna since he was a lad watching them march through town, spears raised, banners flying. He'd defied Aengus Og, his foster father, for them. It was all he'd ever wanted.

"Is this to be Grainne all over again?" Finn asked gently.

The sound of her name on Finn's lips startled Diarmid, reminding him of his guilt and regret. Everything he'd promised to make up for.

This was his punishment, and he deserved it. "I'll do as you wish."

"As I wish," Finn repeated mockingly. "Aye, 'tis what I wish. The love I bear you makes me stupid, I fear, but killing you for disobedience as I should would only ruin morale, and I can't lose a good man now. We all love you—I wish you would remember it."

"And you need me for the *geis*." Diarmid couldn't resist a touch of sarcasm.

"Yes," Finn agreed. "You'll thank me for this when the time comes to kill her. 'Twill make it easier if you're not resisting out of love. Because she *does* have to die, Diarmid. For us. For our people. Her death will release a power that will win us anything—*everything*."

Goddess power. Uneasily, Diarmid asked, "Do the Fomori know about the triune?"

Finn shook his head. "Not as yet, according to our spies. But 'tis certain they'll discover it soon. You'd best find the lass quickly. And Diarmid . . . betrayal *will* mean your death this time. If I have to bind your hand to mine to take her life, I'll do it. And then I'll slit your throat as well, however much I love you."

Diarmid knew his captain meant it. He and Finn *were* at odds; they had been for years. He had no choice but to put his feelings for Grace aside. If she had goddess power, keeping her alive was not an option. Such power released upon her death . . . Finn was right: the Irish people were what mattered. Restoring the honor of the Fianna. Saving the Irish from the Fomori.

But . . . how had he not felt such a power in her? Had he been so distracted by desire and love that he hadn't seen it? Or was it that she was unformed still? Untrained, unfinished?

When Finn dismissed him, Diarmid went to Aidan, who was slumped against the wall, his white face and shirt appearing disembodied in the shadows. Diarmid squatted beside him, saying quietly, "Finn just told me that he thinks Grace has goddess power. When you told me she isn't as she should be, is that what you meant? Is that what you think?"

Aidan raised haunted eyes. "Why ask me? Does it change what you feel for her?"

"It changes everything," Diarmid said bluntly. Everything he must do, everything he must feel. *Fate is ever-changing.* He felt it working upon him now, moving things about, a giant game in which he was only another pawn. "I have to find her. You said you felt a connection to her. She said she spoke to you in her dreams. Where is she now? What do you feel?"

"I don't feel anything."

"You don't?" Diarmid asked suspiciously.

"She's gone. I felt a storm of fear, and then it stopped, just like that. As if things were cut off. As if she fell between worlds. I don't feel her. I don't hear her. She's gone, Derry." He gave Diarmid a baleful look. "And perhaps it's better so."

Aidan had obviously overheard his conversation with Finn.

Diarmid wished he didn't agree.

SIX

The first morning (sidhe *time*)
Grace

I woke to warmth and the stink of gas from the lamps I'd left burning, and a copper tub filled with steaming water set in the middle of the floor. The gilded trunk was open to reveal a confusion of colorful scarves and stockings and petticoats and ribbons and gowns.

I sat up warily. I'd heard no one, and I was alone. I didn't know how these things had come to be here. Magic or too-silent servants—I didn't like either thought.

I pushed aside my hair, surprised at how stiff it was, until I remembered the fight on the pier, that boy's blood spurting. *Sarnat. Where is she now? Is she safe?* I glanced down at the now filthy bedcover I'd been sleeping on, noticing in the same moment that my shoulder was so brown with blood, it looked as if I'd been the one stabbed. I rubbed at my cheek; flecks of dried blood came off in my hand.

After that, there was nothing on earth that could keep me from that bath. The blood had soaked through to stain my corset and my chemise as well, along with salt and seawater, sand and dirt and sweat. I'd never been so glad for hot water.

A bar of lilac-scented soap floated in the tub. I washed my hair three times. When I was done, the water was a murky shade of pinkish brown, but I was clean. I wrapped myself in the thick towel folded beside the tub and considered the filthy pile of my clothing. I could not bear to put it on again. But there was the trunk, with clothes exploding from it.

There were scarves of gauzy silk, a satin petticoat edged with lace. A chemise so fine that, when I pulled it over my head, I could see the pink of my skin glowing through. It was the most delicate undergarment I'd ever worn. Another corset; white and new and so stiff, it took me a while to fasten it, and even then, I couldn't tighten it well. There were stockings of gossamer silk—nothing like the coarse wool I'd been wearing— and garters with yellow silk roses.

I rifled through the gowns—there were four: one striped purple, adorned with pansies; a second day gown of sky-blue watered silk that shimmered with rainbows in the gaslight; and a third of a beautiful topaz, with a square neckline and fringe. They were all gorgeous; better than anything I'd ever worn. I'd never even seen Lucy Devlin in such finery. It had been so long since I'd had anything pretty.

Then I got to the fourth one.

It was pink silk, a ball gown, and one I recognized—the silk roses and the trailing ribbons, the puffed sleeves decorated with lace. This was the gown I'd had made for my debut— plans that had come to nothing once the Fianna came into my life. *"Pink's a good choice for you. Devlin won't be able to look away."*

I dropped the dress as if it burned. Whatever held me prisoner had enough power to glamour a room to tease me and to call up my debut gown. How had it known? Was it in my head even now? Even Sarnat had been frightened—the same girl who had taken down a dozen gang boys without flinching. I remembered the feel of the furred animal—or whatever it was—against my fingers last night, the brush of bone, that unsettlingly sentient dog, the darkness and the maze of a shop.

I had vowed to be clever, to find a way to escape, and instead, I'd bathed in what must be enchanted water and used enchanted soap, and now, I was half-dressed in enchanted clothing. I knew what glamoured food and drink could do to non-fairies, but did the rest of it have the same effect?

It was too late if it did. *Very clever, Grace.* I'd already made so many mistakes . . . I'd practically handed myself to whatever this was. Diarmid would be furious with me. I was furious with myself. But whatever spell was cast, I'd already fallen into it. Now I must deal with the consequences. I took a deep breath and turned to reach for my abandoned dress, stopping short when I saw that the stained red silk coverlet on the bed was gone, replaced with a golden one.

And the pile of my clothes was gone.

My skin prickled, but now there was no choice. I couldn't walk around in my petticoats. Slowly, I picked up the topaz gown. The dress fit perfectly—a little tight about the bodice because of how loose the corset was. The fringe danced at my shoulders and along the skirt with the slightest movement, and I knew the color complemented me—they all did. Spelled for me. Glamoured for me.

Now what? What was I to do? Snap my fingers? Scream at the walls and demand to speak to my captor?

I stepped over to the door and turned the knob. To my surprise, it opened, and I found myself staring out at a hall that formed a U around a central set of stairs. The wooden railings gleamed in the light of gas sconces. Everywhere were tall piles of dusty things, all looking as if they hadn't been touched in years. Trunks and lampshades and piles of books teetering crazily on upturned chairs, creating jigging, narrow corridors in the already narrow hall. The smell of dust and must and foxed paper filled my nose.

I made my way through, careful not to touch or brush against anything—it all looked so precariously balanced. I had no idea how Roddy had brought Sarnat and me through this last night without it all crashing to the floor—and in such profound darkness as well. *Sarnat, where are you?*

Doors lined the walls, and carved out of the chaos were pathways to each of them. But every door I tried was locked. The stairs were narrow, made more so by things crowding the edges. Books mostly, among them Poe's *Tales of the Grotesque and Arabesque*, novels by Fanny Fern, Elisha Kane's *Arctic Explorations*, red-covered travel guides, textbooks, and poetry. There were so many, I couldn't imagine anyone finding the time to read them all.

I doubted anyone had. It was just a motley pawnshop collection, like everything else: old boots and sheet music, hats and broken furniture, silent clocks, birdcages and stuffed birds, a stuffed lizard and some moth-eaten stuffed cats who seemed to follow me with their creepy glass eyes. I felt I was being watched, but perhaps it was only the taxidermy, because I heard nothing but my own footsteps.

When I reached the bottom of the first landing—which branched onto another U-shaped hallway set with doors and crowded with towers of things—I paused, listening for the archdruid's music.

I heard the sound of tiny bells.

I thought of that animal brushing up against me in the dark, and Roddy's *"It's too late,"* and Sarnat's fear. This stairway went straight down; it was nothing like it had seemed last night, with its endless corridors and twists and turns. I thought about going back to my room until I was sent for, but then . . . what if I wasn't?

So I continued down. The bells in my head grew louder, though the house was as silent as ever. I smelled that elusive perfume again, a familiar scent—where did I know it from?

It looked as if the staircase just ended at a wall, but as I reached it, I saw a corridor branching off to either side. One side was completely blocked by a tangle of chairs. The other was open, leading into darkness.

It was either go forward or go back, and so I took the only path. *Like a lamb to slaughter—such a comforting thought.* The walls were very close—barely my own width. The corridor seemed to go on for yards and yards before I saw a light at the end of it—silvery and glaring. The bells jangled in my head, the perfume teased.

I steeled myself and stepped into the light.

It was blinding. I put my hand to my eyes to shield them.

"Ah, I was hoping for the pink."

The voice from last night. I struggled to see. "Who are you?"

"I'm as you see."

"I can't see you! I can't see anything. Show yourself!"

"Oh, aye. Pardon, I'd forgotten your affliction."

The light faded and then disappeared. I lowered my hand, blinking into the room we'd entered last night. It was as full as the rest of the shop, with windows that looked out on Cherry Street, and "Roddy's Grotto" painted upon the glass.

At the far end, near a counter piled with knickknacks and a glass case full of jewelry, stood a stag, lowering its head to point its antlers at me, and beside him a young man about my brother's age, glowing faintly silver.

But what a young man. I'd never seen anyone like him. His hair was black and long, hanging in knotted curls below his shoulders. He wore an ancient-looking linen tunic embroidered with gold and purple and red around the collar and sleeves and hem, and a capelet of feathers—black as his hair, shining faintly blue—and a pair of leather trousers tucked into boots that came to his knees. Chains of tiny bells hung around his neck, hundreds of them, and he wore gold hoops in his ears. His wrists were circled with tattooed bracelets, another tattoo scrawled across his collarbone, peeking from beneath his shirt. His jaw was square, his cheekbones sharp. A full lower lip, and deep-set eyes of a strange light amber.

He was odd, but very attractive, too, in that way of the *sidhe*. Handsome and alluring, fascinating and dangerous and intense, as if they'd been made for the kind of temptation that led to ruin.

Perilous.

He stared at me as I stared at him. I felt that draw that always came with the *sidhe*, the urge to step closer. His song was different—not *let me touch you, touch you, touch you*, but instead the music of those bells calling me onward, so that I wanted them for myself. I wanted a chain of them around my neck. I wanted to dance. To dance and dance and never stop.

The whippet-like dog came out from behind him, the stag backed restlessly away, and from the corner, I heard a sniffling and snorting. A boar emerged from a stack of crates, its evil tusks gleaming.

It was all I could do to hold my ground, not to run toward the young man or away to the door. Neither would do me any good. He smiled—such straight white teeth—and came toward me. The perfume was stronger now, and I recognized it. It was the Druid Tuama's scent—*the Druid Tuama?*—a Druid scent on a *sidhe* boy. I wasn't certain which confused me more, that impossible combination, or the fact that I knew it.

He reached out; I felt paralyzed as he lifted a curl of my hair, rubbing it between his fingers the way Finn had once done. Like Finn, he stared at it as if he were trying to sight a secret. The cape shimmered and fluffed its feathers the way a bird does when it bathes. It was frightening—and mesmerizing.

"Don't touch me," I whispered.

He looked up at me, raising a dark brow. "I've no wish to steal your power. Yet." The feathers ruffled and preened. "Do you like what you see, *veleda*?"

"I want to go. Where's my friend? Where's Sarnat?"

"I don't know. Around here somewhere, I think. 'Tis hard to find things sometimes. Perhaps she's lost."

"I want to find her and go."

"But you can't," he said lightly, dropping the strand of my hair. "Not until you're done with me."

"You can't just keep me prisoner. There are people looking for me—"

"No doubt. But how will they find you? Battle Annie will not break a vow. Did you tell anyone else where you were going? Can you even feel your brother?"

I started.

"You see? I know a great deal about you." His golden eyes gleamed. He brushed his finger over my jaw. I felt a shiver, a sting—my power responding to his magic—and I jerked away.

He smiled; it was faintly threatening. "Do you like your room? I was uncertain which would torment you more: your Fenian white knight or your Fianna warrior. Do you think I chose well?"

"They see what you most want."

"Who *are* you?" I tried to keep my voice from shaking. "What do you want with me?"

He shrugged. The feathers shivered, and the bells tinkled with the motion. "You tell me. You're the one who's come searching."

"For an archdruid."

"Then 'tis a happy thing you've found him."

I remembered Roddy, wild haired, mad eyed. "You've drained his power."

"That I have," he said, again with that smile.

"So he's of no use to me. Tell me where Sarnat is. Let us go."

"If I do that, you'll never find the answers to your questions."

"I won't find them now," I said bitterly. "Roddy knows nothing. He remembers nothing. How can he help me?"

"Perhaps he can't. But perhaps there's someone else you can ask." He pointed at the ceiling. I looked up.

There were branches of twisted oak twined with mistletoe, a cage of branches above our heads. I stared at it, puzzled. A bolt of pure red lightning zapped into it, sending sparks flying. I gasped and ducked, but they were already gone, leaving only smoke and the smell of electricity in the air.

The lightning came from his fingers.

"You're a stormcaster!"

He looked smug. "Among other things."

"What other things?"

"Spell casting. Divination. Dream reading. I can work the elements. And of course, like all my kin, my trade is illusion. But *my* glamours are indistinguishable from truth"—he glanced at me—"which is good for you, else you'd be naked to me or anyone else."

I crossed my arms over my breasts.

He grinned. "You'll have to trust me on that one."

"Trust you? I don't even know who you are!"

"Iobhar." He bowed slightly. "At your service."

"I didn't know *sidhe* could do any of those things. I mean, beyond glamours."

"They can't," he boasted. "Not usually. But I've never known one who could drain an archdruid alone either. 'Twould be overwhelming for most of the others."

"But not for you," I said.

"I am as you see."

Battle Annie had said that taking power only sated the appetite for a time, and then one was hungry again. "You're telling me that you've drunk the archdruid's power and knowledge—and kept it to use yourself? I didn't know that was possible."

"It was a surprise to me as well. When I found him, I'd only thought: well, here's enough feasting for a year. 'Twas a shock to find I could make rainstorms in the dining room."

So carelessly cruel. "You didn't care what it did to him?"

"I don't care what it does to anyone."

Yes, perilous. Be careful, Grace. Be clever. "Does having such power sate your wish for more?"

"Not in the least," he said. "I feel yours from where I stand, *veleda*. 'Tis most tempting. I think it wouldn't take long. Come and kiss me, and we'll see."

There it was again, the music of bells, that tempting perfume. I saw a vision of myself stepping into his arms, taking the bells, dancing and dancing and dancing . . .

"No, thank you."

"I'm light on my feet, I've been told."

"You said you didn't want my power."

"I said I didn't want it *yet*. But that was an eternity ago, wasn't it? Things change every moment, don't they? Just as fate does."

I remembered why I was here, what I wanted. "You say you have the archdruid's power and knowledge."

"Ah, here it is at last. I'd been told you were clever, but I was beginning to wonder."

"You *do* have it?"

"He does." Another voice came from the shadows at the back of the room. Roddy emerged from a doorway half-hidden by a glass-fronted armoire filled with ornaments. He was dressed in a shirt and trousers and a gray coat so worn the folds of the cuffs were white. His elbow poked through a hole in the sleeve. "And I trained him myself." The old man's brow furrowed. "Didn't I?"

"Aye, you did." Iobhar put his arm around Roddy's shoulders. Roddy shuddered but looked at Iobhar with a doting affection, and I understood that, too, the touch you wanted to fall into, the delirium of the draw of power.

I wasn't ready for this. Iobhar was more than dangerous. He'd so easily overcome an archdruid. I couldn't be clever enough to withstand him and the temptation of those bells.

But still I said to Roddy, "Do you remember anything?"

"No," he said wistfully. "Or . . . sometimes. 'Tis like a dream I once had. You should flee, milady."

"She can't flee," said Iobhar. "Her questions keep her prisoner."

"*You* keep me prisoner," I corrected.

"Do I?" He looked surprised.

"You said you did. You said I couldn't leave. Not until you were done with me."

"I said until *you* were done with *me*."

Was that what he'd said? I felt confused and stupid. I remembered Diarmid telling me to listen, that their words had more than one meaning.

"You're telling me I could walk out that door if I wanted to?"

"You can leave," said Roddy sadly. "But you won't."

I backed toward the door, keeping my gaze on Iobhar. The stag came across the room and walked with me. The dog watched with his compassionate eyes, as did the boar.

I put my hand on the doorknob. Both Iobhar and Roddy watched me without a word, but Iobhar's eyes gleamed compellingly beneath his dark brows. The storefront windows overlooked a street full of delivery wagons and stevedores unloading crates and barrels, sailors loitering outside saloons. Ordinary life. The life I wanted to return to. One untouched by *sidhe* or Fianna or Fomori or prophecies that meant you had to die at seventeen . . .

But that wasn't my life. Not anymore.

Roddy's gaze was pleading. I knew he wanted me to go. I knew to stay could be the most dangerous choice I'd ever made—more dangerous even than loving a Fianna warrior destined to kill me.

Iobhar said, "Go back to your world, *milis*. Find what you seek there."

My world. Except that my world held no answers. What I was seeking was right here. I dropped my hand from the knob.

Iobhar smirked. "You see? You are your own prisoner, *veleda*."

I knew he was right.

SEVEN

August 5
Patrick

*H*e lay on the forest floor, on a carpet of leaves that smelled *of a dry autumn, dirt and browning grass. Fallen acorns poked into his back, and he shifted in discomfort and stared up at the cage of intertwined, bare branches festooned with mistletoe. He fingered the golden sickle in his hand as he waited for night to fall. It was the sixth day of the moon, the time to harvest mistletoe. His legs were bare beneath his white robes—the air was cold and growing colder. He wished he had not taken on this task; there were others who could have done it. But he'd felt there was something to discover here, something he should know, a vision that might come to him beneath this sacred tree.*

Bile, father of the gods, tell me where she is.

There was nothing, as there had been nothing. No matter what potions he drank or how long he inhaled oracle smoke, he found no answers. The veleda *was gone; there was no Seer who could find her, no divination. All anyone saw was danger.*

The sky darkened. Not night—it was too dark and too fast. A Druid storm.

His skin prickled; his hair stood on end.

A bolt of bloodred lightning split the branches. He rolled away just before it struck the dirt—just to the left of where he'd been. The air smelled of burning. Thunder filled his ears. He scrambled to his feet. Red lightning, Druid lightning, but from where?

"Where are you?" he shouted. "Who are you?"

The world went dark.

Patrick woke with a start, bathed in cold sweat, his heart racing, and the smell of electricity in his nose. He leaped out of bed, huddling against the wall, waiting for the lightning to strike. Whoever cast it wanted him gone.

Suddenly he realized he was in his bedroom, cowering half-naked in a corner. The lightning wasn't real; it was only another dream.

He straightened, raking his hair with a trembling hand. His worries over Grace and her brother intruded even in his sleep. The river pirates. *Sidhe.* Time passing differently . . . Wearily, he went to the washbasin and splashed his face until he felt himself again. The air still felt heavy and ominous. That red Druid lightning . . . He'd seen Aidan throw purple bolts, and Tethra, the Fomori god of the sea, shoot blue, but the red was somehow even more terrifying.

Just your imagination. Patrick glanced in the mirror. He looked tired and pale. Like Mrs. Knox, who was so ashen she was like a red-headed ghost haunting his hallways, offering samples of wedding invitations for his approval, or menus for a wedding supper that changed every day. *"I've decided against the salmon, Patrick. Do you mind? I'd thought duck instead...."*

Plans for a wedding that seemed less likely every hour, given that the bride was compelled to love another and destined to die if he didn't find another spell. Though of course he couldn't say that. Mrs. Knox knew the stories, but she didn't believe them, and he had no stomach for forcing her to see the truth.

What was worse was Grace's grandmother. Her coma had deepened. They could no longer get her to swallow anything. *"I think it's time to let her die, Mr. Devlin,"* the nurse had told him, and Mama had said the same. *"It would be a mercy, Patrick. I'm certain Maeve will come to see it too. And Grace, when she returns."*

But he couldn't agree. He had to keep Grace's mother well and her grandmother alive until Grace came home. *If she comes home.*

He pushed the thought aside and dressed. He was halfway down the stairs when the old tapestries on the walls shivered and grew bright—no longer threadbare relics. He smelled smoke; from the courtyard came the clanging of swords. Patrick gripped the railing hard, lightheaded, waiting for the hallucination to pass. Instead, he saw Aidan at the bottom of the stairs, as ghostly as his mother—no, more so. Truly an apparition. *A summons*, Patrick realized. *From where? How?*

I hate this.

Patrick hurried down the stairs to the back door, weaving through the busy servants and surprised cook in the kitchen out into the garden.

"I need some air," he said to the Fomori guard. Patrick pushed aside the trailing, thorned vines of the climbing rose twining over the trellis gate, which hid the park from view. He crossed the square to the gazebo.

There, just as he'd expected, was Aidan.

Patrick stepped into the gazebo. "You can't just send a note like other people?"

"This is easier."

"Why are you here?"

Aidan leaned back against the bench. "Two reasons. Well, actually three. We got your message about keeping Grace away from the city. I want to know why you sent it. Is there something new?"

"I was worried, but now I think I may have been mistaken."

"Mistaken about what?"

"The riot—that boy who tried to kill you?"

Aidan frowned. "What about it?"

"I'd ordered the Fomori to leave you unharmed, and I thought they were betraying me. But I was wrong. That is, it *was* the Fomori, but only Miogach, who thought he was protecting me."

"I see," said Aidan slowly.

"I didn't want Grace in the city until I'd figured things out. But I've changed my mind. I feel . . . danger. I'm worried. So please . . . bring her back."

"We can't. Grace has disappeared."

Patrick realized he'd known it already. This was what his dream had been telling him. "How?"

"Derry left her—safe, he thought—so he could help rescue Oscar. But when he went back for her, she was gone. He thinks she was taken, because she wouldn't have left him."

"Grace has a mind of her own."

Aidan said gently, "He's used the lovespot, Patrick."

Patrick had known this too. Oscar had already said it, and there was no reason not to believe it true. None but a foolish hope.

But the spell would fade. Patrick thought of his sister, Lucy, whom Diarmid had also bespelled as a way to get close to Patrick. Her love was turning to anger—slowly, but it *was* turning.

"I hope it doesn't change how you feel about Grace—"

"It doesn't. I love her. I know she loves me too. What she feels for Diarmid is a lie, and she *will* return to me." Patrick had to believe it, or he would go mad.

"I'm glad to hear that. Because you're right, she's in danger. We've been . . . connected. Strange, I know, but until recently, I've been able to hear her. I feel her."

Another thing that didn't surprise him. "Until recently?"

"I can't feel her anymore. It's nothing but confusion in my head usually. My grandmother's visions and my own and all these things I can't possibly know—God, it's a nightmare most of the time. But Grace was clear. Until she wasn't."

Again, Patrick felt the niggling sense of wrongness: Aidan
had more power than he should, and Grace had less. But . . .
there was the Fianna's conviction, and Simon's: goddess power.
"Simon MacRonan thinks as the Fianna do about Grace's
power. But he saw something else too. The Otherworld. Not
death, though."

"No, it isn't death," Aidan agreed. "I felt it too. Whatever
it means, it's where she is. I felt her fear, and then she was just
. . . gone. We need to find her quickly. Derry thinks the *sidhe*
have something to do with her disappearance."

Patrick said, "The Fomori believe she's lost in time. A
sidhe glamour, perhaps."

"That makes sense. She made a bargain with the river
pirate queen. No one knows what it was."

The strongest fairy the Fomori had felt in centuries, Patrick
remembered. "But Grace knows what the *sidhe* can do to her."

"You know Grace. Once she's set on something . . ." Aidan
shrugged.

Unfortunately true. It made his job so much harder, and
had for years. *His job? Years?* Patrick pushed away his confusion. He paused before he said, "Aidan, your grandmother's
worse. I don't know how much longer we can keep her alive.
And your mother . . . her worry over you and Grace is eating
her alive."

Aidan's expression shuttered. "Mama's stronger than you
think."

"She's barely eating—"

"She's stronger than you think," Aidan repeated. He glanced toward a man walking his dog at the edge of the square. People were beginning to appear on the paths. "There's one more reason I'm here. Grace and Derry found an ogham stick with a prophecy that echoes my grandmother's words. You're the expert in ogham and Celtic relics."

"Was it on wood or stone or bark?"

"Wood."

"What did it say?"

"'The sea is the knife. Great stones crack and split. Storms will tell and the world is changed. The rivers guard treasures with no worth. To harm and to protect become as one, and all things will only be known in pieces.'"

To harm and to protect become as one.

Those words sounded familiar . . . or no, they *felt* familiar. As if he *should* know them. But he'd never heard them before, had he?

Aidan said, "I don't know what any of it means, but it's important. I've been trying to figure it out. Before Grace disappeared, she understood at least part of it. Does it make any sense to you?"

Patrick felt as if things were rushing past him, things he should be grasping. "I don't know. Perhaps."

Aidan rose, glancing about. "I've got to go. Let me know if you discover anything."

"How am I to do that?"

"There's a telegraph pole on the corner of Eighth Street and Fifth Avenue. Leave a message there. Just pin it up. Someone will get me word."

The telegraph poles were always covered with broadsheets and advertisements. No one would notice another.

Aidan started down the steps. "Take care, Patrick."

"Wait. Do you know anyone who casts red lightning?"

"Red?" Aidan shook his head. "No, why?"

"Nothing. Just a dream I had."

But Patrick's mind was spinning as Aidan left. His dream. Danger and confusion. The lovespot. Grace's connection with her brother. Triune power and his own doubts.

Patrick hurried to his study and stared down at the amulets and bowls and statuettes in the glass cases. Many of these things his father had collected. Some of them had been in his family for generations. A Druid egg—a crystal the size of an apple, clear as spring water. Amulets of quartz in blues and greens. A silver torc and bronze shield, a silver goblet. He was more aware than ever of what was missing: the ogham stick that helped the Brotherhood call the Fomori. Diarmid had stolen it, and Patrick had not seen it since, and though he had no more need of it, the collection felt incomplete without it.

Acting on a whim, Patrick opened the first case and passed his hand over each of the items inside. He couldn't say what he was searching for. He went to the second case and did the same thing. By the time he got to the third, he was feeling foolish. There was nothing in that amulet or that statuette. Not in that plate or that bowl—

He stopped as a vision flashed before his eyes. A bowl like this one, steaming in a room filled with smoke. Delicate hands holding it out to him.

The bowl wasn't particularly beautiful. It was small and of bronze, cast with wrens. He couldn't remember its story, nor if it even had one. It was very early Celtic and probably once belonged to a Druid who used it to drink potions that brought visions. Patrick reached for it. The moment he touched it, it stung him—only static electricity—but when he curled his fingers around the bowl, it seemed to hum in his hand. He had to be imagining this, but it felt so familiar. He knew every line, every dent in the bronze, though his father had done the cataloging for this piece. Patrick couldn't remember ever touching it before.

As he stood there, bemused and marveling, his dream returned and settled deep, the branches like a cage above his head, mistletoe dangling, and red lightning scorching the air.

EIGHT

The first morning (sidhe *time*)
Grace

You know who I am," I said to Iobhar. "And so you must know what I have to do."

He waved my words away. "Prophecies are tiresome. 'Tis as if you Druids meant to torment the whole world."

"The oldest magic is that of blood and sacrifice," said Roddy, pulling a chair from a pile without seeming to dislodge anything else, like a massive game of pick-up sticks. He sat. "We Druids did not invent it. We only use it."

"So you've said, but it matters little. 'Tis the problem with mortals, your insistence on absolutes." Iobhar fingered the bells around his neck.

Their music crept into my head; when I looked at him, he smiled as if he knew its temptation.

"Who is more worthy? The Fianna or the Fomori? I can think of nothing less important than a question of worth. Arrogance and pride sometimes bring the best of changes, and good intentions often bring the worst." Iobhar gestured to the animals. "Take my friends here—all of them lead a better existence now, though my intentions in changing them were anything but"—Iobhar gave me a wicked smile—"good."

"You *changed* them? You mean—?"

Iobhar pointed to the dog. "Cuan was a man who tried to cheat me. He's become quite loyal. As for the stag . . . ah, let me think . . . oh yes, Stag was a sailor. Very drunk and unwilling to listen to reason. But he was a handsome enough lad that it seemed a pity to make him something less noble."

In horror, I asked, "And the boar?"

"The boar was . . . well, a bore. A thief I did some fencing for who didn't know when to be quiet. Still a fault, isn't it, Torcan?" Iobhar shrugged. "There were others. I had some stuffed when they died, because I grew to like them. They're around here and there. Perhaps you've seen them?"

The cats and the lizards and the birds on the staircase. Those creepy eyes. I shuddered. "What makes you think they like this existence better?"

"They eat, don't they? And I'd allow no one to hurt them."

"They can't talk—"

"Thankfully."

"Or . . . or leave—"

"They can leave if they like. But why would they? Stag wouldn't last a day on the streets. Torcan either. Perhaps the dog would do better—people here seem not to eat dog meat."

I felt sick.

Iobhar went on, "Two of them would have been hanged by now; 'twas their nature and unlikely to change. The sailor—perhaps shanghaied. Or buried at sea. Or dead of drunkenness or disease in a foreign port."

"It would be their choice at least. You've taken away their free will."

"Free will is important to you?" he asked.

"Of course. It is to anyone."

The feathers on Iobhar's shoulders ruffled as if in a breeze. I smelled that Druid perfume. Again, he fingered those bells around his neck. I took two steps toward him before I realized what I was doing.

He said, "What free will have you? Your pretty little life was only a prison. Bound by what others told you must be done. By *oughts* and *shoulds*. And then, the moment you escape it, what do you do? You bind yourself with love and lies and promises. You think so small, *veleda*, like any mortal. You disappoint me."

I felt the truth of his accusations. "But I've come here to learn. To be trained. To change my fate."

The sound of rushing footsteps. Sarnat raced into the room, a pile of books tumbling to the floor in her wake. "*Veleda!* You're all right?"

"Yes, I'm fine. Where have you been?"

"Trying to find my way through this confusion." Her light eyes blazed. She pointed at Iobhar. "You will let us go at once."

Iobhar leaned against the counter and said to Roddy, "You see now why I prefer to live away from my own kind?"

"I thought 'twas out of fear of competition," said Roddy.

"Sheathe your claws, little girl," Iobhar said languidly. "She's chosen to stay."

Sarnat looked at me, and I nodded. "For now. He's the archdruid."

"Archdruid? He's nothing of the kind. He's fooled you, milady. We've heard tales of strange things happening here, but we've never sensed any power at all."

"You can't sense it because it's *in* me," Iobhar explained. "And I'm one of you."

Sarnat advanced on him. "I don't know what you've told her, or what glamour—"

A jagged fork of red lightning shot from his hand, cracking at her feet, raising smoke and sparks. Sarnat jumped back with a gasp.

"She's said she wants to stay," Iobhar said. "But you can go."

"I'm to stay with her."

"Unless you want her incinerated, *veleda*, I suggest you ask her to keep her distance," Iobhar said.

"Leave him be, Sarnat," I said.

"Very well. *For now*. But if I see he means to hurt you—"

"Such devotion you inspire, *veleda*," Iobhar said. "What a force you would have been once. Armies dashing toward death for you. Fianna raising spears and swords."

"That isn't what I want," I said.

"Perhaps you should want it. The things I could teach you . . ." He fingered those bells. The music chimed seductively in my head. "An archdruid and a *veleda*. Think of it. We could rule the world, you and I."

I saw armies charging, spears raised, the Morrigan's three aspects—Macha, Nemain, and Badb—inciting frenzy and hatred, ravens screaming, and the clash of swords. As in my dreams, lightning flashing purple and red. Cyclone winds and thunder so loud it was as if the earth roared. I saw myself standing in a giant hall, clad in red, Patrick beside me in a white tunic, and Diarmid bowing as he laid his bloodied spear at my feet, while Iobhar smiled from the throne we shared.

And then . . . the vision wavered. Again, I heard the bells, that lovely temptation, but now there was a discordant note within it, a minor key, singing gloom and sorrow. The vision melted away. The dream was the past, and the past must stay the past.

I met Iobhar's challenging gaze. "Tell me how I can change my fate. Tell me how to change the prophecy and the *geis*."

Iobhar tilted his head as if in thought. My hope rose, stark and painful. Whatever he said next would change everything. My whole future—everything I wanted.

"The prophecy is already in motion, as is the *geis*. There is no changing it. The *veleda* must die, and Diarmid Ua Duibhne must kill her or die himself and send the Fianna into the void. There is no other way. This will be done. This is the word that was spoken."

Only Sarnat's quick hand on my arm kept me from sinking to my knees.

"No." My voice sounded far away. "No. Please."

"The veil between worlds will open on Samhain," Iobhar went on ruthlessly. "And the sacrifice will release your power to your choice. There is no other spell, *veleda*. Your people did their work well. 'Tis your fate. And that of your lover."

"But fate is ever-changing, isn't that true? And I can change this. I have to change it."

"The cycle is already half-done, *veleda*. What you must do now is complete it. If you do not, the world will end in chaos. Not that it matters to me, particularly."

I heard the power of the truth in his words. "Did the Fomori lie to me? Did they know there was no other way?"

Iobhar shrugged. "Is hope a lie? Blame your ancestors, and not the old gods and warriors, who are as bound as you are. Your people knew what they deeded you, and they cared nothing of the price you would pay. 'Twas more important to them to have the last word. They could not resist making the Fianna feel their power, as needless as it was. All men eventually pay for the consequences of their deeds. The Fianna would have learned their lesson at the hands of those who despised them. 'Twas what they deserved. No more than that. And no less."

"And so I have to die."

Iobhar came to me, his amber eyes glittering. "'Tis a hard thing for a mortal lass. I could help you, if you wish."

"Help me? How?"

Sarnat's hand tightened on my arm.

I pulled away. Iobhar's music made it hard to think. He leaned close, whispering, "Let me drink you up, *veleda*. None of this will matter if your power is gone. Your Diarmid will be relieved of his task and his pain. The Fianna do not belong in this world. Let them die."

A kiss and it would be done. A long drink of power, and I would be relieved of my choice, and I would be free.

Oh, it was tempting. I found myself lifting my hand, reaching to touch him—

A bad chord intruded, corrupting his music. I heard the wrongness of it. I saw the Fianna disappearing, crumbling to dust. I saw Diarmid calling to me. I saw myself, eyes blank, as drained and mad as the Druid we'd met at Coney Island.

"No," I said. "No, not that."

The bones in Iobhar's face took on harder edges. "Then you will indeed die."

Bright sunshine slanted through the large front windows, the bustle of life that had nothing to do with Druids and spells. Except it did, didn't it? Stories told us how to survive a complicated world, how to know right from wrong, good from evil. Stories said that what we did mattered.

Patrick was willing to sacrifice his life for Ireland. Diarmid had pledged himself to the Fianna, to a service bigger than himself. I could choose to run. I could surrender to Iobhar and turn myself into a madwoman, let the Fianna die, and chaos rule. Or I could make a difference in the world.

I took a deep breath. "Train me, then. Teach me the incantation. Teach me what I need to know."

Iobhar cocked a brow. "Are you certain, *veleda*?"

"I'm certain," I said.

August 22
Diarmid

Diarmid had been in every warehouse and two-cent stale-beer dive and saloon on the waterfront, every shop and restaurant. He'd spoken to sailors and stevedores, gang boys and thieves. His face was still plastered everywhere, and he risked that someone would recognize him, but it would be worth it if he found news of Grace.

Battle Annie and her *sidhe* were nowhere—no one had seen them or heard from them. The other river gangs only said things like, "Try Brooklyn," or "Ain't seen 'em in months, and good riddance."

But Brooklyn had already been tried; Keenan and Goll were over there every day. They were growing desperate. It had been almost a month since she'd disappeared.

He turned down an alley he'd already haunted a dozen times, because at the end of it was a ten-pin bowling alley the gang boys liked. It was twilight, the change of worlds, when the *sidhe* were most comfortable, though he hadn't seen any tonight. The crash of pins falling and scattering came from a tenement at the end of the street. He stepped aside just as a bowling ball thundered out the open door, slowing to a stop only a few yards behind him.

A boy chased after it, waving to Diarmid before retrieving the ball and lugging it clumsily back. "Hiya, Derry. Care to play?"

Diarmid shook his head. "Anyone new up there today?"

"Nope. No one."

Diarmid rubbed his eyes, trying to banish his exhaustion and disappointment.

Where is she?

He debated whether to stay out tonight, as he had the last two, searching for her in the darkness along the riverfront. The discontent and violence grew worse with every passing day, but he preferred it to being in the basement flat with the others. Preferred it to Finn's watchfulness and his own anxiety and Aidan's hostile gaze.

Yet he needed sleep. His exhaustion was starting to win out over his good sense. He was on edge, as willing to start a fight as to avoid one. Better to go home, to rest.

He slipped into one alley, through a crowded dive, and out a cardboard-covered back door. At the street, he paused, looking for policemen.

Instead, he saw Aidan.

Diarmid drew back into the shadows, wondering why, even as he did so. He should be doing exactly the opposite. Aidan was alone, which he shouldn't be. He was too valuable.

Finn had asked Aidan to keep one of them with him at all times.

Grace's brother looked jumpy. It was obvious he didn't want to be seen. Who was he hiding from? The *sidhe*? Or the Fomori?

Or the Fianna?

Diarmid wanted to find out, and Aidan needed protection, so he stepped from his hiding place. He went up behind Aidan, clapping him on the back. Aidan started so badly, he stumbled.

"Damn, Derry, you frightened me."

"You should be more careful. I snuck up on you easily. I thought Finn told you not to go out without a guard. The *sidhe* are everywhere."

"I haven't seen a single one tonight. Anyway, I can protect myself." Aidan split the walk with a thin bolt of lightning.

"The *sidhe* are quick. They'd be on you before you knew it."

"I don't want a guard."

"'Tisn't your decision to make."

"I'm not like you. I'm no slave to Finn's whims. The rest of you won't make a move without his approval."

"He's our captain."

"And he's right about everything, is that it?"

"No, but questioning him makes us vulnerable. We have to act together."

"As one. Indivisible." Aidan laughed sarcastically. "Even when he asks you to do something you know is wrong?"

Where is this going? "I've vowed to follow him."

"So when he tells you to let him seduce my sister, whom you claim to love, and then he orders you to put a knife to her throat, you'll do it?"

Diarmid's heart clenched. "'Tisn't that simple."

"What happens if you don't do what Finn wants?" Aidan stopped, turning to face him. "Death? But you've died before, haven't you? Was it so terrible that you're still afraid of it?"

Tell me how it feels to die.

"I'm not afraid of death," Diarmid said. "But I don't want to die for nothing. I'm *Fianna*, Aidan. D'you know what that means? I've vowed to serve the Irish, to protect them with my life if I have to."

"A vow that was easy to put aside once, wasn't it?"

"I never put it aside. I just forgot what it meant. We all did. And that was a long time ago. We've changed."

"Have you?" Aidan asked scornfully. "I've heard the tales, you know. How beloved the Fianna were. Exalted. Gods, even. But you were corrupted by tributes and women. You're just as arrogant and ruthless as the tales tell. All of you."

It shouldn't have stung, but it did. "If that's what you think, why have you joined us?"

"When I was a boy, I wanted to be one of the Fianna too. I believed in things like blind loyalty."

"You didn't answer my question," Diarmid insisted. "Why choose us now? Why not fight for the Fomori if you think we're arrogant and blind?"

"Because I can see a future with the Fianna," Aidan said. "Ireland . . . I couldn't care less about it. Ireland's done, but this is my city, and *here* we can find a place for ourselves. These gang boys have been searching for something to believe in, and the Fianna have given them that. I want to help. But I won't follow blindly. And you haven't always. You went against Finn once before for the love of a girl."

"It was a mistake," Diarmid said. "I was compelled. There was a *geis*."

"You're saying you had no free will? That you don't have it now?"

"I'm bound. You know it as well as I."

"But you broke those bindings once. You defied Finn."

"And I'll regret it every day of my life. It tore the Fianna apart. The only thing I'd ever really wanted to be part of. I'd thought the Fianna could never be divided, but I managed to do it. *Me.* I did what no one else had ever done, what no one ever thought *could* be done." Diarmid didn't try to hide his misery. "Finn was everything to me, and I let a lass come between us and all I cared about. So don't tell me I should be defying him for love. I won't tear apart the Fianna again. I can't."

"So it's redemption you're looking for?" Aidan's blue eyes were electric. "Perhaps Finn will forgive you at last, but how will you forgive yourself? Or was it a lie when you told me you loved Grace?"

"'Tis no lie," Diarmid said.

"Then I hope your honor will be comfort enough when she's dead."

Diarmid said hopelessly, "You don't understand."

"I understand that you'll kill her to win Finn's favor, even if you love her. I suppose you believe in her goddess power, too, and what it can bring you—"

"By the gods, I don't care about her power!" Diarmid erupted. "I'd give anything to keep her alive, can't you see that? I'd sacrifice myself to save her. But it isn't just me. Other lives depend on this." He felt such grief and regret and sorrow, he could hardly say the rest. "She asked me once to change the world for her. I've tried. I'm *trying*. The archdruid is the only hope I have."

"Another spell, you mean," Aidan said quietly. "Do you think there is one?"

"No. But 'tis the only thing I can think to do."

Aidan reached into his pocket, taking out the ogham stick.

"Does Finn know you have that?" Diarmid asked.

"He gave it to me. It belongs to my family, after all. I think the prophecy written on it has something to do with all this. I'm trying to figure out what Grace understood about it. I think if I can decipher it, I'll know where she's gone."

"She hasn't *gone* anywhere," Diarmid said. "She was taken. She wouldn't have left me."

Aidan looked at him thoughtfully. "You were really raised by the god of love, Aengus Og?"

"Aye."

"I'd expect you to know more about love, then. Or perhaps it's simply Grace you don't know."

"I feel like I've known her the whole of my life," Diarmid said.

"But I *have* known her nearly the whole of mine. And I think you're wrong. No one took her. She set off on her own to look for the archdruid. But what she found . . . I don't know." He paused. "Do you remember that night you came upon me in the gambling hell?"

"Aye."

"You saved my life that night, though you didn't know it," Aidan said. "And then Finn saved it doubly when he saw what I was. I'm grateful to both of you. More than I can say."

Diarmid hadn't known that. It made him vaguely uncomfortable. "Why are you telling me this now?"

"Because as grateful as I am, I'm not willing to follow a debt into hell—unlike you. It doesn't matter what I owe you; I won't trust you until you earn it. So I want you to know: I'm going to find my sister, and when I do, I'll keep her safe, whatever it takes. Whoever I have to call upon."

"What does that mean?" Diarmid asked.

Aidan's expression hardened. "Just remember it. You do what you feel you must. So will I, and hope to God we agree."

TEN

The first week (sidhe *time)*
Grace

I don't understand how this is teaching me anything." I stared down at the game board, set with gold- and bronze-colored pieces, on the table between us.

Iobhar moved one of his pieces to block mine. "Fidchell is wooden wisdom, *veleda*."

"It's wasting time." I moved my piece. He blocked it again. "Shouldn't I be learning spells or something? I only have a few—" I couldn't say the word. I didn't even want to think it.

"Days?" Iobhar provided with a cruel little smile.

My stomach dropped. "I was going to say weeks."

"A week, a day, a year, a century. What does time matter?"

"I suppose it doesn't to an immortal."

Roddy glanced up. He was sitting at the counter, dusting each piece of jewelry in the glass case. "Most Druid teaching takes . . . what was it I told you?"

"Fifteen to twenty years," Iobhar said.

"Years?" I asked in disbelief. "I don't have years."

Iobhar moved a piece, neatly surrounding my *banán*, the king piece whose escape was the entire goal of the game.

Sarnat rolled a ball for Cuan, who chased it and brought it back, tail wagging. I said to Iobhar in a low voice, "Do you suppose he really enjoys that?"

"He's been a dog for some time. And he was never clever to begin with. Your move."

"I don't want to play. I want to learn. Spells and incantations, whatever it is I'm supposed to know."

"You're supposed to know fidchell."

"You beat me every time."

"We could go on to divination, if you like. We'll begin with animal entrails. Those of a dog are easy, and we've one here, so . . ."

I looked at him in horror. "You couldn't mean to kill Cuan!"

He shrugged.

I glanced at Sarnat, who mouthed: *Let's leave this place.* I shook my head and turned back to the game. I shoved a piece to a square that looked good. There was no rhyme or reason to the one I chose; the game was nearly a mystery to me.

Iobhar sighed. "I begin to despair of you, *veleda*. How can you not know what to do?"

"I've only just discovered I *am* the *veleda*. Until a few days ago, I'd hoped . . . I'd thought . . ." I trailed off, not knowing what to say.

"That you were just a lass with a strange power that meant nothing?" Iobhar leaned over the table, those eyes golden with intensity. "Play the game as a *veleda* born and bred, not as a fearful commoner."

I looked down at the board, trying to find the escape route, the right strategy. He had already left me with nowhere to go.

He mocked, "You try to *think* it out. *Listen*."

I tried. But all I heard was his music, that tempting melody. I blocked it and moved a piece.

Iobhar said, "You've lost."

"I hate this game!"

"Set it up again."

I rose. "No. Let's move on to something else. I haven't the time for this. I don't have fifteen years."

"If you fail this, you'll fail the rest."

I sagged back into the chair. "I didn't expect it to be so hard. Or so stupid."

"You rely on your mind and your eyes, the senses most easily deceived. 'Tis your power you must harness, and that doesn't come from the mind, but from here—" He tapped his heart.

"You make it sound easy."

"Nothing worth doing is easy," he said contemptuously. "How disappointed your ancestors would be. A long line of powerful priestesses ending in *you*. The great Neasa seeding nothing but a shallow-rooted weed."

I pushed aside the board so that the pieces scattered. "If that's what you think, why are you bothering with me? Why not just drink my power and be done with it?"

Sarnat said, "Milady—"

"Perhaps I will yet," Iobhar said. "It seems you're worth little more than one or two days of feasting. You *are* nothing."

I glared at him. "How am I nothing if the fate of the Irish hangs on my choice?"

Iobhar's gaze was so cold I shivered. "You are nothing *to me*. These are mortal affairs, and I care little for them. I'm doing you a favor, *veleda*—don't forget it. I would drain your power in a moment if I tired of you."

Roddy stiffened, and Sarnat threw me a warning look. Iobhar's threat raised the hair on the back of my neck. I swallowed hard.

He rose. "Come with me. Not your watchdog, just you."

"Where to?"

"Another test," Iobhar said. "And do not fail this one."

He took me to an empty room—that there even *was* an empty room in this place was shocking. It was small, with no window. He asked me:

"What is blacker than a raven?"

"What is whiter than snow?"

"What is sharper than the sword?"

I guessed wrong each time, but he didn't seem angry, or even concerned. He only said, "He who holds must first have discovered. He who has discovered must first have sought. He who has sought must first have braved all impediments."

"Could you be more confusing?"

His eyes narrowed. "Sit on the floor."

I did. My palms were damp with sweat.

"Now you must find the breaking of time."

Perfect. "I'd been hoping for something easier. Like putting out the sun with my bare hands."

He didn't smile. "Think of nothing, *veleda*, and keep thinking of nothing until time and space fall away."

Then he left me.

With the door closed, and no window, the darkness was pressing, the silence unbearably loud. I clenched and unclenched my fists and tried to think of nothing. I listened for music, for my brother. I thought of my family and Patrick, the Fomori and the Fianna, but it was as if a wall had been put up between me and the rest of the world. I closed my eyes, imagining Diarmid's touch, his kiss. The *geis.* Suddenly it was all I could think of.

I was going to die.

I rushed to the door. I couldn't find it. I ran my hands up the wall, as far as I could reach and then down to the floor. No door. Not on this wall, nor the next, nor the next. I was trapped. My own gasping breath filled my ears. I felt a kiss on my lips, another at my jaw, a hand tangling in my hair, holding me still, and then I saw the flash of a knife. Searing pain and blood gushing hot. My death. The dream I'd had so long ago.

I am going to die.

All the things I would be leaving behind: Mama's hand on my forehead smoothing my hair from my face. My grandmother's dark eyes brightening as she told my favorite stories. Aidan holding me tightly, promising never to betray me.

Stroking the silver chasing on the *dord fiann,* Finn's hunting horn, as I dreamed of faraway lands and battles and white knights. Kissing Patrick.

Diarmid.

Diarmid.

I sank to my knees. *The mirror crack'd from side to side . . . "I am half sick of shadows," said the Lady of Shalott.* I remembered telling the story to the fairy Deirdre and her followers in a Brooklyn warehouse. When I'd told them that the Lady of Shalott chose death over living life through a mirror, Deirdre had asked: *"Do you think she regretted her choice?"*

"No," I'd said.

No.

I lifted my head from my hands and stared into the darkness. I'd always felt as if I'd been meant for something special, something that belonged just to me. I'd longed for romance and adventure, and now legends had come alive before my eyes. Finn and Ossian, Keenan and Conan and Goll. Oscar's white-blond hair shining in the sun in Battery Park, his teasing smile. Miogach's sympathetic gray eyes and his reassurances, Lot's startling beauty, and Daire Donn laughing over something Patrick had said, and then the way Patrick had turned to me with love in his eyes, the kind of love I'd never thought to see.

I remembered lying in Diarmid's arms and telling him I could never regret what had happened between us, because loving him was part of me.

"There's only going forward."

These things would never have been mine without the prophecy that meant my death now. Not the Fianna nor the Fomori, not adventure and romance. Not love.

If I could go back, would I choose to give them up? How could I? How could I regret the very thing that had given me what I'd most desired? A song was made of many notes— without the melancholy, there would be nothing to measure the sweetness.

What is blacker than a raven?
Death.
What is whiter than snow?
Truth.
What is sharper than the sword?
Understanding.

My fear disappeared, and in its place came a beautiful, peaceful calm, an acceptance that dried my tears. I was going to die, and it would be all right. It would be as it should be.

I settled into the darkness, which was clear and bright as the moonlight that had once called me to follow it.

Time and space fell away.

ELEVEN

September 30
Patrick

The sea is the knife. Great stones crack and split. Storms will tell and the world is changed. The rivers guard treasures with no worth. To harm and to protect become as one, and all things will only be known in pieces.

The words whispered in Patrick's ear during the day; at night, he heard them murmured through the smoke of oracle fires. Familiar and not. Obscure and yet somehow . . . not. He thought of them whenever he looked at the bronze bowl on his dresser. The bowl was connected to the words. He knew it, though not why or how.

It was only one of many mysteries. It had been two months since Grace had disappeared, and there was still no sign of her. They all felt the strain of passing time. Now Patrick stood in the basement of the clubhouse, staring at four insolent *sidhe*. Three boys and a girl, all strikingly beautiful.

Miogach was saying, "'Tis only information we seek, nothing more. You have never before cared for the troubles of mortals, why do you insist on taking a side now?"

"We've taken no side," said one of the boys. "We know nothing."

"You know nothing of any archdruid?"

They were silent.

"We know there's one in the city."

"Then follow your own clues," said another boy. "Why torment us?"

"Have you felt a *veleda*?" interjected Patrick.

The girl frowned. "We have. But no longer. She is gone."

Patrick struggled to hide his fear. "Where's Battle Annie?"

"She has never been our concern," said one of the boys. "We don't serve the river queen."

Miogach let out his breath in frustration. "By the gods, I'd like to cut your throats."

"We feel Druids all over the city," said the girl. "Some with more power than others. You have one here now. Let us speak with him. We'll tell him what we know."

She spoke of Simon MacRonan, Patrick knew, who was upstairs. But it was too dangerous to let the *sidhe* near any Druid.

"They know nothing, 'tis clear," said Miogach wearily.

Patrick agreed. "Let them go."

Then he went home. He felt useless. There must be *some* news of Grace. If only he could think a little harder, be a little smarter . . . It was up to him to find her—he was the only one who could.

Patrick wasn't certain why he believed that. But he knew, absolutely, that it was true.

————— ✥ *That evening* ✥ —————

He stared out the French doors into the twilight garden while his mother and Lucy and Mrs. Knox discussed wedding decorations. The roses were nearly gone now. He remembered Grace standing among them the first time he'd kissed her; and so when Mrs. Knox said, "Lot and I thought lilies," he said, "Roses. Please. Not red ones. Yellow and pink."

They stared at him. He'd been silent for so long, he supposed they'd forgotten he was in the room.

Lucy asked, "Has there been any word?"

He shook his head.

"Why haven't they arrested that gang boy?" Mama complained. "He must know something of her whereabouts. Why, he's the one who kidnapped her!"

Patrick heard what she didn't say—his mother believed Grace had run away and become a gang girl.

Mrs. Knox said, "Lot believes we will find her safe and well."

"They *should* arrest Derry," Lucy said angrily. "Why, I wish they'd hang him!"

"Have they searched the rivers?" Mama asked.

Mrs. Knox's hand went to her throat.

Patrick glared at his mother. "There's no reason to search the rivers. Grace isn't dead."

Lucy put in, "Everyone believes Derry's hiding her somewhere. Just yesterday, Liza McGowan said she wouldn't be surprised if they found Grace already with child in some tenement—"

"Lucy, please!" Mama said in horror.

"I'm just telling you what I've heard. I'm sorry, Mrs. Knox, but you know how people gossip."

Mrs. Knox said firmly, "Grace would never do such a thing. She would never throw away her future."

Unless she was under the spell of the ball seirce. But Patrick said only, "No, she wouldn't. And Lucy, you shouldn't be passing along such talk."

"Why *don't* they arrest him?" his mother asked. "What's wrong with the police in this city that they can't find a gang boy who's done such a terrible thing! There are posters everywhere! You can't tell me *no one's* seen him!"

Patrick said, "He belongs to a gang the immigrants think are heroes. They protect Finn's Warriors."

"They should rip Derry's heart out instead," Lucy said.

"My dear!"

"I'm sorry, Mama, but I can't help it. I hate him."

Which was better than grieving him. Lucy and their mother kept arguing. Mrs. Knox rose restlessly. She came up beside Patrick, staring at him as if she were seeing him for the

first time. Her eyes looked odd—blue darkening to indigo—
and distant.

Patrick frowned as she grabbed his arm. "Mrs. Knox?"

She clutched him, nails digging through his sleeve, and
whispered, *"Eubages, brithem, vater."*

"What? What did you say?" Patrick asked.

She blinked at him. "Why aren't you with her?" she asked
in confusion. "You should not have abandoned her." Then her
eyes rolled back in her head. *"Éicse."*

He caught her just before she hit the floor.

The second week (sidhe *time)*
Grace

C hest!" Sarnat shouted.

I shoved my elbow into the boy's chest. He gasped.

Sarnat ordered, "Foot!"

I stomped on his instep.

"Nose!"

I spun, shoving my hand into his nose. The boy yelped and went down, disappearing, the glamour evaporating like smoke.

I turned to Sarnat. "Well?"

"At least you're no longer helpless." It was the most praise I was likely to get from her. She'd been teaching me defensive moves in the afternoons, when Iobhar was busy with the shop. Today was the first time I'd managed to bring my opponent to his knees.

Roddy appeared in the doorway. "Iobhar's ready for you now."

Sarnat said, "You'd do better to train with me than with that mountebank."

"He's no mountebank."

"He's no archdruid either. Just a boastful fairy. I don't sense Druid power anywhere in him."

"But I do," I said, hearing the archdruid's song mingling with Iobhar's bells. "He says you can't sense it because he's *sidhe* too."

"Or perhaps he's teaching you nonsense. How would you know?"

I didn't try to explain how I knew I was supposed to be here, that this was what I was meant for.

Iobhar was behind the counter, opening drawers, searching, muttering as he slammed one shut and then another.

"What are you looking for?" I asked.

"A Druid egg. 'Tis doubtful you would recognize one, but—"

"I know what they look like. Patrick had some. Crystals the size of an apple."

Iobhar nodded. "Aye. Go see if 'tis in the study."

I sighed and gestured for Sarnat to come with me. "If I'm not back in a year, send someone for my body. Though you might not find me in that mess."

Iobhar said, "Leave your warrior here, even though every moment in her company tempts me to turn her into a cat."

She glared at him. "Searching for a Druid egg would be more interesting than listening to your riddles. Milady, you're not his servant. Let him find his stupid egg himself."

"I need it for the next lesson," Iobhar said.

I resigned myself to a pointless search and went through the narrow, dark corridor to the stairs. I'd grown used to the way the shop seemed to expand or contract depending upon the task Iobhar set for me, but the chaotic mess of it never changed.

Iobhar's study was on the second floor. Inside were globes and amulets, maps and books, skeletons of tiny, fragile birds and lizards, skulls of sheep and cows and horses and two human ones as well. His raven-feathered capelet, tossed over a chair, ruffled as I came in, releasing his strange Druid-*sidhe* scent, and I shuddered.

I began my search for the Druid egg. It was unlike Iobhar to send me looking for such a thing. As he said often, *"I can make a world just by thinking it."* Why not just create a new crystal? This one must be very important.

I heard a low growl behind me. "It's all right, Cuan," I said without turning around. "He knows I'm here."

The growl again. I looked over my shoulder. There was no Cuan. Nothing at all.

The growl was louder, threatening, in front of me. I jerked around. No dog. I heard it again, more than one dog now, filling my ears and echoing in the beams. A cloudy presence whirled and pulsed in the corner, spinning faster and faster, and then it coalesced into red, glowing eyes and teeth sharp as razors, dripping saliva. Long snouts and bristling fur.

The hounds of Slieve Lougher.

In terror, I spun and ran from the study. They were right behind, snapping at my heels, howling and snarling. I raced for the stairs, but the stairs had disappeared; there was only darkness before me, and the hounds of hell were nearly on me. There was nowhere else to run. I plunged into the darkness.

Into a cave.

I stumbled, gasping hard. The hounds hadn't followed. The cave was soundless, but . . . *a cave?* It must be a glamour, an illusion, just as the hounds had obviously been. If I turned around, the hall would be behind me. *Just turn around.* But when I tried, there was only stone. I knew it wasn't real, but still I felt myself panic. *Don't. You'll fail the test.*

Before me, the cave opened, a low arch leading into a tunnel. I ducked through and followed it down and down and down, slipping on loose pebbles. From below came the roar of the sea, waves upon a rocky shore. The tunnel was short; in only a few yards, it opened into another, smaller cave, walls hewn by water, cupped and smooth. And then the walls shivered, the sandstone shifting, dissolving into rivers of sand that flowed to the floor and then gathered and shuddered, transforming into figures, into boys. Gang boys, one after another, their eyes glowing. They looked at me with a hunger I recognized, and I turned to run, but the tunnel had closed behind me. There was no going back. Only forward. Philosophy made real. The irony was not amusing.

"Hey, little girl." A singsong chant. Started by one, and then others joined in. *Hey, little girl, hey, little girl.* They drew around me as they had on the East River dock only a few nights before. My mouth went dry. Sarnat had trained me well, but I was no warrior. I might escape one or two, but twenty?

There was a light, another pathway opening beyond them. Escape. But to get there, I had to go through them.

I took a deep breath and launched myself into them, stabbing my fingers into the eyes of one, my elbow into the throat of another, kicking the groin of a third. I told myself they were only an illusion, but they felt as real as Sarnat's glamoured boys, grabbing at my hair, my arms, my clothes; scratching, biting, and twisting. I pummeled my way through, my skirts tangling about my legs and my corset biting into my ribs. They gave chase as I broke away and scrambled down another narrow tunnel, so low in some places, I was doubled over.

The walls shifted again, the tunnel making an abrupt turn, and unexpectedly, standing before me was Bridget, the woman who'd harbored me and Diarmid in Brooklyn. Her older daughter, Molly, lay still on the ground beside her. Her younger, Sara, wept.

I skidded to a stop, and as I did, the visions of the boys faded, and men—soldiers—took their place, lifting rifles with bayonets, running over grassy fields toward other soldiers in British uniforms, toward the Hill of Tara. Ireland. Irish men convulsed on the ground, groaning. The dead stared blindly at the sky. Others were bloated from hunger. So much desperation and fear. "We need the old gods," one of them said beseechingly to me, and I knew he meant the Fomori. "Choose them. They can help us."

Another grabbed my ankle, his fingers curling in a death grip. "Help us," he croaked. "Help us. Help us." The flesh melted from his hand, a skeletal manacle. Behind me, the shouts of the gang boys came loud and close. I jerked my foot loose, shattering the bones so they rolled chittering across the dirt. I raced on.

All around me, men and children were fighting and dying. Now the streets of New York City, a ragged militia, boys clutching at me with hot, sweaty fingers. "Help us! Give us heroes!" Their pleas tugged hard at me, but I kept running, into another chamber, thankfully empty and still.

I slowed. Someone stepped from a shadowed cranny. A giant of a man wearing an eye patch.

Balor. I didn't know whether to feel relief or fear. He lifted his eye patch, and a ray of light shot from his eye, a bolt of pure electricity splitting the ground just beside my foot. I jumped away, and he was gone, and there was Lot, blond and beautiful, a gown tied over one shoulder, one breast exposed to show a horrible mouth with black lips and rows and rows of gnashing, needlelike teeth. I stumbled back, and she held out her arms to me and said, "My darling, don't be afraid. We need you. We can save them if only you'll choose us." In her eyes, I saw rolling, verdant fields and men cheering in victory. I saw the flag of Britain lowered, and the harp and green of Ireland raised.

And then she disappeared, too, and there stood Finn holding knives dripping blood, and Oscar, his white-blond hair bright in the dim light. A boy with a slit throat lay at his feet.

"Don't be afraid," Finn said. "Believe in us. We can help them, if only you'll choose us." And in his eyes, I saw Bridget's children in clean new clothes, the Dun Rats in a schoolroom, men going to work, pride in their step.

None of this is real. Finn's hand was on my arm. Here was my childhood hero, the leader of the men I'd spent a lifetime dreaming of, and yet . . . "Come with us," he begged. "You know we are your destiny."

It took all of my strength to break free, to dash past him and Oscar into yet another dark tunnel. Voices filled the blackness. My best friend, Rose, plaintive and afraid, *Where are you, Grace? You should be here with me. Please come back.* Lucy Devlin's anxious pleas, *You belong with Patrick, Grace. You know you do.* My mother's voice. My brother's. My grandmother's. *Grace, come home. Grace, choose us. Choose us, choose us, choose us.*

I tore down the tunnel, racing around a corner, nearly barreling into a man who stepped in front of me.

Patrick.

He was haloed, his hair golden and his eyes so green. *Only an illusion*, but still, everything in me surged toward him. It had been forever since I'd looked into those eyes. He smiled and reached out his hand. "Choose me, Grace."

And then another stepped from the shadows. I knew before I turned who it was, and my heart set up this hammering beat. Dark haired. Blue eyed.

Diarmid.

He smiled; that long dimple in his cheek cut deeply. He held out his hand. "Choose me, Grace."

I could not move. I could not choose.

Footsteps pounded behind me, gang boys cursing, the hounds of Slieve Lougher growling. All around me were the cries of the Irish and the immigrants.

"I don't know," I whispered. "I haven't learned enough yet. I don't know—"

Patrick pulled a knife. And then Diarmid. Knives that flashed impossibly in the dark. An eerie chanting reverberated from the stone walls.

Both reached out to me, and I knew whoever touched me would kill me. I had to escape. I had to find the way out of this place. *No going back. Only forward.*

My instincts screamed to run. But where? Behind me waited everything I was running from. But to go forward . . . to face the grim certainty of death in the smiles before me . . .

We all have to wager. Faith or fear?

I felt paralyzed with indecision. I was failing. I'd learned more than this. I knew what I had to do. I just needed to have faith that I could do it.

I closed my eyes, listening until I heard the music of the world beyond, the true world. I let it fill me and surround me. When I opened my eyes again, Diarmid melted into the air like a shimmer on water, and then Patrick did the same. Footsteps behind me silenced; the growls turned to whines and then nothing. The cave walls drew back as if some giant were dragging them apart, and I was staring at a field, and great, vast pyramids of laced branches, three-sided and three-cornered, with seven windows in each. They were on fire, burning fiercely, flames snapping to the sky. The celebration of Samhain in an ancient world. The smoke filled my nose and stung my eyes.

The fires went out, one after another, leaving only darkness and mist undulating like a veil in a breeze. The veil between worlds. The air shuddered as the veil rippled and thinned. A faint silvery glow broke from the earth, and spirits of the dead rose like wisps of fog; and the world felt complete and connected, all part of the same song, just as Diarmid had once told me. The past and the present and the future all tangled together. The way the world really was, if only we could see it. The beginning was the end, and the end was the beginning. I felt power radiating from my fingertips. *This is where I belong. This is who I am. I want to know this. I want to know more.*

The song went silent, and then the darkness lifted to reveal the hall outside the study, the stairs.

I negotiated the jumbled path down to Iobhar.

I said, "The egg is in your hand," and he smiled and opened his palm to reveal the crystal globe.

"You sent her to look for it and you had it the whole time?" Sarnat asked in irritation.

"The end is the beginning, and the beginning is the end," I said.

Roddy smiled. He clapped his hands, slow and loud. *Clap clap clap.*

Iobhar's amber gaze came to me. "We'll start learning the spells tomorrow."

―∽― *The next day* (sidhe *time*) ―∽―

The spells were sacred. They were not written anywhere, but memorized and passed down through generations. Every word had to be intoned perfectly.

Iobhar cleared a place in the study and set a porcelain basin decorated with rosebuds on the floor. It filled with steaming water on its own.

"You must bathe in that without letting a single drop hit the floor. And you must do it neither naked nor clothed."

Impossible tasks. Again. I was beginning to think I was an idiot for expecting them to get easier. "How am I to do that?"

"'Tis not my task, but yours, *veleda*." He leaned against the wall and crossed his arms.

"You mean to just stand there and watch?" I asked.

"How else am I to judge if you've done it well?"

Not a drop on the floor. Neither naked nor clothed. Another riddle.

I glanced around, looking for a clue. Books and bones, globes and maps, Iobhar's raven capelet.

The feathers fluttered as if they sensed my intention. I took the capelet from the chair. Iobhar said nothing. I unhooked it, spreading it flat on the floor. The feathers shrugged in protest.

I took off my boots and my stockings, and stood barefoot on the feathers, which were stiff and slick.

"Might I have a cloth?"

It materialized in Iobhar's hand before I'd finished saying the words. He tossed it to me, and I caught it easily. Then I stared down at the steaming basin. *Neither naked nor clothed.*

I heard Diarmid's words from when we were searching for the *sidhe*: *"They like dawn and twilight—the change of worlds."* Neither day nor night, but both. *"The river's a good start. The edge of things."* Neither the shore nor the water, but both.

I unbuttoned my bodice and struggled out of my gown. I felt my cheeks grow hot as I took off the corset. Turning my back to Iobhar, I lowered one sleeve of my chemise, baring one shoulder, one breast. I felt Iobhar's unblinking watchfulness and knew my face was bright red with embarrassment, but I made myself concentrate. Carefully, I used the cloth to bathe one side naked, and then I wet my chemise until it was soaked to my skin, bathing my other side through it. Water dripped down my skirt, over my bare feet, pooling on the raven feathers, which fluffed and held the water close, not allowing it to touch the floor.

It took forever, but I washed one side naked, and the other clothed. When I was done, I set the cloth back into the basin and pulled up my chemise to cover myself again. Not that it mattered particularly—it was soaking wet and transparent. I turned to face Iobhar.

"Well?"

His expression gave nothing away. "Good enough."

In disappointment, I said, "Only good enough?"

"If 'tis compliments you're working for, you've failed already."

I went hot again, this time with humiliation. I *had* wanted to impress him.

"The gestures are as important to the spell as the song of it. Without them, the incantation will not work. This is a spell for the *eubages*, the Seer aspect of the *veleda*."

His movements were very deliberate. A hand posed just so, ending with a chop that passed into a kind of swerve, a dash across the hips. "Move as the sun rises and sets for good intentions"—he paced out a circle—"and the other direction for satire and curses."

I memorized everything. Every movement, from the slightest lift of a brow to the exact angle of a wave. Every Gaelic word he spoke—each one lilted or emphasized or whispered. In finishing school, I hadn't the talent for watercolors. French conjugations baffled me. I was an uncertain dancer. But these spells were like reading poetry, with its rhythms and deeper meanings. I had a talent for them, and I liked it. I wanted to keep learning forever.

"Good," Iobhar said, after I'd performed the spell to his satisfaction three times. "Go to your room and dream. And when you wake, tell me what comes to you."

I did as he asked. And what dreams came?

None.

I woke disoriented and confused. Not a single dream. Only deep sleep. But perhaps that was the point. I didn't yet trust myself to know. I went to tell Iobhar, and any hope I'd had faded when he frowned.

"No dream? But that's impossible. Think hard, *veleda*. Perhaps you don't remember."

"I only slept."

Iobhar's frown grew. "Then 'twas something done wrong. Show me the spell again."

I tried, but the spell had so completely left me, it was as if sleep had wiped the slate clean. Impatiently, Iobhar said, "Come now, *veleda*. We've little time. Show me the spell."

"I'm trying."

"Start again."

"I was so good at it, and now I can't remember it at all!"

"'Tis a spell that belongs to the *eubages*, which is in you. Reach deep for it. Again."

It was useless. Finally, Iobhar said, "We'll try again tonight."

So that evening I relearned it. Just as before, I knew it inside and out. Iobhar said with satisfaction, "You'll dream tonight."

But I didn't. And in the morning, I could no longer remember any part of the spell.

Iobhar said, "You're not trying hard enough."

My head ached with effort. "I *am* trying. Do you think I enjoy this? Are you certain it's the right spell?"

"Do you doubt me?" Iobhar asked softly.

Roddy said, "He's done it right, lass. Or at least it seems that way to me."

"But you wouldn't know, would you?" I challenged. "You can't remember what the right way is."

"I told you he was nothing," Sarnat said. "Why you should trust one such as him, I don't know."

Iobhar raised his hand, and Sarnat's future as a stuffed cat flashed before my eyes. Hastily I said, "Iobhar, no. Please. I'm sorry. I'm certain you've taught me well. I thought I had it right, but perhaps . . . I'll try it again. Show it to me again."

"I think we'll try something different." He led me into a room filled with birdcages of all kinds and framed mirrors stacked one against the other. He angled one of the mirrors so I could see myself, full-length, within it.

He handed me a hawthorn branch and took me through the steps of another spell, this one designed to divine in mirrors. When I'd learned it perfectly, I stared into the depths of the glass, waiting for the visions.

Instead, all I saw was myself, my dark eyes wide and worried, my hair unkempt and hanging loosely over my shoulders, the violet stripes of my gown looking black in the light.

"Do it again," Iobhar ordered. "And this time, listen for the music."

That was something I *could* do. I performed the spell again. I listened for its music, searching for it beyond the songs of Iobhar and Roddy and Sarnat. I sent my mind deeper, winding it into the words I chanted.

And I heard the discord. An off note. Two. My inflection hadn't been perfect after all. "I have to do it again."

This time, I kept the music in my head as I spoke the incantation, and once more, I heard the jangle of missed notes.

I broke off in the middle of a word. "I thought I was saying it right."

"You were," Iobhar said.

"The music says I'm not."

Iobhar fingered his necklace of bells, sending them tinkling. "Try it again."

We spent the rest of the afternoon trying. I was near tears, and Iobhar's gaze was stony. He pointed to a nearby birdcage. A yellow canary appeared within it. "For every time you fail, another appears."

I didn't realize what that meant until I kept failing. More canaries materialized in the cage. Yellow and blue and green, crammed together, pecking one another in aggravation.

"Iobhar—"

"You've the power to stop it."

I tried again and again. The birdcage filled. The little birds shoved up against the bars, tormenting me with their frantic chirping. I tried to concentrate on the spell. No matter how I said it, or how often Iobhar insisted I was doing it right, the music said otherwise.

My eyes blurred; the bright feathers became only smears of color. The canaries began to die. Horribly and cruelly, smeared with blood from fighting, and then slowly suffocating.

"Stop! Please stop. I'll never get this." Obviously, I *wasn't* meant for this. I was stupid and clumsy. "How can I do the ritual when I can't even get this spell right?"

The birds in the cage vanished. Iobhar's anger turned thoughtful. "'Tis clear there's a problem."

"Yes. The problem is that I'm a failure."

He stalked from the room. I dropped the hawthorn branch. Already the spell was slipping from my mind. What kind of *veleda* couldn't remember a simple spell?

My power answered—vibrating beneath my skin, humming in my veins. Still there. Still mine. What made me think that I could perfect in days what it had taken other Druids years to learn? I didn't have long, but I could not be impatient. I would learn this. I would be good at it. I had to be.

I went in search of Iobhar, ready to begin again.

THIRTEEN

October 19
Diarmid

It had been nearly three months since Grace had disappeared. Samhain was only days away, and they were all anxious. Finn kept the rest of the Fianna busy organizing their rapidly growing militia when they weren't looking for Grace, but he'd refused Diarmid the permission to train.

"You're the one who lost her, so you'll spend every hour searching," Finn told him with a thin smile. "If she's not dead—and you'd best hope she's not—you'll bring her to me."

She wasn't dead. Diarmid knew it; he would *feel* it if she were. But what she *was*... that was the fear that haunted him, that he couldn't get past.

Every day Diarmid went out, and every night he returned, restless and irritable. Finn's watchful concern was like an itch between his shoulder blades, and Aidan's growing hostility didn't help either.

"Play a game with me," Oscar said, motioning to the chessboard that Goll had made from scraps of wood, using corks and stones for the pieces. "'Twill ease your mind."

"I'm in no mood for it," Diarmid said.

"Aye, you're grouchy as a mean-tempered boar, but I'll take you on. You won't bring her here by sulking."

"Have you not noticed how close we are to Samhain?"

Oscar just rolled his eyes. "Come and play, Derry."

Diarmid sighed and gave in. Aidan sat in the corner, glaring at him. This made it hard to concentrate, and the game went poorly.

The third time Diarmid glanced at Aidan, Oscar said, "What is it between you two? You rarely take your eyes off him. I'd say you were sweet on him, but then . . . 'tis clear you'd rather kill him than kiss him, and he's no better."

"You've a true gift for the obvious." Diarmid moved a bishop. "He's angry with me for Grace."

Oscar captured the piece. "You can't blame him. You compelled his sister and stole her virtue. No brother can like that."

Diarmid scowled.

Oscar only grinned. "So 'tis true then? You *did* steal her virtue?"

"None of your business."

"Ah, I see. Well, so that explains Aidan. What reason have you to dislike him?"

Diarmid lowered his voice to ask, "Do you trust him?"

Oscar shrugged. "Aidan's served us well in the battles he's fought. Without him, we never would have escaped the

Tombs, and I'd still be fodder for the Fomori. He's risked his own life to help us. We need him, Derry."

"Just . . . there's something about him . . ."

"He's the brother of the lass you love. 'Twould be better to make him your friend than your enemy."

"Why does it matter what Aidan thinks of me? There's no future for me and Grace. You know it as well as I do."

"Aye, but 'tis good to hear you admit it," said Oscar. "I confess, I wondered if you ever would."

Diarmid made a final, futile move, and shoved the board away, leaning back against the wall. Slimy water from a seeping leak wet though his shirt. "Well, now I have. So you and the others can stop wondering whether I mean to betray you."

"We don't wonder it," Oscar said. "But you're hard to be around these days, Derry, and we all miss hearing you laugh. You'll have a future without this lass."

"If we find her, and she chooses us," Diarmid pointed out.

"We *will* find her, and she *will* choose us. We've got the *ball seirce* and Finn on our side." Oscar rose, ruffling Diarmid's hair. "Of course, 'twould be better to have me working on her as well, but no one wants to overwhelm the lass."

"Thoughtful of you," Diarmid said.

Oscar laughed and went to join the others, and Diarmid went back to brooding. When midnight came, he went to his pallet, but he couldn't sleep. He missed Grace. He wanted her with him. He knew it was stupid. Everything felt wasted and useless. No one had seen her. No one knew where she was.

Creak.

Diarmid opened his eyes just in time to see Aidan disappear up the stairs.

Diarmid rose to follow. One or two of the others stirred, but relaxed again when they saw it was him. Once Diarmid was out the back door, he glimpsed Aidan moving quickly through the broken gate into the alley. Diarmid drew into the shadows, keeping a good distance between them. Twice, Aidan shot thin bolts of purple lightning into the shadows, each followed by a *thud*. An old man with a broken bottle and a younger one with a knife. So Aidan was paying attention. It reassured Diarmid somewhat.

Aidan went over to Broadway—more dangerous for both of them, and there were plenty of policemen and people about, but at least it was dark, and it was easy to avoid the glow of streetlamps. Diarmid had thought perhaps Aidan meant to go to the Knox house, which was abandoned now that the rest of the family was living with Patrick Devlin. Diarmid hoped not. There were Fomori guards there constantly, and the Fianna had men watching it, too, hoping for Grace's return. But Aidan skirted that street, and with dread and disbelief, Diarmid realized Aidan was headed to Devlin's house.

Why?

Aidan cut through Madison Square. Diarmid paused at the edge of the park, hiding among the trees, watching. He expected Aidan to go right to the Devlins' back gate, but instead Grace's brother went to the pavilion in the middle of the park.

Then, the *squeak* of a gate, the *clank* of a latch falling shut, and Patrick Devlin hurried from his yard into the park.

Aidan was a spy for the Fomori.

What other reason could there be for him to sneak out at night to meet with Patrick?

Diarmid heard the murmur of voices, and he moved closer, creeping low until he was at the back wall of the gazebo, crouching out of sight.

"Have you discovered anything?" Aidan asked. "It's two weeks until Samhain."

"I know," Patrick said tightly. "Don't you think I know that? I've been thinking of the prophecy. I think you're right. It's trying to tell us something."

"I dream about it every night. I'm on a ship in the middle of the ocean, and it feels as if I'm disappearing as we get farther and farther away. From what, I don't know, but 'the sea is the knife,' just as the prophecy says. It's severing me from something important, something I need to do. There are storms, and lightning—"

"Red lightning?"

"No." Aidan lowered his voice. "Why do you keep asking me about it?"

Patrick answered, a murmur, and at the same time a dog barked, so Diarmid heard only ". . . Grace."

Diarmid froze.

"She did *what?*" Aidan asked.

"She swooned speaking Gaelic."

"Gaelic? She doesn't even know it."

"She said *eubages*, *brithem*, and *vater*. Then she asked why I'd abandoned her. She said *éicse* just before she swooned."

"What does that mean?"

"*Éicse* was the ultimate goal of the Druids," Patrick explained. "It means poetry and knowledge, wisdom and divination. Sort of a combination of all things. The truth of the world, I suppose, is the best way to describe it."

Diarmid's mind spun. Gaelic words, and *éicse*. Grace.

Patrick said, "Does it tell you anything?"

"Not really." Aidan paused. "But she's all right? She's safe?"

"Yes. My mother and Lucy were there, but they didn't hear what I did. They think she swooned because we were talking about Diarmid. It hasn't happened again. I've told no one else. But she may have mentioned it to Lot. They've become friends. Have the Fianna discovered anything?"

"Not yet. They're—" Aidan stopped. "I feel . . . something." He rose, his shadow disturbing the darkness.

Diarmid held his breath, not daring to move.

"I have to go," Aidan said. His footsteps thudded across the gazebo's hollow floor, and he rushed down the steps.

Diarmid couldn't follow until Patrick left, and then it was too late. Aidan was gone.

Diarmid's mind would not be still. Aidan was dreaming Grace's dreams. Ships and the sea. *She* had swooned chanting Gaelic while they'd been talking of him. *She* was friends with Lot. *"She's safe?"*

Who else could it be but Grace?

Patrick had Grace, and Aidan knew it, and the two of them were keeping it secret.

Diarmid didn't know whether to feel relief, exhilaration, or dismay. Patrick Devlin had her. She hadn't disappeared at all, and by keeping it secret, Patrick guaranteed the Fianna would waste time looking for her—time better spent training a militia.

Had she been with Patrick the entire time? Three months? What had happened between them?

Nothing. It has to be nothing. Diarmid had seen the love-spell in her eyes. He hadn't mistaken it. Grace was no common lass. She would never have lain with him if she hadn't at least believed she loved him. Which meant that if Patrick had her, she was being kept against her will. *Unless the spell has worn off already.*

It was all Diarmid could do not to break into the house this moment.

But there were guards everywhere. He would be captured or worse. He couldn't endanger the others by forcing them to rescue him. No, better to tell Finn and come up with a plan.

Diarmid stared at the Devlin house, at the windows glowing against the night, wondering which one was hers. He thought of touching her again. Kissing her.

Handing her over to Finn.

Diarmid felt sick. He couldn't bear the thought of it. Watching Finn seduce her and being able to say nothing, do nothing . . . *Leave her with Patrick. She would be safer. It would be better.*

Except it wouldn't. Patrick said that she and Lot had become friends, and Diarmid knew what a good liar the Fomori goddess was. Grace had been half taken in by them already. All her talk of Miogach's reassurances and Daire Donn's charm—Diarmid couldn't trust that Grace could see the truth. Samhain was coming. A choice had to be made. Diarmid had a job to do.

"Are you one of us?"

"Aye," he whispered. "Aye."

He kept the vow in his head the whole way home.

FOURTEEN

The third week (sidhe *time*)
Grace

S ome things remained. Iobhar taught me the movements of
the stars and the planets, and I remembered those, along
with their meanings. I could go into a trance at will, and I
found meaning in the most convoluted of Iobhar's riddles.

But I couldn't do divination, no matter how often I tried,
nor could I shoot lightning from my fingertips or bring a rain-
storm or raise tornados.

Most importantly, I could not work the spells for the Seer.
No matter how often I said them, the music told me I was
doing them wrong. I had no dreams or visions.

Iobhar threw ogham sticks and read the movements of
crows, searched for answers in my palms and breathed oracle
smoke. He called pigeons and twisted their necks, disembow-
eling them to read their entrails while I turned away, horrified and nauseated.

Each time, nothing. He cursed whatever it was he didn't
see, glaring at me as if I were deliberately trying to vex him.

I'd warned Sarnat to keep her distance. Torcan and Cuan and Stag seemed to know to stay away. Roddy muttered as he ceaselessly cleaned brooches and rings. We all walked on eggshells—sometimes chairs turned into snakes as we passed, and deep pits opened in the floor without warning. Red lightning lit a stuffed cat on fire, and when I shouted at Iobhar to put it out, he brought a hurricane. Little tornados spun down the stairs, creating all new corridors and mazes.

There was much I *could* do, and my power grew day by day. But I was frustrated and angry, relearning the spells, trying new ones.

One day, as I beat another of Sarnat's glamoured gang boys, I said, "At least *you* haven't wasted your time."

"That remains to be seen, doesn't it?" she asked. "These are only glamours. Who knows what a real boy would do?"

"You mean you're not clever enough to know?" I teased.

"I don't think like a mortal, milady, nor would I wish to. 'Twould be like asking you to think like a worm. Who knows that they think about anything at all?"

Iobhar entered the room, gesturing for me to come with him. "We're going to try the incantation itself."

I went cold. "*The* incantation? For the ritual?"

"You think you are not ready for it?"

"No, I—"

"Then come."

I followed Iobhar to the study. When I was done with the ritual cleansing—the half-dressed bath I'd grown used to—he handed me a small bowl full of a steaming liquid. "Drink this."

I eyed it dubiously. It smelled bitter and foul. "What is it?"

"An infusion."

"Is it poisonous?"

"Mildly. But 'twill bring visions."

Dying sounded no better accompanied by dreams, however good they were. "Do I need it for the ritual?"

"No. 'Twill only make you more receptive."

I swirled the potion in the bowl. It didn't help.

Iobhar ordered, "Drink it."

I took a careful sip. It tasted as nasty as it smelled, and I almost spit it out again. I held my nose and drank the rest of it quickly.

Iobhar held a knife with a sparkling jeweled handle. "'Twill require some blood before the sacrifice itself, enough to show your willingness to die. I won't cut this time, but you must learn each step." He took my hand. I felt the tingle of his magic calling to my power, but it was controlled, at least for now.

He ran the point of the blade lightly down the pulsing vein of my wrist. "You'll cut vertically."

The potion hit me then, a wave of dizziness, the sting of his magic, potent now. Iobhar released my hand. The stinging stopped. He gave me the knife and said, "Show me."

I repeated the movements, and as I did, he spoke Gaelic, words I should not have been able to understand, though I did. They translated themselves in my head: "'The Erne shall rise in rude torrents, hills shall be rent. Every mountain glen and bog shall quake.'"

"Say it," he told me.

My head pounded; the room seemed to whirl around me. "The Erne—"

"In Gaelic, *veleda*."

The words came as easily as if I'd been speaking English. He took my hand again, curling his fingers around my wrist. Again the sting of him, the burn. His scent swirled around me. His eyes became a kaleidoscope, a hundred different hues of brown and gold, whirling and tilting, scattering and coming together.

He spoke again. "'This is my choice. I deem it worthy and just. I deem it mine.'"

I repeated the Gaelic after him, singing as he had. I felt the bright fire of power stirring in my veins.

"'I am the *veleda* chosen. Long the journey I have made from yesterday to today. The Erne I passed by leaping, though wide the flood.'"

I knew the melody of these words as if I always had.

Iobhar laid my hand flat, crossing it with the knife. "You will blood it," he explained, showing me how I would smear my blood over the hilt, my wrist, and hand—a circle in blood.

"'I have seen and weighed. Great stones crack and split. Storms will tell and the world is changed. I release my power to the chosen. This is the word that is spoken. This is complete.'"

The words from the prophecy. The room spun. The colors in Iobhar's eyes reeled, and I was in a cyclone, images leaping and crossing and blurring, the *dord fiann* in my hands and Patrick leaning to kiss me, Diarmid glowing and my brother casting lightning, Miogach smiling at me and my mother saying *"There is no veleda. It's just a story. Just a story ..."*

Great stones crack and split. Storms will tell and the world is changed.

The images fell into darkness. I fell into nothingness. The spell splintered around me, prophecy and music, a cacophony in my ears, nothing but noise and noise and noise. *Great stones ... Storms will tell...*

Everything stopped.

My head cleared; I heard a gasping breath—my own. "Those words. I know those words."

"Not well enough," Iobhar said.

"No, I mean ... the storms will tell—"

"There's no point saying it again." He turned to leave.

"You don't understand! Those words—about the storms and the rocks breaking and the world changing ... those were part of the prophecy."

Iobhar turned again to face me. "The incantation has passed from *veleda* to *veleda* throughout time. Of course you know them."

"Not that prophecy," I said. "I mean the other one. The prophecy Diarmid and I found on an ogham stick on Coney Island."

"The potion's effects will leave you soon. You should rest."

"Listen to me! The ogham stick belonged to a Druid. He said it needed a key to decipher it, and then ... Diarmid was the key and I ... it was what brought me to you."

Iobhar paid attention at last. "How so?"

"Part of it said, 'The rivers guard treasures with no worth,' and when I listened to the music, it told me where to find you. The stick told me you were here."

Iobhar scowled. "What else did the stick say? Tell me. Leave nothing out."

I did.

"'All things will only be known in pieces,'" Iobhar repeated.

I remembered my brother's words, my grandmother's. "Everything's broken. That's what my brother says."

"Your brother?"

"Aidan. He's a stormcaster."

"He's a stormcaster? Your *brother*?"

"Didn't you know that? I thought you knew everything."

"That managed to escape me," Iobhar said wryly. "What color is his lightning?"

"Purple. Why?"

"Curious." Iobhar strode to the door.

"Why does it matter what color his lightning is? And what about this prophecy? Do you think it has something to do with why I can't manage the spells?"

He paused at the doorway. "I think it has everything to do with it."

"What?"

"I don't know," he said. "Yet. But I mean to find out."

October 20
Diarmid

"You're certain of this?" Finn asked.

Diarmid said, "I know what I heard. Devlin's got her, and Aidan knows it."

"'Tis worth a search, if nothing else," Finn said. "You'll take Oscar with you tonight. If the two of you find the lass, you'll bring her here directly. Understood?"

Diarmid nodded. He wouldn't let himself think of what Finn meant to do, nor how he felt about it. "Aidan can't know."

"Aye. I'll leave it to you and Oscar to decide how to proceed. And Diarmid . . . don't get caught. We haven't the resources just now to rescue you."

Diarmid knew that already. There had been several fights in the last few weeks, and they were all tired and bruised. That the Fomori fared no better was small consolation.

He tried not to feel giddy at the thought of seeing her again. Holding her, touching her. He couldn't be thinking about those things. It was no longer about what he wanted. What mattered was finding her and bringing her to Finn.

Aidan's earlier words burrowed like a guilty secret. *"I won't follow blindly."* But Aidan didn't know what it felt like to betray one's brothers. Diarmid refused to think of his own hopes. Grace's rescue first, the rest he could deal with later.

He was tense with nerves and excitement as he and Oscar made their way to the Devlin house that night.

"She'll be under heavy guard," Oscar said.

"You've said that a hundred times. Afraid?"

"Not as long as Lot and Balor are far away. And Tethra too. I've no wish to be skewered by lightning or struck dead by an eye."

Oscar whistled "Yankee Doodle" as they approached the Devlin gate, which was shrouded by the tangled yellowing vines of a climbing rose. He flipped the latch, saying loudly, "Curse you for stopping for that beer. We should've been here ten minutes ago. Hope the master don't have our heads."

"What else should he expect, calling for us so late?" Diarmid followed Oscar into the yard, letting the gate clang shut behind him.

"Who goes there?" The Fomori guard, a rifle at the ready, stepped from the shadows.

"The master called us down from the stables," Oscar said.

"What for?"

"How do we know?" Diarmid said irritably. "Rich men have their whims."

The guard said, "'Tis late for a drive. The master's probably gone to bed."

"We ain't too happy about the time ourselves."

"I don't know anything about any stableboys called down."

"I guess he forgot to tell you," Oscar said.

The guard peered at them through the darkness. "No. I think not. Why don't the two of you just turn around and go—"

Oscar struck the guard on the temple with the hilt of his dagger and then cut his throat. Together, he and Diarmid pulled the dying man beneath a bush near the back stoop.

"It'll be awhile before they see him," Oscar whispered with satisfaction, wiping his bloody dagger on the grass. "If we're lucky, morning."

"Don't count on it." Diarmid tucked his own dagger back into his belt as he went up the stoop. He looked through the small, wavery window into the dark kitchen, and then tried the door, which opened easily and soundlessly. There was no one inside. When he knew it was safe, he motioned for Oscar to follow him. Grace was here, somewhere. In minutes, he would see her again.

Diarmid led the way into a hall. To his left were the servants' stairs. Stealthily, he and Oscar went up. At the top, Diarmid slowed, peering around the corner. There was no one in the hall, only closed doors on either side. He reached around, twisting the key on the sconce. The gaslight sputtered out.

He tried to remember which rooms were which. Patrick's at the end of the hall, next to an adjoining room meant for a wife. It had been empty the first time Diarmid had broken into this house. Was it still? An adjoining room, where Patrick could have access to her at all hours . . .

Don't think it. Not now.

If he were Patrick, he would have guards posted at her door, but there was no one. Not in front of that room, nor the other that he knew to be a guest room. Odd. Or stupid. It didn't make sense, but Diarmid couldn't leave until he checked.

He motioned to the two rooms, and Oscar nodded. They crept down the hall. Diarmid reached for the nearest doorknob; Oscar moved in close.

Behind them, a door opened.

He and Oscar threw themselves against the wall. The open door cast dim yellow light into the hallway. A woman stepped out with it. She wore a dressing gown. A long blond braid fell over her shoulder.

Lucy.

Her gaze went right to them. She froze, gasping—she was going to scream.

Diarmid flung himself at her, clapping his hand over her mouth, pressing her back into the bedroom. Her blue eyes widened in recognition, and she stopped struggling. Oscar came in behind them, closing the door.

Diarmid whispered fiercely, "Lucy, lass, we mean no harm." He looked for the lovespell in her eyes and found it. He said gently, "I'm going to take my hand away. Don't scream. D'you understand me, lass? D'you promise?"

She nodded. Slowly, Diarmid took away his hand, prepared to silence her again in a moment.

"Derry," she breathed. "You came. I told them you would."

Oscar said, "Just tell us where she is, and we'll be gone."

"Who is *he*?" Lucy asked.

"A friend of mine. Look, we can't stay. We're just here to find—"

Lucy laid her hand against his chest. "I can't believe you're really here."

He drew her hand away. "'Tis good to see you, lass, but we have to go. If your brother finds me here . . ."

She licked her full, perfect lips. "You stayed away so long. Everyone said you'd abandoned me. You must promise not to go away like that again, Derry. I've missed you so. I can hardly stand to be without you."

Oscar snorted. Diarmid glared at him. "I promise," he lied. "Now, if you could just tell me where she is . . ."

"She?"

"Grace," he said, still gripping her hand. "Tell me where your brother is keeping Grace. Which room, *milis*? Quickly now, we haven't much time."

Lucy blinked as if she'd suddenly awakened. She jerked away from him. *"Grace?"*

"Sssh. Not so loud," he said.

"You've come back for Grace, not me." Her voice rose. "They were right. Everything they said. She eloped with you. It's Grace you're in love with!"

Frantically, Diarmid tried to cover her mouth again. She pushed him away in a fury. "Don't you dare touch me! How dare you come here!"

"Lucy, please—"

"She's not here!" she shouted. "She's gone. I hope she's dead and you never find her!"

"Someone's coming," Oscar said urgently.

"Help!" Lucy screamed. "Help! Help!"

A slamming door, racing footsteps. Lucy screamed again. There was only one way out. Diarmid dashed for the window, Oscar on his heels. He jerked it open. A two-story drop. He slung himself over the sill. Just below was a small roof over a bay window.

Oscar yelled, "Jump!"

Diarmid heard Lucy's door crash open, and he released his hold on the sill. He hit the roof below hard. The shadow of a guard raced into the yard. Diarmid clutched the edge of the bay roof and dropped when Oscar landed, his boots scattering bits of shingling over Diarmid's shoulders. Patrick Devlin leaned out the window above, shouting, "Stop them!"

Diarmid hit the ground just as the guard reached him. He grabbed his dagger from his belt, shoving the blade into the man's gut. The guard fell, but there were others rounding the corner of the house, more than a couple—where had *they* come from?

Oscar landed, and they ran out of the yard, into the park, the guards close behind. The shadows of the park seemed to mass and move; it was rapidly alive with policemen—Fomori warriors—and he and Oscar were running for their lives.

They dashed down the back streets, past the middle-class homes. The streets were mostly empty here at this time of night, which was good, because despite their deformities, the Fomori were fast. Diarmid's lungs burned.

Oscar gasped, "This way," and dodged down an alley, through a pile of emptied kegs, sending them rolling across broken cobblestones. The fetid contents of the gutters splashed over Diarmid's boots.

They spun down another alleyway, skidding around corners. The buildings turned to slums. More and more people about, drunks and homeless mostly, starting awake as they raced past. The police and the guards were gaining, the Fomori shouting, "Stop them! Stop them!"

Diarmid felt as if he'd been running forever. They were near the East River, Corlears Hook. If they hadn't lost the Fomori by the time they reached the piers, there would be nowhere else to go. Someone fired a shot; Diarmid heard it whizzing by him, a high whine in his ear.

Oscar looked wildly about. "There," he rasped. A pawnshop. Probably a fence used to evading the law. Diarmid and Oscar crashed through the door.

The place was a madhouse, piles of junk everywhere, and at the far end, a glass-enclosed counter where an old man stood. He looked blearily up at them.

Diarmid slammed home the bolt on the door. Oscar shouted, "We need a place to hide. Quickly!"

The old man jerked his head to a door in the back. "We don't want any trouble."

Diarmid and Oscar hurled themselves into the storeroom, which was tiny, barely big enough to hold them both. Diarmid got a glimpse of sagging shelves holding old wooden boxes, rusted tools, and jars of nails before Oscar shut the door, closing them in darkness. The smells of oil and dust filled his nose.

They listened for footsteps, voices. It was profoundly quiet. Eerie even. Diarmid's skin prickled. He didn't like the feel of this place. There was something off. Something . . . wrong.

"I don't hear anything," Oscar said finally. "I think we've lost them."

"Let's get out of here," Diarmid said.

"Another moment yet. Let's be sure."

The eeriness only intensified as they waited. By the time Oscar said, "I think it's all right now," Diarmid would have braved the hounds of hell to get out of the room.

Oscar cracked the door, peeking out, before they emerged.

"They ran on by," the old man said. "I think you're safe enough."

"Thank you," Oscar said.

There was something familiar about the old man, although Diarmid knew he'd never seen him before. At his side stood a thin whippet with unsettlingly watchful eyes. The man put a distracted hand to the dog's head as if he meant to calm it.

His gaze went beyond them, behind. Diarmid looked over his shoulder but saw nothing.

The old man said, "Are they? Are you sure of it?"

The hair on the back of Diarmid's neck rose. Oscar rolled his eyes and mouthed, *Crazy*. He jerked his head toward the door.

Diarmid said, "We owe you a debt. If you've ever any need of Finn's Warriors—"

"Ah, that's who you are?" The old man's bleary gaze sharpened, and again Diarmid felt that disconcerting sense of familiarity. "'Tis you it all settles on, is that it?"

"I don't know what you're talking about." Something brushed past him, a fleeting touch that coursed through him like fire, rocking him. But there was nothing there.

The old man stared past him again, as if he were listening to someone. "Do you want me to keep him?"

Diarmid grabbed Oscar's arm. "'Tis time we're gone."

Oscar nodded. "Aye. Thanks again."

Diarmid half expected something to keep them from reaching the door, and when they were out of the shop, he felt an overwhelming relief.

Oscar glanced up and down the street. "Let's circle back before the Fomori figure out they're chasing no one."

Diarmid followed Oscar, but escaping the Fomori seemed less important than escaping the pawnshop and that fiery, ghostly touch.

"The old man was mad as a hatter, wasn't he?" Oscar said when they finally slowed.

"Did you feel it?" Diarmid asked.

"Feel what?"

"That touch . . . 'twas like . . . I don't know. A spirit maybe, but—"

Oscar laughed. "You've been spending too much time with the *sidhe*."

And then Diarmid realized what had been so familiar about the old man. He'd seen that look before. On Druids sucked dry by the *sidhe*. It was what had felt familiar about the pawnshop, too, the aura of lingering Druid magic, the presence of the *sidhe*.

"We have to go back there," he said.

"Go back? Are you mad? We can't go back now. The Fomori will be all over!"

"That old man was a Druid who's been drained. What if he can help us find Grace?"

"How can he, if he's been sucked dry?"

"He must know something," Diarmid insisted.

"Why should he?"

"Oscar, don't you think it odd? A drained Druid no one's heard of—"

"And you've been right about everything so far, have you?" Oscar pointed out. "When it comes to her, you're grabbing at shadows. If he does know anything, he'll still know it tomorrow, when there aren't a dozen Fomori looking for us. Come *on*, Derry. 'Twas too narrow an escape for my liking. Tomorrow, if you still want to, we'll come back."

Diarmid had been wrong about Grace being in Patrick's house, and he might be wrong here. But something told him he wasn't. A drained Druid, the feel of the *sidhe* . . . No, it wasn't a coincidence. But Oscar was right. They could not go back now. But tomorrow—

He prayed it wouldn't be too late.

SIXTEEN

That same night (sidhe *time*)
Grace

When the door jerked open, and Diarmid came running into the shop with Oscar, I'd thought him another of Iobhar's tests. Everything I felt for him—love and fear and desire—rushed back like Cliodna's Wave, threatening to sweep me away.

"Give them what they seek," Iobhar directed Roddy. When they disappeared into the storage closet, I leaped to my feet. My skirt caught the corner of the fidchell board, sending pieces scattering.

Iobhar said, "Stay, *veleda*. 'Tis none of your concern."

"It's Diarmid! And Oscar."

"I know who it is. You were running from him when you came here, were you not?"

"Yes, but—"

"You should be running from him still. Sit down."

"I can't," I said helplessly.

"There they go," Sarnat said, glancing toward the window. A group of warriors—Fomori—ran past.

I missed Diarmid; I yearned for him. But at the sight of his pursuers, I remembered why I had left him, and Iobhar was right—my reasons hadn't changed. But to see him again, to touch him . . . how could I resist it?

I waited with nervous joy for the door to open. When it did—and Oscar stepped out, and then Diarmid—I said, "Derry."

He didn't turn around.

I said more loudly, "Diarmid."

Again, he didn't seem to hear me. I looked at Iobhar in confusion, but he only said to Roddy, "They're Fianna."

Roddy said, "Are they? Are you sure of it?"

Diarmid looked over his shoulder. His eyes were such a deep blue, they made me shiver. I remembered that last morning with him, how loved and desired I'd felt. How strong. But now he looked right past me as if I were invisible. It hurt more than I could have imagined.

"I don't understand," I whispered. "Derry—what is it? What have I done?"

"He can't see you, *veleda*," Iobhar told me. "You're glamoured. He sees only the shop and Roddy. He can't hear a word you say."

"Then unglamour me," I demanded.

Iobhar regarded me steadily. "No. There are things you must do yet, *veleda*. This warrior has no part in it. He'll only distract you. Nothing has changed. Not the choice, not the *geis*."

Roddy said to Diarmid, "'Tis you it all settles on, is that it?"

Diarmid said, "I don't know what you're talking about."

I wanted to hear him say my name in that deep voice. I could not bear being so close without his knowing it.

"Please," I said desperately to Iobhar. I touched Diarmid's arm, and he brushed at his sleeve. "Look, he can feel me."

"As if you were a breath. You're behind the veil, *veleda*, invisible to those who would use you for their own ends." Iobhar's amber eyes glimmered. "Which will win, I wonder? His love for you or his honor?"

Roddy said, "Do you want me to keep him?"

Iobhar waved a hand. "Send them on their way."

I was going to let him go. I was. Iobhar was right. I wasn't ready. I still felt too much for Diarmid, and there was still so much training to be done. But then he and Oscar started for the door, and I hurried after. I wanted him to see me, at least; and outside the shop door, I would be visible again.

But when I tried to follow them into the night, a force stopped me. A wall between me and the world.

"I can't go out," I said.

Iobhar's smile was self-satisfied.

"You told me I wasn't a prisoner here."

Sarnat snarled, "He's a spider, and he's got us caught in his web. I told you he was a liar."

He pointed at Sarnat.

"Don't hurt her," I demanded.

"So many orders," he said lightly. "'Unglamour me, let me go, don't hurt her.' What is it you want, *veleda*?"

"I don't want to be a prisoner," I said.

"Your own fate keeps you so."

"You told me I could leave when I was done with you."

"Which you are not, are you?"

I heard the tinkling of his bells, his music, his temptation. "You can't keep me forever."

"Your warrior cannot help you now." His eyes turned dark, and I was afraid, though I couldn't say exactly why. "You will see I'm right when 'tis done."

I looked out the window. Diarmid and Oscar were gone. There was no sign they had ever been here. Even now, the whole thing seemed not quite real, like a vision brought on by one of Iobhar's potions. Except . . .

I felt Diarmid still. He was an ache in me that never went away, no matter how often I told myself we had no future. And now it was worse, because I felt the weight of the task I'd set myself more intently than ever, and I realized there was a part of me that had hoped for his rescue.

But Iobhar spoke the truth. The task was mine, and there could be no rescue. I was alone—and I had to remain so until it was done.

Whatever it cost.

SEVENTEEN

Later that night
Patrick

The house was in turmoil. It was 2:00 a.m., and every lamp was lit, servants rushing around in robes and nightcaps, Mama urging everyone to take a cup of tea as if it could cure all the world's ills. Mrs. Knox looked troubled; Lucy was alternately sobbing and railing.

That two of the Fianna had managed to bypass the guards and break into the house, that one of them was Diarmid, and that they'd thought Grace was *here*, seemed impossible.

"Your guards," Patrick said again to Bres, who looked as weary as any man awakened in the middle of the night to deal with unexpected chaos, "how the hell did they get past your guards?"

"Our warriors won't let them escape now." Bres's eyes were dark with determination. "They've been told to track them to the ends of the earth if they must. And they will. Or pay the consequences."

Patrick glanced across the room to where Lot, beautifully gowned and coiffed regardless of the hour, had her arm around Mrs. Knox. They'd become fast friends. It was good, he supposed. It meant that Mrs. Knox was on his side and could help persuade Grace—assuming they ever found her. He buried the thought, along with his despair.

There had been no repeat of her swoon, and she'd said she had only been overwrought. As for the Gaelic . . . *"Mother spoke it. Some words must have stayed with me."*

Perhaps that was true. But there had been something disingenuous in her tone, though he didn't know why he thought so. He'd said nothing of the incident to the Fomori—what was he to tell them when she shrugged it off that way? Still, it made him uncomfortable. That, and the fact that he'd begun to notice the way she watched him sometimes, as if she were afraid . . . of *him?*

And his dreams . . . No. He didn't want to think of those just now.

Bres said, "I want to hear again what happened."

"Is that truly necessary? Lucy's already beside herself."

"Perhaps we've missed something."

Patrick rubbed his face and nodded. He went to Lucy, who stood, red eyed, by the French doors, staring out as if she expected Diarmid to materialize from the shadows. "Bres wants to hear what happened again," he told her softly.

She said, "Fine. As long as he brings Derry back so I can stab him in the heart myself."

Patrick sighed and led her back to the Fomori leader.

"So you heard a noise." Bres steepled his fingers beneath his chin. "A scuffling."

"I told you. I thought it was rats." Lucy clutched the fringe of the huge paisley shawl she'd thrown over her already voluminous chenille dressing gown. "I was going to find John so he could do something about it. I hate rats."

"But it wasn't rats you saw when you stepped out."

"Oh yes it was. A particularly large and nasty one." Lucy's face contorted. "And I was so *overjoyed* to see him. I thought he'd come back for me. But it wasn't me he was looking for. It was *Grace*."

"He asked for her specifically?"

"He said he was here to find her. He wanted to know where my brother was keeping her."

"And you told him . . ."

"That she wasn't here." She glared at Patrick. "I told him I hoped she was dead and he never found her."

"Lucy," Patrick admonished.

"I *told* you she was in love with him. I told you she'd run off with him. And you wanted to think she'd been *kidnapped.* Sometimes you're so naive, Patrick."

"You're the one foolish enough to think he came for you," Patrick shot back.

Bres mused, "What I find most curious is the fact that he thought she was here. Why would he think that, I wonder?"

"I don't know," Patrick said.

"You've no idea?"

"None." It was true. Aidan knew she wasn't here, and Patrick assumed he'd told the Fianna.

"Curious. You've been most helpful, my dear Miss Devlin. And I assure you, we will find this young man who's wronged you. He will get his just punishment. Perhaps then you may find some measure of peace."

Lucy's big blue eyes filled with tears. "That's all I want. I don't want to think of him anymore."

"That, too, will pass, though it may not seem so," Bres said kindly. Again, Patrick saw the compassionate smile that had won the loyalty of a country, the king that Patrick wanted to believe in. "We have all suffered in love, and we all survive to realize how foolish we've been."

"I can't stand to think of how Grace betrayed me." Lucy scowled.

"Perhaps 'twas not a betrayal. Blame the lad, if you must blame anyone. Miss Knox is to be your sister-in-law, I believe. 'Twould not do for sisters to dislike each other. I hope you can find it within yourself to forgive her. After all, it seems clear this lad has abandoned her as well. She will need your kindness."

Lucy favored Bres with a thin smile. "We'll see."

When she left, the kindness in Bres's expression fled. "Sit down, Devlin. You make me nervous, hovering about that way."

"I don't feel like sitting."

"I suppose not. Your fiancée is missing, and the Fianna traced her here. I imagine you have a great deal to be anxious about."

Patrick started. "You think the Fianna *traced* her here?"

"They had a reason for believing you held her."

"I haven't seen her since the day before she was kidnapped! I don't know where she is any more than you do."

Bres glanced at Mrs. Knox and Lot. "Perhaps the Fianna suspect that she will return to her family soon. Her *morai* is still comatose?"

"Worse than that. It's all we can do to keep her alive."

"And the mother . . . she still says nothing?"

Beyond Gaelic words she shouldn't know? "She doesn't believe the legends."

"I wonder what the Fianna know that we don't?"

Patrick wondered that as well.

The Fomori king paused. There was something about it that filled Patrick with dread. "We cannot find another spell to save her."

"*What?*"

"No such thing exists. I'm only being honest with you, Devlin. You should have no false hopes."

"But then . . . you're saying she'll die?"

"Yes, but—Lot may have another solution. A bargain, perhaps, with the Otherworld. A favor for a favor."

Patrick's hope warred with his foreboding. "What kind of a favor?"

"Aengus Og kept Diarmid's soul after he was killed on the plain of Ben Bulben. Lot believes she can do the same thing, though she has never attempted it."

Patrick remembered the legend well. "But it wasn't permanent. Aengus Og only brought him back from time to time."

"Aye. But we could keep her soul tethered until we can find another solution."

An icy cold filled Patrick's chest. "And if you can't?"

Bres smiled—the smile of a king, and one Patrick didn't know whether to believe. "If anyone can find a way, 'tis Lot. Have you forgotten she's a goddess? And a very clever one. You should have no fears on that score."

It was not the reassurance Patrick wanted, but it was better than nothing. Better than death. They would tether Grace's soul and find a way to bring her back permanently. They were *gods*—or at least Tethra and Balor and Lot were. Bres was right; if anyone could do it, it was Lot.

Patrick was so busy convincing himself that he forgot to ask what favor the spirits of the Otherworld might ask in return.

—∾— *October 21* —∾—

The Fomori lingered until nearly dawn. When they were finally gone, Patrick started for his bedroom. He was halfway up the stairs when he heard, "You do realize that the Fomori are our only hope of saving Grace."

Mrs. Knox stood at the bottom of the stairs, her hand resting on the newel post, and there was a defiant determination in her expression that was so different from her usual distraction that, for a moment, Patrick thought he must be dreaming.

"The Fomori?" he echoed. He came back down. "But I . . . You said you didn't believe the old stories."

"I never *wanted* to believe. I thought if I just ignored everything, it would all go away. But Lot has shown me that I'm only hurting Grace by refusing to see the truth."

"Lot?"

"She's helped me understand so much." Mrs. Knox winced as if in sudden pain, putting her hand to her temple. "I feel that Grace is in grave danger. Lot says they can still save her. She can bring Grace's soul back to us, Patrick. But only if Grace returns and chooses them. We *must* find her before the Fianna do."

The words spilled out before Patrick could decide what not to tell her. "Grace found an ogham stick with a prophecy. Aidan says she was following it when she disappeared."

"Aidan?"

"He's with the Fianna, Mrs. Knox, but he wants to save Grace too. He tells me there's a connection between them. That he can *feel* her—or he could, anyway, before . . . I know it's odd, but—"

"Odd? Not in our family. What does this prophecy say?"

When he told her, she frowned. "How familiar it sounds."

"That's what I thought too."

"It's in a story . . . somewhere." Her frown deepened. "I can't remember where."

Patrick said, "There's something else you should know. Even if we find Grace and bring her back . . . she's been with Diarmid Ua Duibhne. You remember he has the *ball seirce*. That's a true story, unfortunately."

Mrs. Knox grabbed his hand. "I know. But I also know Grace loves *you*, Patrick. She must not be allowed to ruin her future because she believes in a lie. I will do anything I can to keep that from happening."

Assuming Grace had a future. Or that souls could be brought back and made to stay. But Patrick didn't say that. He wanted to believe. He wanted it more than anything. "The *ball seirce* is very strong. You've seen what it's done to my sister."

"Grace will do what's right in the end. I know it. We'll save her life, and she'll do what's right."

Patrick remembered Aidan saying that his mother was stronger than she looked. Patrick saw that strength now. He didn't feel so alone. "You should get some sleep, Mrs. Knox. It's been a long night."

"I trust you, Patrick. I know you will find her."

Patrick was relieved that she knew the truth, but her trust was a heavy burden. She seemed so certain he could fix this, and yet he was no longer certain of anything. His dreams never left him; the prophecy murmured in his head. He felt always that he was on the edge of worlds; a single wrong step, and he would hurtle back into time, into another century of swords and Druids and rooms filled with oracle smoke.

They were only dreams, he told himself. But there was a part of him that knew they were more than that, that there was something in them he should understand, something he should remember.

And that was the most troubling thought of all.

EIGHTEEN

That same day
Diarmid

Diarmid cornered Aidan near the stairs. "A word with you."

"Leave me alone." Aidan tried to push past him. Diarmid didn't budge.

"When you met with Patrick Devlin two nights ago, who were you talking about?"

"Ah, so it *was* you I felt. I'd have thought eavesdropping beneath you."

"I'd have thought consorting with the enemy beneath you. Was it Grace you spoke of?"

Surprise flickered in Aidan's eyes. "Grace? No, why would you think that?" He glanced at Finn. "Oh, I see. Let me guess: you thought we were talking about Grace, and you went to find out for yourself. No wonder Finn's annoyed with you again. How many times do I have to tell you that I'm trying to save my sister's life? Why the hell would I want her with the Fomori?"

"You were talking about someone who swooned. Someone speaking Gaelic."

"My *mother*, you addlepated ass. *That's* who we were talking about. Patrick was worried about her, though he shouldn't be."

"How would you know? When was the last time you saw her? Does she even know you're alive?"

"It's none of your concern, as I've told you before," Aidan spat. "Now let me pass."

"Not until you tell me why you were meeting with Patrick Devlin."

"Not that it's any of your business, but I thought he might be able to interpret the ogham stick."

Now Diarmid was surprised. "The prophecy?"

Aidan nodded grimly. "Patrick studies relics, you know. I thought he could help."

"So you gave him the information that might lead him to Grace first."

Aidan let out an exasperated breath. "She's *engaged* to him, which I think you keep forgetting. And he loves her and wants to save her. That's not a lie."

The words were like little blows.

"He's not under a *geis* to kill her either," Aidan added. "So if you're asking me who I trust more to help me save her, I'm going to choose Patrick, whether he's allied with the Fomori or not."

Diarmid shoved Aidan into the wall. "You're dangerous and you don't even know it. If Patrick and the Fomori find her first, she's dead. By the gods, 'tis lucky Grace loves you, no matter that you don't deserve it, or I'd slit your throat."

"Let's not talk of who's deserving, shall we? You're the one who left her. It's because of you that she's in danger now. All I asked was for you to protect her, and you couldn't even manage that."

The guilt worked. Diarmid released Grace's brother. Aidan pushed by, shoving Diarmid hard.

Diarmid could not deny Aidan's words, and he would not wait another moment to talk to that Druid in the pawnshop. The old man had to know something. It was too strange—a Druid in Manhattan that no fairy had yet mentioned. It didn't make sense.

He grabbed the railing, swinging to the stairs. He'd only taken a few steps before Oscar called out, "Don't be going off alone, Derry. Wait until I'm done with training, and we'll go together."

Diarmid winced when Finn asked, "Go where?"

"We found a burned out Druid yesterday," Oscar told him. "Drained by the *sidhe*. Half-mad. We were going to question him today."

Aidan turned around. "What?"

Diarmid ignored him and said to Finn, "I don't want to waste any more time. I'll go alone. The old man won't be any trouble."

"I'll go with you," Aidan said.

"No," Diarmid snapped.

"He might know something about the prophecy."

"I don't want you," Diarmid said bluntly.

Finn waved a dismissive hand. "Take him anyway. Perhaps he can discover something, Druid to Druid. They tend to understand each other."

Diarmid bit back his irritation. "Fine. Come on then."

Neither he nor Aidan said anything as they left the flat and walked through town. They didn't speak until Aidan pushed him into an alley, out of sight of two policemen that Diarmid had been too distracted to see.

"Look, I know you're angry," Aidan said, "but I'd rather not have to tell Finn you've been arrested."

"You shouldn't have come," Diarmid said.

"Finn's right, and you know it. Perhaps the Druid will tell me something he wouldn't tell you."

"You've never seen a Druid like this. We'll be lucky if we get any sense from him at all. The *sidhe* don't leave much behind."

Aidan shuddered. "Were the fairies still there? Did you feel them?"

Diarmid remembered that Aidan had reason to be fearful. "I won't let them touch you if they are there. But 'twould be best if you weren't like your sister, insisting on making bargains that are better not made. They'll tempt you, and you'll find it hard to resist. I'll try to keep you from being stupid, but I'm no miracle worker."

"I'll try to keep *you* from losing your temper and killing him before he tells us anything, but I'm no miracle worker either," Aidan said.

Diarmid laughed reluctantly. "Maybe we could call a truce, aye? At least until we get back."

"Agreed. What matters now is finding Grace."

They said little more as they made for Corlears Hook. The pawnshop was easy to find again. Aidan opened the door and they went into the muffled quiet. Again, Diarmid felt that uncomfortable, eerie heaviness. Already he wished to be gone.

"Do you feel it?" he asked Aidan.

Grace's brother shifted his shoulders as if to relieve pressure. "Yes. Where is he?"

Just then, there was a clicking sound, toenails on floorboards, and the whippet Diarmid had seen yesterday rounded a corner. It growled low.

Warily, Diarmid called, "Anyone here?"

He heard nothing, or—whispers, though they seemed weirdly inside his own mind. Aidan was cocking his head as if he heard the same thing. Diarmid's skin crawled; it was all he could do to call again, "Hello?"

The dog growled once more, and then there was a crash from the back, and the old Druid emerged from the storage closet.

"Ah. 'Tis you again. Not hiding today?"

"We've come to ask you a few questions, if you don't mind." Diarmid stepped toward him. The dog growled, but slunk out of the way.

"Questions're free." The old man went to the glass counter and pulled out a bracelet, which he began to polish.

Diarmid went up to him, pressing his palms upon the glass. "You're a Druid, aren't you?"

"Druid?" The old man looked at him with watery eyes and sighed. "Ah me, no."

"Perhaps not now," Aidan said, coming up beside Diarmid. "But you were once, weren't you?"

His rubbing of the bracelet grew more intent. "Was I? Perhaps. The years pass so—"

"The fairies came," Diarmid reminded him. "D'you remember that? They wanted to touch you—"

"Touch you, touch you," the old man said in a creepy, sing-song voice.

Shivers slid up Diarmid's spine.

Aidan started, looking over his shoulder. "What was that? I heard something—"

"Ghosts," said the old man. "Spirits. Oh, we've plenty of them, don't we?" He laughed; it was a boyish giggle.

Aidan said, "We're looking for my sister. She's a Druid—a *veleda*. Have you seen her? Or heard of her?"

"Why ask me?" The man polished the jewelry feverishly.

Aidan said, "Because you're a Druid, like she is, like I am."

The old man's expression sharpened, distraction gone. "You'd best leave. You're in danger here."

"In danger from what?" Diarmid asked.

The old man said to Aidan, "He waits for ones like you. He'll want to keep you."

"Who is *he*?" Diarmid asked.

"Leave! Go now. I cannot help you."

Aidan frowned. "But my sister—"

"Go!"

Diarmid seized the man's wrist, stopping his incessant rubbing. "Have you seen her?"

"No. No, no, no. If you value your friend, you will take him away."

"You mean the *sidhe* return here?"

Again that childish giggling. Diarmid released the Druid's wrist and stepped back. Aidan swayed, looking over his shoulder in confusion. Diarmid recognized that expression. He'd seen it in Grace, when they'd been surrounded by the *sidhe*.

Diarmid's uneasiness turned to fear. "Aidan, we need to go."

The old man sang, "Aye, they return. Over and over. *Touch you, touch you, touch you . . .*"

Aidan's knees gave way. Diarmid grabbed his arm, keeping him upright.

"Do you hear that?" Aidan asked in a faraway voice. "A song . . . bells."

"Go away," the Druid said. "Don't come back."

Diarmid tightened his grip on Aidan, who was swaying in earnest. "If you hear anything of her, anything at all, send word to Finn's Warriors. Can you do that?"

"There's no hope." The man shook his head. "There's no hope for any of us."

Diarmid pulled Aidan to the door.

"Let go of me. I have to stay." Grace's brother struggled in Diarmid's grasp. "He wants me."

Diarmid shoved Aidan out the door so forcefully, they both fell into the street. Aidan blinked as if he were waking up. He stared at the shop.

"Are you all right?" Diarmid asked.

"Dear God. I've never felt anything like that." Aidan was pale and shaking. "That song was . . . I couldn't resist it."

Diarmid sagged in disappointment. "'Tis bad, I know. Grace felt the same."

"It pulls you in. Like . . . like gravity. Did you feel it?"

"I felt the magic; I didn't hear the song. But I'm no Druid, am I? I'm glad to be rid of the place, but I was so sure . . ."

"What made you think he would know something?"

"I can't even say. 'Twas just . . . odd, don't you think? This place being here, us never having heard of it?"

"There was no reason to hear of it. He's been drained, as you said."

"But the *sidhe* return. They were there. You felt it. Why would they come back if there's nothing to feed on?"

"I don't know." Aidan sighed. "But Grace isn't there."

"No," Diarmid admitted.

"I'll tell you one thing, though. If she ever was, she would never have escaped it." Aidan threw him a bitter look. "Not without you, not alone."

Aye, she was alone. His fault. It was something he could not forgive himself for. Diarmid prayed it would not turn into disaster.

But he feared it already had.

NINETEEN

The fourth week (sidhe *time*)
Grace

I dreamed of Diarmid turning away, deaf and blind to my pleas to stay, and then the hounds of Slieve Lougher were chasing us, their glowing eyes and slathering jaws, those dagger-like teeth, and Diarmid did not wait as I fell farther behind, the hounds nipping at my heels—

I jerked awake with a gasp only to hear that the dream had followed me. Claws scratched at my door. A bloodcurdling howl. Then the howl turned into a whine, and I realized it was only Cuan.

When I opened the door, he gave me a sad-eyed look and turned to the stairs, clearly meaning for me to follow.

"What? Now? It's the middle of the night—"

He whined again. Iobhar would not wait. I grabbed a dressing gown from the trunk and pulled it on, pushing up the huge, draping sleeves, nearly tripping over the hem as I followed Cuan down the stairs. Iobhar was obviously in a temper again—it looked as if a tornado had hit. Piles had been scattered or become mountainous. Six chairs teetered on a mound of crockery. A tower of books stretched to the ceiling, brushing cobwebs heavy with dust.

Iobhar was at the counter with a single oil lamp burning low. Neither Roddy nor Sarnat was anywhere to be seen, but Stag stood to one side, and Torcan rooted about the floor. I glanced at the windows; it was black outside.

Iobhar stared into a bowl of water skimmed with shimmering oil. Lamplight sent rainbows across the surface.

He looked up. His eyes were frighteningly yellow.

"What?" I whispered, drawing back.

"The first day I drained Roddy, there were ten other *sidhe* with me. They held him down while I leeched him. They cheered every moment. He begged me not to stop, but I wanted to torment him. I spent days tormenting him, sucking a little each day. An exquisite torture."

I remembered when the *sidhe* had grabbed me on Battle Annie's boat, how repulsed and terrified I'd been even as I never wanted them to stop. "Why are you telling me this?"

"Is it true?" he asked.

"It sounds like something you would do."

"Is it true, *veleda*?"

I felt suddenly tired. "Yes."

"Is it *true*?"

His tone was so urgent, I was surprised.

"Listen. Tell me if it's true."

I understood then what he was asking. I cast my mind out, envisioning the scene as he'd described it. The music came, true and strong, and then . . . no. A wrong note.

I said, "No, it isn't. At least not all of it. There were no other *sidhe*. You were alone. You meant to leave him because you were afraid it was too much power. But he begged you to stay. He said he was old and tired. He offered to teach you, and you wanted to learn."

Iobhar didn't confirm or deny. He said only, "Here's a simple spell I want you to try. 'Tis the way to call someone to you. Put yourself in a trance."

I closed my eyes, as he'd taught me, breathing deep until my fingertips and my toes began to tingle, and I felt the hum in my blood. Iobhar whispered, "Imagine who you want to see. Sing: 'Mountains and seas I have braved for you. The air moves aside as I pass. Now come to me and come and do not tarry. The earth waits not, nor do I.'"

Who I wanted most to see was the one I should not call— not that he would see me anyway. Instead, I envisioned Sarnat. I sang the words, feeling them deep within me, in the hollow of my skull, reverberating in my ears.

But the notes were wrong. My voice would not sing them correctly. When I came out of the trance, I knew it would not work, and I knew that Iobhar had suspected that it would be so.

"'Great stones crack and split,'" he murmured. He rubbed his full lower lip with his thumb. "There's a number comes up ever and again when I cast divination for you, *veleda*."

"Three," I told him. "You're always muttering 'three.'"

He nodded. "The *veleda* was given three powers: the power of the *eubages* to see the future; the power of the *brithem* so she could tell truth from lies; and the *vater*'s power of sacrifice, that she might give her power to the worthy. 'She sees, she weighs, and she chooses.' The Seer, the Judge, and the Prophet. Threefold. The *veleda* should be able to do any spell meant for one of her aspects."

"And?"

"You can't."

"Why not? Is there something wrong with me? Am I *not* the *veleda*?"

"You are the *veleda*. 'Tis no doubt of it. And there is something most definitely wrong with you. Know you of any kind of magic worked upon your family? You should be able to cast lightning. The purple belongs to you. The visions. The dreams."

"I did have dreams for a while, where I saw battles and—" I broke off, remembering the ones about Diarmid that had brought us closer. *Give in.* "But when we . . . when my power was released, they went away."

"Did you lose anything else? Or gain anything?"

"The music grew stronger. And . . . I could hear and feel my brother as if he were part of me. Part of my thoughts. That's gone now. I suppose that's because of your wretched glamour."

"Did you feel such a connection with anyone else? Besides your Diarmid?"

My Diarmid.

"No. No, but . . . but there *was* someone. Another presence. Always watching and waiting but silent. Whoever it was wouldn't answer or show himself. But that's gone too. You know, Aidan is the one with all the power. Perhaps—"

"Your brother is a male. The *veleda* must be female. 'Twas always so. Nothing is strong enough to change that."

"Then why can he do the things I should be able to do?"

"Because the *veleda*'s been split into its three parts. *Eubages*, *brithem*, and *vater*. It shouldn't be possible. I can think of only one thing that might have caused it."

"Which is what?"

Iobhar ignored my question. "That your brother—a male—has been given the power of the Seer is meant to be a punishment."

"Well, it's not as if he doesn't deserve it, but—"

"The punishment isn't for him, but for the one who incurred the curse. To remove the power from the rightful heiress, to give it to a male . . . 'tis the work of angry forces. Nature herself has been betrayed. Do you know of Cormac's Cup?"

"Yes. When Cormac the High King died, the *veleda* became the cup personified."

Iobhar murmured, "A lie spoken over it . . ."

"Broke it into three pieces," I finished.

"As the *veleda* is broken into three."

"I've lied, Iobhar," I said in a rush. "Over and over again, but . . . I didn't think it was so bad. I mean, just little lies, to bill collectors and my mother, and—"

"'Twasn't you who put it into play, but an ancestor. And it could have been done only by the most powerful kind of lie: a broken vow."

"But it if was an ancestor, then why should Aidan and I be punished for it?"

Iobhar's smile was cruel. "Blame your Druids. Consequences are far-reaching, and they meant for punishment to hurt. Which is more painful: what happens to you, or to those you love? You, as the *brithem*, should see this already."

"I'm the *brithem*?" I said uncertainly.

"Aye. Those are the spells you *can* do. You're the one who weighs, who can tell truth from lies."

Given how often I'd lied myself, it seemed a little too ironic.

"Your brother is obviously the Seer."

"Then who is the Prophet?"

Iobhar shrugged. "Someone in your family."

"But . . . there's hardly anyone left. My brother and me. My mother. My grandmot— Oh, *Grandma*. She knew the stories. She told me I was the *veleda*. She *said* there was a curse. She said we were broken, and she told me to find you." That hovering, silent presence, not speaking because she *could* not. The coma held her tight in its grasp. *Of course.*

"Then no doubt 'tis her."

"But what does this mean for the prophecy? It says the *veleda* must die. Does that mean . . . all three of us?"

"Perhaps."

"No," I said in horror. "No. Not my brother. Not my grandmother. I'm the one who's accepted it. It belongs to me. There must be a spell that can put us together again—"

"'Twas a curse. You cannot make it right or change it."

"But it's not fair! Why should all three of us have to die?"

"You forget the world you're in, *veleda*. Many things have been lost. Curses are meant to punish. The most awful outcome possible . . . that is the true one."

"But this is my family. We're all that's left."

"Which may be the point," he said.

"Iobhar, I have to go home. I have to tell Aidan. I have to ask my grandmother. Perhaps she knows what happened. Perhaps she knows a way to fix things."

"Do you really think she does, *veleda*?" Iobhar's amber eyes seemed to glow. He came around the counter, close enough that I was nervous. He stroked my cheek, and I felt transfixed. The spell of him was mesmerizing. "I've a better idea. Let it all go. 'Tis a new world. Such old things no longer belong in it. Stay with me. Let the Fianna and the Fomori go to whatever awaits them."

I whispered, "I can't."

"But you can." He brushed his lips across my jaw. It burned like fire. "Come now, kiss me."

I wanted to. The temptation to forget it all, to let it go, to stay here under Iobhar's spell. *Why not?* It was suddenly hard to remember why I cared about anything ... or what anything meant. I wanted to surrender ...

"The more you want something, the more it will cost." I was doing exactly what Diarmid had warned me not to. I was letting fear make me stupid.

I jerked away from Iobhar. But still I heard that music, the danger and the magical draw of him. My awareness of what he could do, of what he could make me want, shimmered between us.

"Let me go," I said.

Iobhar laughed. "You are still weak, *veleda*, and untrained. If I were to let you go now, my kin would make short work of you."

"I'm stronger than you think," I said.

"Not strong enough. When you are, you will be able to leave. Until then ... you belong to me."

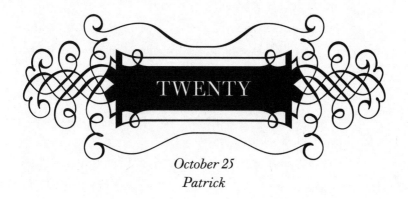

October 25
Patrick

Patrick tapped on the door and stepped into the room. Grace's grandmother lay motionless. The lamp on the night table was turned low, the curtains drawn, the room thick with the smell of unwashed skin and sickness.

The nurse jumped to her feet. "Mr. Devlin."

He closed the door behind him. "Is there any change?"

"No, sir. None."

He hadn't expected there would be, not really.

"I'd like a moment alone with her," he said.

The nurse left, and he sat in the chair beside the bed. Brigid Knox was skeletal, barely breathing. The truth was that she should be dead already.

And yet she wasn't.

He took her cold, white hand. "What does it mean?" he whispered.

Of course, there was no answer.

He felt a fool, but still he continued. "I've been having dreams about ancient times. I'm a . . . a Druid, I think. But now the dream is all around me, even when I'm awake. I know Grace is in danger. I feel that I should be able to *see*, but I can't. Nothing makes sense."

The woman couldn't answer. She probably didn't even hear. But Patrick couldn't stop.

"Grace is more powerful than they'd imagined. They aren't trying to save her, because they need her death. I've turned the prophecy around and around, but I can't figure it out. Grace says you know things, and I . . . I suppose I'd hoped that you could give me a sign, that you could show me something. I'm a fool, I know. I should just—" He bowed his head, feeling desperate and alone again.

Her chest shuddered, a sharp intake of breath. Her whole body shook. Fearfully, he leaned close—

And he fell into time.

The air was thick with smoke. All around him were biers with men upon them. Finn and Ossian. Oscar and Conan. Keenan and Goll and Diarmid. The archdruid, Tuama, stood in the middle of the circle, touching each of the Fianna with a hawthorn branch while a slight girl stood next to him.

Neasa's daughter, whom he, Glasny, had vowed to protect, as he'd protected her mother.

Tuama chanted the spell; Neasa's daughter repeated it. The roots of the rowan tree writhed beneath their feet. Neasa's daughter brought down strikes of purple lightning, and the earth opened, swallowing the Fianna and then closing again, leaving no scar. The spell was complete. It had worked; the future of the Irish was tied to the Fianna.

Neasa's daughter said, "'Tis done, Glasny. I did it."

The scene melted away; he was in a room, empty but for a pallet on the floor spread with furs. He held a bowl in his hand—cast bronze, decorated with wrens, and inside was a potion—he smelled vervain and wormwood and ylang-ylang. He lifted the bowl to his lips, drinking, waiting for the visions. . . .

Suddenly Patrick was back in the bedroom, staring down into an old woman's face. He broke out in a cold sweat, nauseated. It took him a moment to remember who and where he was. Quickly, he pulled his fingers from hers, rubbing his face, raking back his hair.

He still smelled the potion, tasted it. Somehow, Grace's grandmother had given him the message and shown him what to do.

He yanked open the door so violently, the nurse in the hall jumped. "I need vervain," he told her. "And ylang-ylang. Wormwood."

"And where am I to get that, sir?"

"Ask the kitchen, and tell them I don't want excuses. Tell someone to get it all and bring it back here, as quickly as possible."

Patrick went to his bedroom and grabbed the bronze bowl on his dresser. He took it to his study, leaving instructions for the butler to bring him the herbs the moment they arrived. Then he waited.

It seemed to take forever—it was hours, certainly, before John came to his study with his hands full of small jars. "We could only find them dried, sir," he said apologetically. "I hope it will serve."

So did Patrick. There was a ewer of water on his desk, and as soon as John left, he opened each jar and sprinkled the correct proportion of the dried leaves and stems into it—*how could I know this?* But he did. He waited for the potion to steep, pacing to the glass cases against the wall, staring unseeingly down at the relics, thinking of the vision, the Fianna, the earth shuddering beneath his feet. *Glasny*, Neasa's daughter had called him, and it troubled Patrick that he knew the name already, that he knew *her*. The whole thing had been like a memory—though how could it be his?

By the time the potion was ready, it was twilight. Instinctively, he knew it was the perfect time. The infusion was muddy looking, the leaves and stems bloated. He poured the potion into the bowl and nervously brought it to his lips, taking a careful sip. It tasted like dirt, chased by a strange, faintly herbal flavor. Not pleasant but not horrible either. He drank until it was gone and then sat, closing his eyes, waiting for . . . he didn't know what.

When it came, he didn't even realize it. The words of the prophecy wound through his head, spinning like dreams, waves washing upon a shore and a ship deck tilting beneath his feet, red lightning cracking though oak branches strung with mistletoe. *The sea is the knife . . . great stones crack and split . . . the rivers guard treasures with no worth . . . the rivers guard treasures with no worth . . .*

The rivers guard treasures.

Patrick opened his eyes.

The fireplace was before him, but what he saw was a ramshackle building and Grace standing at a window, her hands pressed against the glass, "Roddy's Grotto" painted upon it, and red lightning flashing in the room behind.

He knew how to find her.

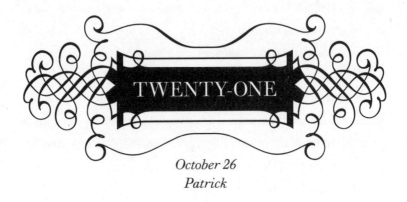

TWENTY-ONE

October 26
Patrick

A pawnshop on Cherry Street?" Aidan asked, looking strained.

Patrick glanced around the café. No one was paying attention. Still, he leaned closer. "I know it seems strange, but I tell you, I saw her there."

"You saw her? When was this?"

There was no logical way to explain it, and Patrick didn't try. "It was a vision I had."

"A vision?"

"I know, I know. It sounds so foolish, I hardly believe it either. But I drank a potion, and—"

"A potion?" Aidan's eyes widened. "Since when have you become a *deogbaire*?"

Cupbearer. Potion maker. Patrick was surprised Aidan knew the word. "I'm not, not really, but I dream about her all the time—"

"Stop. Please. This is my *sister.*"

"Not that way," Patrick said impatiently. "At least, not always. I'm in ancient times, and I'm not myself . . . or I am, but I'm more than me. All I know is that Grace is in danger. I don't understand any of it. I visited your grandmother, and I had a vision when I was with her that told me how to make the potion. So I made it, and drank it, and . . . and I saw Grace in the pawnshop, with red lightning flashing behind her."

"The same red lightning you were asking me about before?"

"I've seen it a few times now," Patrick confessed. "I know you don't believe me—"

"It's not that I don't believe you." Aidan took a deep breath. "It's that . . . this pawnshop you speak of . . . I've been inside. Recently. And Grace isn't there."

Patrick stared at him. "What?"

"Derry and I discovered that the owner was a Druid. But the man's been drained by the *sidhe*, Patrick, and he's half-mad. The place is full of *sidhe* magic. It was all Diarmid could do to get me out of there."

Patrick remembered Aidan in Battery Park, the hungry-looking *sidhe*. Aidan swaying toward them. *Protect him. Do your job.*

Aidan said, "I don't think I could have resisted it if not for Derry. I can't go back there. The place is dangerous as hell for any Druid. If Grace was ever there—and we saw no sign of her—I don't want to think what's happened to her."

"She's there," Patrick said, unwavering. "I'm going to get her. I hoped you would come with me."

"I can't go into the place," Aidan said. "But I'll come with you. I'll help however I can. But just so you know, Derry's been following me. He knows I meet with you. He overheard us talking the other night about my mother. He thought we meant Grace."

"That's the reason he broke into my house?"

"A rescue attempt," Aidan said wryly. "He's hotheaded, but you know that. He may well show up today. Just a warning."

"Perhaps we'll be lucky, and he'll fall down a well or something." Patrick rose. "Let's go."

Once they were outside, Patrick paused to search for any sign of Diarmid or the others. "It looks clear."

"That means nothing. He's sneaky. But he wasn't around when I left, so perhaps we will be lucky."

"Out recruiting more hoodlums?"

Aidan's glance was pointed. "I can't tell you our plans, so don't ask."

They walked quickly toward the East River. The pistol in Patrick's suit pocket was a reassuring weight, but it didn't ease his apprehension. Aidan was tight-lipped and pale, his blue eyes dark.

The neighborhood grew rougher. Patrick saw the curious stares and felt uncomfortable, even though he'd been in worse places in Ireland. Well, not worse, perhaps. Threadbare children played in puddles of sewage while pinched-faced mothers watched them wearily. Homeless men followed them with hostile gazes. In Ireland, Patrick had been a savior. Here, people blamed him for their troubles for no more reason than his good clothes. He wanted to tell these people what he hoped for, everything he was fighting for: Ireland and justice. Their homeland. If these people knew what he'd done, they would think him a hero too.

But then, he remembered the tenement the Fomori had burned in the search for the Fianna, the families they'd left homeless. Bres said they'd found them all better places to live, but Patrick realized he'd never made certain of it.

"It's not far now," Aidan said.

Corlears Hook. The waterfront bustled; steam rose in great gray plumes over the busy harbor. They turned the corner of a narrow, crowded street, and Aidan stopped. "There it is."

Just as in his vision. Patrick felt both nervous and giddy. "You're certain you won't come in?"

"Not if you want me to come out." Aidan looked drawn and ill. "If you're not back in an hour, I'll find Derry. We won't leave you there."

Patrick nodded. The pawnshop door was like any other, and yet he had the sense that once he went through it, everything would be changed. He hesitated, but in the end, he knew what he had to do. He had always known.

Patrick opened the door.

TWENTY-TWO

The fifth week (sidhe *time*)
Grace

*Y*ou belong to me."

As much as I hated being caught in this glamour, under Iobhar's spell, I knew that he was my only hope to learn more about my power. He'd told me that I could escape him when I was strong enough, and so I dedicated myself to being stronger. As long as I was here, I would learn everything he could teach me. I would learn until I could win.

"You are too attached to the world," Iobhar told me. "Until you put your allegiances aside, you will always be hindered. Remember, *veleda*, break space and time. Be part of the world, but apart from it as well."

Neither, nor. Both. Iobhar's amber gaze followed me everywhere. His music never left my head. I knew he was waiting for me to fail, to surrender. I was only one-third of the *veleda*, only a third of what I should be. And what of Aidan and my grandmother? I struggled with my fear and my frustration, while Iobhar tempted me to forget it all.

But there was more at stake than just myself or my family, and I couldn't turn my back on Diarmid—or Patrick.

"You are strong enough now," Sarnat whispered to me as we sat waiting for Iobhar to appear. Roddy rearranged brooches and necklaces and rings the way he did every morning. Torcan rooted around in a corner, and Stag nibbled at a bucket full of hay. Cuan curled up near Sarnat—his favorite person, as far as I could tell. He seemed to like her even more than Iobhar. "I'll help you. Together we can leave this place. He would say anything to keep you prisoner. We will go to my queen. She'll protect you."

I didn't answer. We'd argued this already. Listlessly, I moved a piece on the fidchell board.

The front door opened. I paid it little attention; people came into the shop all the time, thieves and sailors trading with Iobhar or redeeming what they'd pawned. He could make himself seen whenever he wanted, but his glamour kept me invisible, and I'd stopped being curious.

"Grace?"

The voice was so familiar, it was a moment before I realized it wasn't coming from my memory.

Patrick.

He stared right at me. Another of Iobhar's tests meant to teach me to separate myself from those I loved. But he looked so real.

"Grace!" He raced toward me.

"*Sever your allegiances*," Iobhar had said. I could not fail this lesson.

"You're here." Patrick stopped just before me. "Aidan and Diarmid said you weren't, but I was so certain . . ."

I stared dumbly at him. He was as perfect as my memory: gray-green eyes, nearly blond hair, a mouth that looked always ready to smile. He reached out. Sarnat hurled herself between us, forcing him back. "Don't touch her."

"Grace, tell her who I am. Grace? What's wrong? Tell this girl to stand down. I've come to take you home."

He said just the right things. Everything I would have wanted him to say. Iobhar was so clever.

I forced myself to look back at the game board. "A *veleda* can have no allegiances."

He tried to push past Sarnat, who shoved him. Patrick stumbled. Then he was holding a small pistol. He pointed it at Sarnat. "Get out of my way."

The pistol startled me. It seemed out of place, too modern for a glamour. Cuan whined. Stag pawed the floor. Roddy rose from his stool in protest.

"Put down your weapon," said Iobhar, appearing as stealthily and quickly as he always did. The raven capelet fluttered at his shoulders. His eyes blazed. I expected a snap of his fingers, and the vision would disappear. I did not expect him to address it.

Patrick tightened his lips and lifted the gun, more steady, more determined. "Not until you release her."

This was no vision.

"Wait— Patrick . . . you can see me?"

He frowned, but he didn't take his eyes from Iobhar. "Of course I can see you."

"You're not a glamour?"

"Hardly. Are you all right?"

"She is more than when you knew her," said Iobhar quietly. His bells tinkled as he moved forward.

Patrick leveled the gun. "Not another step."

"And what will you do?" Iobhar mocked. "Shoot me? Do you truly think it can stop me?"

Patrick looked momentarily confused. Then he gestured to Sarnat. "Then her."

Iobhar pointed.

I shouted, "No!" just as the bolt of red lightning whipped through the air. It caught the gun; Patrick jerked back, dropping it, crying out in pain. The pistol, melted into a misshapen lump, thudded to the floor.

Patrick stared at Iobhar. "You're the one."

I said, "He's the archdruid, Patrick. And one of the *sidhe* as well. He's very dangerous."

Iobhar said silkily, "Aye, very dangerous."

"I've an entire troop of soldiers just outside. Let her go, or I'll call them."

Iobhar laughed. "I could fry a troop of soldiers to a crisp before you said a word. But you've no soldiers. Only yourself and a Druid youngling who knows better than to come inside. Perhaps your rescue will not be a rescue at all." Iobhar laughed again. "Even if you could save her, what would you gain? Her allegiance? Are you so certain of your powers of persuasion?

Who will she choose in the end, do you think? You? Or the warrior she loves?"

My face went hot. "Iobhar, no—"

"Or perhaps 'tis not so simple. The warrior could not see through the glamour as you do. Why is that, I wonder?"

"I don't know. But I'm tired of games." Patrick reached out his hand to me. "Will you come with me, Grace?"

"I won't be able to get out the door. I'm not strong enough to leave."

"Release her." Patrick's voice was hard and cold.

"Patrick Devlin," Iobhar taunted. "Would-be savior of the Irish, burner of tenements, servant to the Fomori. Your very existence is a paradox. You brought the prophecy to life by calling the Fianna, and made the fight what it is now against the Fomori. Thus you've endangered the *veleda* whom you are sworn, through blood and time, to protect." Iobhar's grin was contemptuous. "Behold your illustrious protector, *veleda*. There has always been one, and there will always be."

I remembered Diarmid's story of my ancestor Neasa's protector, Glasny. He'd told me every *veleda* had one. "Patrick?"

"Listen," Iobhar ordered.

I heard Iobhar's bells and the Druid's music, the faint, eerie hum of the glamour. But there was a new song, and though I had not heard it before, it reverberated deep within me, familiar and beloved. Sweet and comforting, like hot chocolate beside a fire on a cold winter's day. *Safe*, and I realized why I had always trusted Patrick, why I loved him.

Because I was meant to.

He was my protector. It was why he could see me even through the illusion of the glamour—

An illusion. Something that both existed and didn't. Iobhar had given me the clue, and I had not been clever enough to see. The glamour was a lie, and I was the *brithem*, trained to see it. *Neither, nor.*

Suddenly, the world was a giant puzzle whose pieces came together as they never had before. I listened to the hum of the glamour, to the weft and weave of it, the way each note fit with the others, and this time I heard the discord. The shop was just a pawnshop, overfull and dusty, smelling of mildew and old leather. There were no hallways leading off to stairs or floors that didn't exist. No tangle of oak branches above, no knots of mistletoe. The lie melted away before my eyes.

Iobhar's gaze sharpened, a wry smile curved his lips. "Very good, *veleda*."

Patrick said, "What bargain will you make so I can take her out of here?"

"There won't need to be a bargain," I told him.

"I can no longer hold her," Iobhar acknowledged. His gaze held mine. "Remember this, *veleda*: in silence is your only safety. You remain in grave danger. I cannot protect you. Nor, I think, can he, though he will try."

I understood. I must keep secret what we'd learned about the splitting of the *veleda*. "But what about my—"

Iobhar stopped me with a shake of his head. "The path is uncertain. I cannot see it. Do not trust anyone. You are weak yet, and your training is incomplete. If you choose to leave now, I can do nothing to help you."

Patrick gestured roughly. "Come on, Grace, let's get out of here before he changes his mind."

I looked at Iobhar, struck by how much I didn't know. How much he could still teach me. I was tempted to stay. To learn. To drink up all his knowledge—

"Aidan is outside," Patrick said.

My family. The split *veleda*. The Fianna and the Fomori and everything that depended on my choice.

I took Patrick's hand. He was as warm and reassuring as he'd always been.

Iobhar said, "We will see each other again, *veleda*. You will need my help."

"If I do, it will be on my own terms," I told him.

"It has always been on your terms, and if you were stronger, you would know it. Now, go. And take your wretched *sidhe* slave with you before I turn her into a cat."

None of us had to be told twice. I followed Patrick to the door, Sarnat hurrying behind. But just before I stepped out, Iobhar said, "The danger you walk into is greater than the one you leave."

I stumbled. Sarnat whispered, "No stopping, milady." Patrick pulled me over the threshold into a sharp, bright day.

I was back in the world again.

TWENTY-THREE

Earlier that day
Diarmid

Diarmid kept returning to the pawnshop, despite the fact that Grace wasn't there. He'd spent days circling it, thinking about it, sometimes without realizing he was doing so. Today was just the same. It was as if he woke from a trance and found himself again on Cherry Street. He didn't know why, or what he meant to do. He was irritated with himself and turning to go, when he saw Aidan.

Grace's brother stared into the pawnshop window. Every alarm in Diarmid's head went off. He should have known Aidan would come back here. He was a Druid, after all. When Aidan started toward the building, Diarmid ran at him full speed.

"By the gods, Aidan, no!" He grabbed Aidan's arm, jerking him back into a pyramid of barrels. When Diarmid pulled Aidan upright again, Grace's brother zapped him with a small lightning strike.

Diarmid yelped in pain. "What did you do that for?"

"Why the hell are you here?"

"'Tis a good thing I am. I just *saved* you, if you'll notice—"

"I don't need your help. Just go, will you?"

"Not without you. Finn won't take kindly to a drained stormcaster. Not that I care, but he'll blame *me*, and I've suffered enough for you and your family."

"I'm not going to be drained." Aidan glanced nervously at the building. "I'm not going inside, I promise you. Now get out of here before you ruin everything."

"Ruin everything? What are you talking about?"

Aidan's glance leaped back to the building. The pawnshop door opened. Diarmid saw Patrick Devlin come out—*by the gods, Aidan's betrayed us*—and then—

Grace.

Found. Alive. His heart stuttered with relief and joy. *Grace.* He took a step toward her.

Aidan grabbed his arm. "Wait, you fool."

Grace looked up, catching sight of him. Then, she deliberately looked at her brother as if Diarmid were a stranger, as if he meant nothing to her.

"Aidan!" She rushed across the street, her blue silk gown flashing rainbows in the sun, her dark hair flying out behind her as she hurled herself into her brother's arms. The shock of it paralyzed Diarmid. He stood watching, numb and sick and invisible. It should be his arms she was running into. Why wasn't it so? Why wouldn't she look at him? It made no sense. He waited in growing fear and misery.

"What are *you* doing here?" Patrick demanded.

Diarmid tore his gaze from Grace and Aidan. Patrick glared at him. Behind Patrick stood a pale, blond girl with fathomless *sidhe* eyes.

"I was in the neighborhood," Diarmid said tightly.

"You're one of the Fianna." The girl's tone was accusatory; he would have bristled if he hadn't been so aware of Grace in her brother's arms. Ignoring him.

"You let a fairy near her?" he asked Patrick.

"I had nothing to do with it," Patrick snapped. "Grace has been here all this time. Held prisoner by some *sidhe* archdruid."

The girl said, "Battle Annie sent me to protect her, which I have done, while you were far away, Ua Duibhne."

"Battle Annie?" The cursed fairy queen. Diarmid had known she'd had something to do with Grace's disappearance.

Then Grace pulled away from Aidan and said, "I didn't expect to see you here, Diarmid."

The sound of his name coming from her lips sank through him—his weakness, and worse now because of her distance. She wouldn't meet his eyes.

"As you can see, we've found her, which none of the Fianna could do," Patrick said to him. "Alive and unharmed. Why don't you run back to Finn and tell him the news?"

Diarmid didn't look away from Grace as he said, "There's no chance I'll let you take her back to the Fomori."

"It's where she wants to be," Patrick said. "With me."

"Perhaps you should ask her," Diarmid said steadily. "Because it looks to me like she's attached to her brother. Who's with us. Or was, at any rate."

"I still am." Aidan's arm tightened around Grace's waist.

"Then why is Patrick here?" Diarmid asked. "Why did you try to get me to leave?"

"Patrick's the one who figured out where she was," Aidan said.

"He's my protector. My Glasny." Grace smiled at Patrick, and his answering smile made Diarmid want to stab something.

But the smile left Patrick's face when he said to Diarmid, "Yes, I'm her protector. But you knew that already, didn't you? The *veleda* protector, bound through time. We belong together. I'll keep her safe. You sent her into danger. Why should she go with you?"

"I'd hear it from her," Diarmid said, his heartbeat loud in his ears. "Grace, please . . . come with me and Aidan. We can protect you. You know we can. You know *I* can. I have."

She still avoided his gaze, saying to Aidan, "I need to see to Mama. And Grandma. You understand, don't you? I *have* to."

Aidan looked troubled.

"No," Diarmid said.

"She's made her choice," Patrick told him. "How many times must she say it?"

"Grace, look at me," Diarmid said anxiously. "Aidan, you can't let her do this. Tell her. Tell her what will happen if she chooses the Fomori. Grace, by the gods, will you just *look* at me—"

"I'm not choosing anyone yet." This time she did look at him, a brief flicker of a glance that staggered him. "Until I do, I want you to leave me alone, Derry. Please. If you care for me at all, you'll do so."

The words were like stones, and everything in her tone told him she meant them. But that glimpse of her eyes had been enough for him to see the lovespell, though she tried to hide it. He knew she was lying.

What he didn't know was why.

"Aidan, stop her," he said.

"It's not his choice either." Patrick held out his hand; Grace took it. "Now I'll thank you to do as she asks. In fact, I'll do what I can to make certain of it."

Diarmid was rocked by a storm of jealousy and rage and confusion. "I won't let her just walk into danger."

"I'm her *protector.* Do you really think I'll let any harm come to her?"

"Deliberately? No. But your foolishness may."

Aidan put his hand on Diarmid's shoulder. "She wants to go with him, Derry. Let her go. It's best for now."

"Thank you, Aidan," Patrick said with a smug smile. He walked away, pulling Grace with him. She went without a backward glance, and Diarmid's heart went with her. She belonged with him, with the Fianna, with—

Finn.

"It's best this way for now," Aidan said again. He looked gray and sickly, not at all like a man who'd just been reunited with his long-lost sister.

"Are you all right?" Diarmid asked.

Aidan blinked as if calling himself back from a daydream. "There's something wrong."

"There's something wrong, and you let her go with him?"

"It's nothing to do with that. It's . . ." Aidan shook his head. "Never mind."

Diarmid stared after Grace, the sway of her skirts, the rainbows chasing themselves over the washed silk, the bounce of her curling hair against her back. He willed her to turn around. *Look at me. Smile at me.*

She and Patrick and that *sidhe* girl turned the corner and disappeared.

Even so, one small hope burned. The love that had flickered in her eyes before she forced it away. She loved him still, and she was hiding it. Hiding *something*.

And he would not rest until he found out why.

TWENTY-FOUR

That same day
Grace

I had nearly run to Diarmid before I remembered why I'd left him. I loved him and I could not love him. There was more reason to stay away from him than ever. Everything was so uncertain. It might be that Diarmid held the destruction of my entire family in his hands.

His loyalty belonged to the Fianna, not to me. It wasn't Diarmid who had seen through Iobhar's glamour, but Patrick. Patrick was my protector. My heart had known it from the beginning.

But walking away from Diarmid today had been the hardest thing that I had ever done.

My steps were heavy as I followed Patrick and Sarnat. Patrick hailed a carriage. As I started to climb in, Sarnat said, "This is where I leave you, milady."

"Leave me?" She had been my only friend these last days, and I was nervous at the thought of being alone with Patrick. There was so much to say, so much that could not be said . . .

"You've no more use for me now. You're safe with him."

"I've so much to thank you for."

"Aye, you do." She smiled. "But we'll meet again. Good-bye, milady."

I watched her walk away until Patrick said, "We should go."

I got into the carriage. Patrick sat across from me, drumming his fingers on his knee. He was nervous too—it made me feel better to see it.

The carriage started off, and I looked out the window, searching for something to say. So much had changed. I didn't know where to begin or what to tell him. "The trees are losing their leaves early this year, aren't they?"

"Early?"

"It's only September, and that one's nearly bare."

"It's not September, Grace. It's October twenty-sixth."

"But . . . it can't be! I haven't been gone that long."

"Almost three months," he said grimly.

I could only stare at him.

"Have you been with that *thing* all this time?"

"Iobhar," I said distractedly. "And yes. But I would have said it was only . . . I don't know . . . five weeks, perhaps?"

"The Otherworld," Patrick said. When I looked at him in confusion, he went on, "That was what kept coming up in the divination about you. The Otherworld. Daire Donn said time was different with the *sidhe*. That's what Iobhar was, wasn't he?"

October 26. Five days until Samhain.

I'd thought I had weeks to figure out what to do about the split *veleda*. I had only *days*.

"There's not enough time," I whispered.

"I suppose it's too much to hope . . . Iobhar called you the *veleda*. We weren't wrong about that?"

"No," I said.

"Did he know of another spell? Did he know how to save your life?" The hope in his voice hurt. I wanted to tell him everything. He was my protector, the *veleda*'s protector, which meant he was bound to protect my brother and my grandmother as well. He had a right to know the truth.

"In silence is your only safety. . . ."

I had been gone too long. I didn't know what had changed or what anything meant, and now it wasn't just my life at stake, but Aidan's and Grandma's as well. I had to take Iobhar's advice, at least until I understood more.

"He said there was no other spell," I told Patrick. "That the prophecy was in motion and there was no changing it. The *veleda* has to die."

"And the *geis*? Is there any way—"

"No."

"Will Diarmid do it? Or will he refuse?"

I stared out at the passing buildings, at people walking through their lives without a care. "He's loyal to the Fianna."

"And not to you?"

I forced myself to look at him. "Why would you ask that?"

Patrick took a deep breath. "You were with him for . . . for days. I know he used the *ball seirce* on you, Grace. Oscar told us. Aidan confirmed it."

"Why was Aidan with you, when he's joined the Fianna?"

"Aidan and I were working together to find you. He doesn't trust the Fianna to have your best interests at heart. I don't trust the Fomori when it comes to that either."

That was new. "You don't? Why not?"

Patrick hesitated. "It's not really that I don't trust them, it's just . . . they've discovered something odd about your power, and I'm troubled by what it might mean."

"What have they discovered?"

"They think you have the power of the triune. Goddess power. Like the Morrigan."

"*Goddess* power?" How stupidly, tragically *wrong*.

"Have you some reason to think it isn't true?"

I struggled again with the urge to tell him. "I wish it were true. But unless you know of another goddess who can't do a simple summoning spell, I can promise you it's not."

Patrick looked puzzled. "I didn't think so. But why do they keep seeing it? The three, over and over again. And the Fianna's Seer reads the same thing."

"I don't know," I lied.

He was silent. The carriage was no longer jolting over potholed streets. We were coming into a better part of town. Businessmen and women walking with their children. My old world. *Walking with Rose and Lucy. The confectioner's, and sugared violets melting over ice cream.* It felt so long ago.

Patrick said finally, "You didn't answer my question about the *ball seirce*."

I wasn't certain what to say, so I settled for the truth. "It was an accident. He didn't mean for me to see it."

"But you did see it. Yet you just told him to leave you alone."

"There's still the *geis*. I don't trust him."

"Do you love him?" I heard the fear in Patrick's voice, as if he had to ask but didn't really want to know, and I ached for him. He had been a friend to me. He had saved me. He was my protector. I had loved him; I loved him still.

I didn't know what the future held. But why hurt Patrick needlessly? None of this might matter in the end.

"The spell's worn off."

I thought he would be relieved, but he only looked away. Then he said, "We're home."

I glanced out the window. Patrick's house. *Mama.* As if he sensed my nervousness, Patrick reached for my hand. "I know your mother is anxious to see you. Are you ready?"

I nodded. My rescue had been so fast that I hadn't had time to think of what I would tell people, the questions I would have to answer. I had once been so worried about what everyone would think about my disappearance. Diarmid. My destroyed reputation. It seemed so unimportant now, but I knew Mama would not think so.

Patrick helped me from the carriage. When we were inside, he said, "I'll find your mother. Wait for me in the parlor?" I nodded, and he stepped away.

The sliding doors of the parlor were wide open; sunshine from the French doors slanted low and golden into the hall. I stopped short when I realized someone was already there, staring into the garden in a way so familiar that time slipped. As if only yesterday I'd seen her standing there just this way.

"Lucy," I said.

She whirled around. "You! What are *you* doing here? How dare you come back here! How dare you!"

Her fury startled me. "I'm sorry," I managed. "I didn't—"

"I suppose you thought you could just walk in and everything would be like it used to be. Well, it isn't! Did you even think of me once? Did you never wonder how I might feel? And Patrick . . . did you think of Patrick at all?"

"Patrick? Yes, of course I did. I—"

"Don't play your little innocent game with me. I'm not my brother. I'm not going to forgive you. We all know what you did. The whole world knows it!" Lucy glared at me, two points of pink on her cheeks. "I didn't think you'd have the *nerve* to come back here. I thought we'd find you . . . *expecting* . . . in some tenement somewhere—"

It was exactly what I'd feared people would say. I just hadn't expected it to feel so *personal.* Or so embarrassing.

"You knew I loved him, and you ran off with him anyway. I can't even *look* at you!" Lucy spun away so quickly, the ruffles on her gown fluttered.

"What's all this fuss— Oh!"

Mrs. Devlin came through the parlor doors. Her eyes went wide.

"Grace! Oh! Oh, my dear!" She rushed to me, enveloping me in her rose-scented arms, nearly suffocating me in the lace of her bodice. "Oh, my dear."

"How can you welcome her like that, knowing what she did to me?" Lucy cried.

Mrs. Devlin held me out at arm's length, sweeping me with her gaze. "You look well, oh thank heaven for that! None of us were certain. No one knew. But—"

"Is he here?" Lucy asked. "Is he waiting for you? You know there are guards everywhere. He'll go to jail this time, I promise you."

"Lucy, please," Mrs. Devlin said.

"It's not what you think," I said.

"Of course not." Mrs. Devlin clucked and soothed. "We'd despaired of ever seeing you again! To think of everything you must have gone through—"

Lucy snorted.

"The police will have to be notified. I'll send someone for them immediately. They've been so good, searching for you. It will be such a relief to them as well."

I had not thought of the police. I had no idea what I would say to them—or anyone. This suddenly felt so overwhelming. I sagged onto the settee, and Mrs. Devlin sat beside me in an explosion of lace and silk and scent. "It's only that we are so very glad to see you returned, and looking so . . . so *well*. You are well, my dear?"

A not-so-subtle way of asking whether I'd been abused by Diarmid. Raped or . . . or was it as Lucy had said, had I run off in some romantic elopement? Was I ruined? Was I with child?

The absurdity of it all hit me. If only it were that simple. "I'm quite all right." Unless you counted being one-third of a broken *veleda* who had to die in five days.

Mrs. Devlin sighed. "Well, good. Very good indeed."

We all turned at the sound of rapid footsteps from the hall. I rose just as my mother burst into the parlor. She rushed to me, grabbing me so hard we both stumbled. Mama. I knew these arms. I knew her scent. I had missed her so much.

I hugged her back and realized I was crying. She murmured, "It's all right, my darling. Everything's fine at last. You're home now. You're safe. Oh my darling, darling girl." Finally, she drew away, smoothing my hair, which had caught on the wet streaks of my tears.

"I've missed you so much," I said. "I've worried about you and Grandma—"

"Patrick! Grace has returned!" Mrs. Devlin said as Patrick came into the room.

"I know already, Mama. I brought her here directly from the police station." Had I not known he was lying, I never would have suspected it.

His mother looked relieved. "The police know? There's no need to send for them?"

"None at all. Grace has been answering questions for them all morning. In fact, I'm certain she's quite exhausted. We must let her rest."

Mama held out her hand. "Come with me, darling. I'll put everything to rights."

So calm, so self-possessed. Not at all like the mother I'd left. Something had changed. What was it?

I followed her out of the parlor and away from Lucy's baleful gaze—and a world that felt as if it no longer belonged to me.

TWENTY-FIVE

The next moment
Grace

I'd like to see Grandma first," I told my mother at the top of the stairs.

"She's just as she was," Mama said, but she took me to my grandmother's room and told the nurse to leave us.

The changes in Grandma, more than anything else, told me I had indeed been gone a long time. She was sunken, her lips drawn back, skin barely covering her bones. Her hair had gone completely gray. Her breathing was so slight, her chest hardly moved.

I laid my hand over hers where they rested on the bedcovers. "Grandma," I whispered. "Grandma, I'm back. I didn't mean to be gone so long. Time passes differently with the *sidhe*—you told me that in a story once. I'd forgotten."

I wanted to believe that she'd been waiting for me. That at the sound of my voice, she would wake. I wanted to think that the *veleda* connection between us, or even just my presence, would be enough to break the coma. But she slept on. I affected nothing.

Mama placed her hand lightly on my shoulder. "There's nothing you can do, I'm afraid. Nothing any of us can do."

It can't be this way. It can't end like this. But it could. It had. I could not bear the injustice of it.

My mother sat on the edge of the bed, pained with worry. "What happened to you, Grace? Where have you been?"

"You wouldn't believe me if I told you."

"You've been gone three months. You return wearing a strange dress and you're . . . different. Should I call a doctor or . . . perhaps an alienist?"

"You think I'm insane?"

"No. But it would not be unusual for a young girl who's experienced . . . terrible things . . . to need a rest."

"Everything's changed, Mama. *Everything.* But I'm not mad. I'm more myself than I've ever been. I want to tell you what happened, but—"

"I know you've been with Diarmid," she said. "No doubt you believe you're in love with him. He did show you the love-spot, didn't he? He would have been a fool not to, and while the Fianna are many things, they are not fools."

I was dumbfounded.

She took my hands, which were suddenly numb, in hers. "The Fianna will do anything to win you. They are ruthless. That boy is ruthless. They don't want to save you, but the Fomori do. There's no reason for you to die, not for the

Fianna or the Irish or anyone else. The Fomori want to help you, Grace."

I pulled away. "You told me you didn't believe any of this. That none of it was true. You said it was only a *story*."

"I didn't want to believe it. I suppose I thought that if I denied the legends long enough, they would never come true. I never wanted them to come true. Before your father died, his greatest wish was that you and your brother be Americans. He wanted you to have a better life than the one he'd left behind in Ireland. Those immigrants the Fianna care so much for— they're not where your future lies, darling. You're meant to marry Patrick, to have children, to be happy. You can still have that, Grace. If you choose the Fomori, they will do everything in their power to give those things to you." She grabbed my hands again, gripping them. "They have a plan, and I believe it will work. Whatever you think you feel for Diarmid is only a spell. He's used you. He wants you to choose the Fianna, but it won't be the right choice, darling. It won't save you."

The veleda's *split,* I wanted to say. *Can they help with that? What do you know of a curse upon our family?* I looked down at our hands, twined together. "Are you so certain of that, Mama?"

"I know what he must have told you, but he lied. Your heart knows this. You must be true to yourself. Grandma would tell you the same. Once, she made a choice she knew was wrong, and she has always regretted it."

"A wrong choice? What choice?"

Mama glanced at Grandma. "Mother would not mind my telling it, I think. It's your history too. Your Irish ancestors were very well thought of. There was even a time when they were revered."

Neasa.

"Mother's side of the family has always had a reputation for—well, I suppose you would call it the gift of sight. It was the *veleda* power, of course, passed down through the generations. In ancient times, that gift brought wealth and prestige, but then people stopped believing in the old ways. When the British took control of Ireland, our people were reduced to farming. Mother was raised in wretched poverty.

"And then she fell in love. He was a handsome boy. Dark hair and eyes blue as the sky. He swept her off her feet, promising her everything. She fell for those pretty words and that pretty boy."

A little too familiar.

"There was a neighboring farm, a family that had lived beside hers for generations. Patrick's family. The Devlins. Mother had been promised to the eldest son since birth. Devlin boys had often married the girls in our family."

I knew why, of course. The *veleda* protector, passed down through blood. But she said nothing of that, and so neither did I.

"Everyone hoped that the two farms together might survive where one could not. Both families depended on the marriage. Mother loved the Devlin boy. She had dreamed of marrying him. But when this pretty boy asked her to go with him to America, she ignored her duty and followed him."

"And that was Grandpa," I said.

Mama shook her head. "No. Mother discovered she was with child on the journey over. When they landed, this boy deserted her. For days, she searched for him. Weeks. She slept in the street and begged. One day, she was beaten and left for dead. She lost the child. She had no money to return to Ireland, and nothing to return to. Her family had been evicted. Her beloved mother and father died in a workhouse. The Devlins lost everything as well."

I was shocked. "I never knew."

"It's not a story Mother is proud of," Mama said. "I don't think she's ever forgiven herself. That boy was a distraction, a temptation, and she knew that. She was beguiled, but it wasn't love. It wasn't what she'd felt for the Devlin boy. But it was too late. All she could do was go forward." She sighed and looked at Grandma with sadness. "Living with what she did has been a terrible burden. I believe it's guilt that caused her madness."

I stared at my grandmother. It was strange to think she had a history beyond what I knew. Stranger still to think her past had held this.

"Don't make the mistake she did, Grace," Mama urged. "Don't believe Diarmid. Don't allow yourself to be . . . carried away by a pretty smile. Not when there are others who love you truly."

My mother's eyes were so blue in the dim light of the sick-room that they looked unreal. So much had changed, so much to take in . . .

"I won't, Mama. I promise."

She squeezed my hands. "That's all I ask. I know you'll do what's right. You always have."

She rose from Grandma's bed and left me, and I stayed, thinking about the things she'd said. Patrick's family and mine connected by time and blood. My mother's hope when she'd spoken of the Fomori.

Five days until Samhain.

"You'll do what's right." I only wished I knew what that was.

TWENTY-SIX

That night
Grace

I stayed in my room the rest of the day. Mama told me the Fomori had paid a call, but I said I was too tired. I wanted time to myself, time to think. Thinking, unfortunately, didn't help, and I was only more confused when I called the maid to help me ready for bed. But her company felt intrusive, and it had been so long since I'd needed a maid that I sent her away and combed out my own hair, watching my silhouette flicker against the lamplit walls as night came and my room took on deeper shadows. *"The danger you walk into is greater than the one you leave."* What kind of a *brithem* was I, that I could not find answers in anything?

I tried to read the book of Irish poetry that Patrick had given me so long ago, full of blood and thunder and anger. But I kept remembering tiny tenement rooms and boarders filling every space on the floor, swill milk and rotten cabbage and children playing in cesspools, and I wished the Ireland that Patrick worried about wasn't the one so far away from here. I wished he could see . . . but then Mama's words: *"Those immigrants the Fianna care so much for—they're not where your future lies."*

I closed my eyes and saw Diarmid standing in the street outside the pawnshop, his hair falling into his face, his confusion and pain stinging as if it were my own.

No, I can't think of him. I won't.

I listened to the house growing hushed, searching for reassurance in its music. There was Patrick's, those lovely bass notes, subsiding into sleep, and then . . . then a song I'd never heard before. It was an uncomfortable melody, distorted as if notes had been torn apart and scattered. Nauseating. I didn't know where it came from, or who it belonged to, and I tried to push it away and find something else—

A music I knew as well as my own. Fear and love. So close. So . . . close. No, it couldn't be. I'd told him to leave me alone. My eyes flew open just in time to see my bedroom door open.

Diarmid slipped inside, closing the door behind him.

I sat up in surprise. Had I wanted him so much, I'd conjured up an illusion?

"Sssh." He put his finger to his lips. "Quiet, unless you want me to be caught. I doubt I could escape this time."

"What are you doing here?"

"I came in with the coal delivery. I've been in the basement the last four hours."

His face and clothes were streaked with coal dust. Yes, he was real. *Very real.* "Four hours?"

"'Twas the only way I could get in to see you."

I put down the book and rose. "Did you not hear me this afternoon?"

"When you told me you didn't want to see me again, you mean?" His expression hardened. "Aye. But I'm a bit slow, you remember. Best to explain it so I don't get it wrong."

"You have to go. Patrick's just down the hall—"

"Sleeping like a baby. Snoring like a giant too."

"Patrick doesn't snore."

"Now, how would you know that, lass? Don't tell me I've reason to be more jealous than I am."

"I want you to go. I want you to stay away from me."

"The last time I saw you, you were declaring your undying love and promising to wait. You'll pardon me if I'm wondering what happened between then and now."

"I changed my mind."

"You changed your mind." He laughed shortly, advancing, and I backed up against the bedstead. "I came back to Governors Island to find you missing and no clue where you'd gone. For all I knew, you were abducted or dead. I've been searching for you for months." He came close, nearly touching. My pulse, which was already racing, went wild. But his eyes were cold. He was every inch a Fianna warrior now. Ruthless and angry and threatening. "Tell me what happened."

"Don't try to intimidate me. You can't frighten me. I know you too well."

"Then you must know I went half-mad when you disappeared. I've never been so afraid in my life. You owe me an explanation, Grace."

I supposed that was true. "I was in that pawnshop almost from the moment I left the island. The ogham stick told me it was where I would find the archdruid."

Diarmid looked puzzled. "How?"

"I told you, when we ... after we ... my power felt changed. Stronger. I understood that part of the prophecy. It was as if it *wanted* me to find him."

"But you couldn't have been there. I was in that shop. Twice."

"Twice? I only saw you the one time."

"You saw me? And you said nothing?"

"I tried. He held me in a glamour. No one could see me. I tried to talk to you. I touched you, but ..."

"That was you? I felt something, but . . . I don't understand. That old man had been drained. How could he build such a strong glamour?"

"He isn't the archdruid anymore. One of the *sidhe* drained him, and kept the power."

Diarmid frowned. "Patrick said something about a *sidhe* archdruid. I didn't know what he was talking about."

"I've been studying with him. I've learned so much. And there's still so much more—"

"But the ritual." Diarmid's voice was low and urgent. He grabbed my arms, and at his touch, my blood fired in recognition. "Is there another spell?"

"No. You were right. There's no other spell."

"The *geis*?" His voice was barely there.

I had to look away. "The *geis* too. It can't be changed."

"No," he whispered. He pulled me to him, holding me so tightly, I heard the rapid beat of his heart.

I wanted to stay there forever. I wanted to breathe him in. But I gave him a light push. He resisted for one moment, and then he let me go.

I said, "You mean to do it, don't you? You still mean to . . . kill the *veleda*."

"By the gods, how can I?" His voice and his eyes were raw with misery.

"You'd refuse it? You would choose death?"

He looked racked with uncertainty. But I knew what his decision would be. He'd chosen love over duty once before, and it had nearly destroyed the Fianna. I knew how he regretted it. He would not choose love again.

"Please, go now. Don't come near me again." I wanted to be firm, but my voice cracked on the last words.

My hands were still pressed to his chest. He captured one, wrapping his fingers around mine. "What if I don't believe that's really what you want?"

"Diarmid—"

"We have so little time," he said fiercely. "Why not spend it together? I don't want to be apart from you, not even for a moment. Together, we can find some way—"

"There *is* no way." It was so hard not to give in, not to say *yes, yes,* and tell him everything. Diarmid knew Druid ways, *sidhe* ways. Perhaps he would know what to do about the curse. But Iobhar's warning kept me silent. Even an archdruid didn't know what the effect of the split might be. How would a Fianna warrior? And if Diarmid could kill me, the girl he claimed to love, how much easier would it be to kill my grandmother, the *vater*?

"I don't want to be with you," I said. "I don't love you."

"Look at me," he said.

"The lovespell is gone. The archdruid took it away when I asked him to."

"You said it wasn't the spell that made you love me. You insisted on it."

"I was wrong. You were right."

"Grace," he said. "Kiss me."

The words. His deep voice. The spell of him . . . "Why should I do that? I just told you I don't care for you any longer."

"If you want me to believe you, then kiss me. I'll know then if what you say is true."

"I don't want to kiss you."

"Are you afraid?" he challenged.

I was. I was afraid of how much I wanted to kiss him, of everything he would know once I did. I could lie well enough with words, but this . . . I couldn't hide the way my body responded to his.

He leaned close. I felt the warmth of his breath as he said, "If you want me to go, you'll have to show me you don't care. Otherwise I'll never leave you. Not until we're both dead, and even then, if there is an Otherworld, I'll follow you there. I can promise that."

I felt the hand of fate—how was it I could still want him so much, even knowing what must be? *Remember what's at risk. The choice you have to make.* I had to lie to him and make him believe it.

I took a deep breath, gathering my strength, setting my mind against him. And then I kissed him.

I willed myself to feel nothing. I meant it to be a quick, nothing kiss, but even that brief touch sent my blood singing. I drew away. "There, you see? I—"

He dragged me back and kissed me again, and I was lost. My mouth opened beneath his, and his tongue played with mine; his hands were on my hips, keeping me in place, and in the kiss was everything that had passed between us—every other kiss, every touch, lying with him in a storehouse on a bed of straw. He trembled. I felt his longing and love, and it matched mine.

"We have so little time. Why not spend it together?" Oh, I wanted to. I wanted to . . .

But no. *No.* I forced myself to go numb. I made myself think of the lie I wanted him to believe. I didn't love him. I didn't want him. What was between us was over.

It is. It has to be.

I knew when he felt it. He pressed deeper, trying to get me to respond. I wouldn't let myself. He drew back, frowning, and then he kissed me again, fluttering little kisses at the corners of my mouth, my jaw, my throat. I stiffened in resistance.

Finally, he drew away. He looked bewildered and hurt and disbelieving, and I hated it. I hated how wrong it felt.

I made myself say, cruelly, "You see? Does that prove it to you? Now will you go?"

If he heard the tremor in my voice, he said nothing. He gave me a long, considering look. "Aye. I'll go. I won't trouble you again."

"Thank you," I said.

He turned toward the door, and then he turned back. "You know I'll never stop loving you, Grace."

This was so much harder than I wanted it to be. "Just go, Derry." When he reached for the doorknob, I said, "Don't get caught. Please. Be careful."

He looked over his shoulder and flashed that arrogant, cocky smile. "Why, lass, you sound as if you care."

The words echoed—he'd said them before, the last time he'd sneaked into my room, so long ago now that it seemed another lifetime. I was caught in that memory as I watched him slip out as silently as he'd come. I stood there for a long time, listening to the clock on my mantle, the ticking of the minute hand. One and two, then fifteen, then twenty—until I knew he was truly gone.

He wasn't coming back. I had sent him away, and it was best.

It was best.

It is best.

TWENTY-SEVEN

The next moment
Diarmid

S he'd tried to fool him, but he'd seen the love in her eyes and felt it in her kiss, no matter that she'd tried to hide it. Even so, Grace had done something no lass under the lovespell had ever done. She'd sent him away.

Diarmid hadn't thought it possible. The *ball seirce* bound too tightly. It stole a girl's will. Grace should not have been able to refuse him. And yet she had.

How? More importantly, why?

The question nagged at him—along with everything else she'd said—as he made his way back to the others. A *sidhe* archdruid. No way around the prophecy or the *geis*. He told himself that was why she wanted him to go. She was afraid.

But it was more than that. She was changed. She seemed settled in her power, with a newfound confidence he liked. And whatever Cannel said, Diarmid knew she was no goddess. He knew what that kind of power felt like; he'd beheld the Morrigan on many occasions. Such power was terrifying, no matter how well meant. Grace had *something*, but not that.

But what to tell Finn? How to tell him the *veleda* was not only found but in Fomori hands? Diarmid doubted Aidan had said anything. Why would he? He'd been working with Patrick Devlin in secret. He'd practically *given* Grace to Patrick. Diarmid didn't want to think of what Finn might do if he knew.

The basement flat was swarming with people. A party. A fiddler was playing a jig, and everyone who wasn't drinking was dancing, including Oscar, who whirled with some pretty lass. Clapping and shouting and whistling filled Diarmid's ears. At the far end, Conan worked a keg, his bald head shining in the lamplight.

It was the last thing Diarmid was in the mood for. He made his way through the crowd, nodding greetings as he looked for Finn. The music stopped, exhausted dancers left the floor while others took their place, and the fiddler began another song. Some lass grabbed Diarmid's arm and said breathlessly, "Come on, Derry. Dance with me!"

He shook his head and tried to smile. "Later, maybe."

He spotted Finn at last, talking with Keenan. Diarmid headed over. He didn't know what his captain saw in his face, but Finn frowned and clapped Keenan on the back so hard, he nearly choked. "Go on now and look to that lass you've been eyeing."

Keenan left. The music and noise were too loud. Diarmid saw Aidan across the room. Grace's brother looked worried. *Of course he does.*

"What are we celebrating?" Diarmid asked Finn.

His captain eyed him sharply. "Nothing. Just relieving tension. What is it?"

No point in delaying. Diarmid said bluntly, "The *veleda*'s been found."

"When? Who found her?" Finn asked.

"She was in that pawnshop with the drained Druid. Oscar and I couldn't see her because she'd been glamoured by one of the *sidhe* who has taken on the archdruid's powers."

"Taken on . . . how is that even possible?"

Diarmid shrugged. "'Tis true, that's all I know. Patrick Devlin found a way to release her. She's with him now."

"She's with Devlin?" Finn's eyes narrowed. "Why?"

"You remember Glasny? Neasa's protector?"

"I'm unlikely to forget the bane of my existence."

"Patrick is Grace's Glasny."

Finn groaned. "That is not good news."

"Not for us, no."

"You'll have to find a way to bring her back to us."

The music was irritating, the celebration grating. Diarmid's head began to ache. "It's over, Finn," he said. "She's asked me to leave her alone, and she's well guarded at Patrick's. I won't kidnap her again. Aidan might be able to persuade her, but she's done with me."

"She's still under the lovespell, isn't she?"

"She's not just any lass, Finn. She's been training with the archdruid. She's not as she was. She's the *veleda*, and she has a mind not easily swayed by spells. Could you make Neasa do something she didn't want to do? Because that is Grace now."

He was relieved when he saw that Finn understood. "What about the goddess power?"

"I don't think it *is* goddess power. She has power, but it's surely not as strong as the Morrigan's."

"No doubt such things have changed over time. Perhaps more training—"

"I don't think that will make a difference." Diarmid struggled for the right words. "Cannel needs to look at those cards of his again, because he's got something wrong."

"You've suddenly become a Seer, have you?"

"I'm telling you, her power is like . . . like Aidan's," Diarmid insisted. "Not a stormcaster's, but her power's no bigger than that."

Finn considered this. "You didn't see Aidan's power. Why should I trust you about hers?"

"Maybe I didn't feel it then, but I do now. And I feel hers every time I touch her. D'you think Aidan is more than a *eubages*?"

"No. He's a Seer and a stormcaster, but that's all."

"Grace is the same. Whatever Cannel's divining isn't what he thinks."

Finn rubbed his jaw. "Very well. I'll think on that. But we can't leave her in Fomori hands, Diarmid. Tell Aidan I want him to persuade her."

"Me? Why don't you tell him?"

"Because there's something between you two."

"Aye," Diarmid said dryly. "Dislike. And distrust."

"Go talk to him."

Diarmid sighed, uncertain why he was leaving it at that, why he hadn't told Finn about Aidan and Patrick Devlin. Because of Grace, he supposed. *Always because of Grace.*

Smiling as best he could at his neighbors and skirting the dancing, Diarmid pushed his way through the raucous crowd to Aidan, who watched him approach with obvious dread.

Well, good. Let him worry.

"I need to talk to you," Diarmid said when he reached him.

"What did you tell Finn?" Aidan asked warily.

"That Grace was rescued, and that she was with Patrick. I didn't tell him you were involved."

"Why not?"

"I was hoping you could give me a reason not to."

Aidan motioned for him to come closer. "You went to see Grace tonight."

"What makes you think I did that?"

"I feel her, remember? Now the glamour's been lifted, I can feel her again. I feel a connection to you too—and believe me, I don't like it any more than you do. I know you were together."

Aidan knew what Grace felt. It was disconcerting, and not just because Diarmid didn't like Aidan Knox knowing his most intimate moments. The whole thing was odd, wasn't it? That kind of bond? Feeling things as if they were one . . .

"Then you know she told me to leave her alone. Again."

"Do you mean to?"

"I don't know what I mean to do about anything. There's still the *geis*. The archdruid said it can't be changed. I never thought it could, but I hoped . . ." He let the words fall away, too weary to face them. "If I don't do it . . ."

"What happens?" Aidan asked.

"We fail and die. Never to return to any world. But we'll be the lucky ones."

"Why?"

"If we lose, the Fomori will enslave everyone. They won't kill you or Cannel—you're too valuable—but you'll wish they had. They'll force you to use your power to help them until you've gone mad, but they won't let you die, not until they've taken everything they can." After the last war, the Fianna had found prisons full of Druids. Blabbering, reeking, help-less, fingers blistered and bodies racked from overused power. Their minds had been broken; they'd been unable to tell their Fianna rescuers from Fomori torturers. It had been a kindness to give them poison and send them to the Otherworld.

"What happens to Grace if you don't kill her?"

"I don't know," Diarmid said honestly. "But prophecies have a way of working themselves out. And never the way you want them to."

"But you don't know for certain, do you?"

"You're the Seer. You tell me."

Aidan's face creased with worry. "I think, if the prophecy isn't answered, it would be disaster. But it's hard for me to see. When my grandmother's visions transferred to me, her madness came with it. It's all woven through. The prophecy is like a puzzle I have to put together. Some parts don't fit, some don't belong at all. But I can tell you this, Derry: something's happened that no one expected. Grace is keeping it secret, but—"

The music stopped dead; the basement went suddenly, completely quiet. Diarmid glanced up. There, standing on the stairs—

"Who is *that*?" Aidan whispered.

Battle Annie.

She was surrounded by six other *sidhe*, one of whom was the girl who had come with Grace from the pawnshop. She caught sight of Diarmid and whispered something to Battle Annie, who looked right at him.

His breath stopped.

Annie smiled, showing those wicked, pointed teeth. "'Tis you I have need of, Diarmid Ua Duibhne. Come—before I decide to turn your party into a wake."

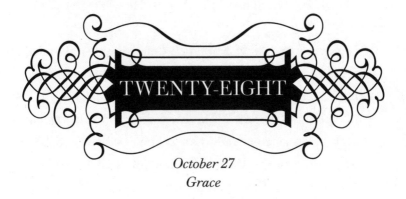

TWENTY-EIGHT

October 27
Grace

Mama came into my room, bearing a large white box. "Look what's arrived. Your debut gown."

My debut. A long ago party for a long ago girl.

"I've no need for that now. I'm surprised you never canceled the order."

"When you disappeared, I couldn't bear to. I didn't want to admit that you might not return." She glanced toward the window, blinking away tears. "Well. It's a good thing I didn't. It will be perfect for the Nolans' ball."

Mr. Nolan was a member of the Fenian Brotherhood, and tonight was his annual ball to raise money for Irish independence. Patrick was obligated, and the Fomori had all accepted, but I hadn't planned to attend.

"I'm not going, Mama."

"Rory Nolan is very important," she said firmly. "And you are Patrick's fiancée."

I laughed. "Samhain's almost here. How can any of that matter?"

Four days from now. Four days before my world ended. How could I think of a *ball?* "The Fomori *will* find a way, my darling."

"There's so little time." *And there's so much you don't know.*

Mama grasped my hand. "Grace, I must ask you to believe that you have a future. Can you do that for me?"

"I don't know," I whispered.

"You must try." She smiled, but I saw a misery in her eyes. "Please, Grace. For me. Don't give in to despair."

Her words echoed a memory. Diarmid on Governors Island just before the storm that sent us running for shelter and . . . and other things. *"Despair is our enemy. . . . You can't give up hope."* I couldn't take that away from Mama. I lifted the gown from the box, and suddenly, I was in my room at Iobhar's, lifting the same gown—glamoured—from a trunk. Numbly, I dressed. A maid came to put up my hair for the first time. Mama said that as an affianced woman, I was officially an adult. After tonight, I would not wear it down in public again.

I felt like an imposter as I stared at myself in the mirror.

"That pink is such a lovely color on you," Mama said from the doorway.

"Devlin won't be able to look away."

I imagined Diarmid standing behind me, his eyes warm, and for a moment, my yearning for him was the strongest part of me.

But you can't have him.

"Shall we go down?" Mama asked.

Patrick and his mother and Lucy waited at the bottom of the stairs. I saw his surprise, as if I were a stranger to him as well. He leaned close to whisper, "You look beautiful."

We got into the carriage, and while Lucy and Mama and Mrs. Devlin chatted and laughed, Patrick and I were silent. I felt his eyes on me and tried not to look at him. I felt guilty enough, because I knew he still loved me, even after everything, and I felt small when I thought of how I'd betrayed his trust. I loved Patrick, but not the way he wanted me to love him.

And if I did have a future, I wasn't certain I wanted marriage to be part of it. At least not yet. I'd only been away from the pawnshop for a day, but already I missed studying and learning, even if my teacher was a lying, dangerous, mercurial villain. I was a *brithem*, after all. Perhaps, if I survived . . .

Well, there was no point thinking it, not unless I discovered what the split *veleda* meant and what I could do about it.

When we arrived at the Nolans', servants took our wraps and ushered us upstairs to the third floor ballroom. Through the crowd, I saw Tethra, with his huge mustache and its pointy waxed ends; Daire Donn, handsome as ever; Lot, her blond hair swept up and shining in the light, her gown a mesmerizing blue. They looked as if they belonged here, as if they'd been part of this society forever. In one corner, a quartet played, and couples whirled about the floor, skirts brushing the floorboards with a *swish* as women smiled into the eyes of their partners.

There had been a time when I longed for this. When I'd wanted to wear my hair up and dance at a real ball. When I would have given anything to have someone like Patrick Devlin at my side. But now, I only felt out of place and sad.

"Shall we dance?" Patrick asked.

"Shouldn't we say hello to the Nolans first?"

"There's a line. We'll be waiting to say hello for an hour. Come, dance with me."

I glanced at my mother, who gave me a reassuring nod as Patrick led me onto the dance floor. He was a good dancer; I barely had to think to follow him, which I was glad for, because I was slowly becoming aware of the whispers. First murmurs, and then louder—meant for me to hear. "How dare she!" "I heard she ran off with that gang boy, and we all know what must have happened *then* . . ." ". . . foolish to take her back."

I felt a flush work its way up my throat and into my cheeks. Patrick's jaw clenched. He squeezed my hand. "Ignore them."

But it was hard to do. I felt people staring; I saw the way they spoke to each other behind their hands. When we went to get punch, the women near the table fled as if I were some terrible disease. I wished Aidan were here. Or Iobhar. A few well-placed bolts of lightning would be welcome, though admittedly, Iobhar might set the whole ballroom afire. Just now, I didn't think I would object.

Patrick said softly, "You and I know what really happened. That's all that matters."

It didn't really help. Then I saw my best friend, Rose Fitzgerald. The last time I'd seen her, she'd been at the Fulton ferry wharf, distracted by Aidan while Diarmid spirited me away. I felt a searing relief. "Look! Rose is here! Thank God!"

Patrick frowned. "I don't know that you—"

But I was hurrying toward her before he could finish.

"Rose!" I called, and she turned. I slowed when I saw the rising panic in her eyes. *No. No, not Rose too.*

Her smile was nervous. "Oh. Grace. I didn't expect to see you here."

"I think no one did." Urgently, I said, "Please tell me we're still friends, Rose. Please—"

"I'm not allowed to speak with you." She looked guilty and upset. "I want to, but . . . my mother's coming. Tell me quickly: are you all right? Did he hurt you? Did he—"

"I'm fine." I could hardly speak past the tightness in my throat. "He didn't hurt me." *Not yet, anyway.*

Rose looked relieved. She glanced past me. "I'm so happy. And I'm so sorry. Please understand, I—"

"Rose, dear, you must come meet Mrs. Getler." Rose's mother came up behind me.

"Hello, Mrs. Fitzgerald," I said, forcing a smile.

She ignored me completely. If not for the fact that her mouth pinched, I would have thought myself still caught in Iobhar's glamour. She gestured imperiously to her daughter. "Come now, Rose."

Rose gave me an apologetic look, and then was swept away. I was left standing alone. Everyone had seen my humiliation. Whispers gathered in force around me. I could have borne it better if it hadn't been Rose. That she felt badly didn't make it better. I wanted her to be braver. To be the Rose she was with me, flouting convention, cursing, kissing inappropriate boys. But I knew that was only the play Rose. The real Rose had been careful not to let anything mar her reputation, and I could not blame her for snubbing me. She had a life to live in society, and I . . . *Oh, Rose!* I wished she would come back so I could tell her everything.

But you can't. And she can't help you. No one can.

An arm came around my shoulder. I was enveloped by the scent of water lilies. Lot. "They've no idea of how important you are. They are nothing but ants beneath your feet."

Not really the comfort I was looking for, though I knew she meant well, in her way. The life I'd been meant to lead had slipped away, and though moments before, I'd been feeling as if I'd outgrown it, I wanted it to be *my* choice whether to keep it or not. I was angry at myself for caring.

I went with Lot to Daire Donn, who took my hands. "Ah, my dear girl! Now you are with the most popular people in the room, eh?" He laughed, flashing white teeth, his chocolate eyes twinkling. "They'll change their minds when they see how much we love you."

"Somehow I doubt that."

"We could make them," Lot suggested. Her smile was light, but there was a menace beneath that made me think of the legends, the gnashing teeth in her breast and four eyes in her back. I was glad she was on my side. For now. "You will be a heroine. There will be statues in your honor."

I didn't want to point out that most statues were for the dead.

She and Daire Donn exchanged a look I couldn't read, and he turned to me. "Come and sit with me awhile?" I nodded. He took me to a cushioned seat by an open window. The night air was chill, but it felt good against the stifling heat of the room. "Would you like some punch?"

"No, thank you."

He made a face. "I don't blame you. Tastes like sweet horse piss." When I smiled, he gestured to the crowd. "The Fianna spread the rumors about you, and made certain everyone here heard them. They will stop at nothing to get what they want. If those in this room knew the truth, they would be more charitable."

"Or perhaps not," I said. "It's not the kidnapping they care about. It's that I was alone with him."

"Ah yes. How do you think of him now, lass? Forgive me, 'tis only . . . the *ball seirce*. Ua Duibhne is quite unscrupulous, as I'm sure you know."

I told him the same lie I'd told Patrick. "The spell has faded."

I didn't know if he believed me, but before he could say anything, Patrick came hurrying over, looking worried.

Daire Donn rose. "I'll leave you to your fiancé."

When he was gone, Patrick sat next to me. "What did Rose say?"

"She's not allowed to speak to me," I said bitterly. I glanced toward Mrs. Fitzgerald, who was preening as she flirted with Tethra. "Her mother cut me. She's known me since I was a child. But now I'm a greater monster than a Fomorian sea god, it seems."

"Grace—"

"I'm sorry. I don't mean that. It's not Tethra who's the monster."

Patrick let out a breath. "Well, I think we've made enough of an appearance, don't you?"

"Showing up was more than enough. But I don't want to hurt your business . . . and neither your mother nor mine will be happy to leave. Lucy will be furious."

Patrick seemed bemused. "You would stay and bear this just because they won't want to go?"

My mother was laughing and talking with Lot. "She looks happy again."

"She and Lot have become very close."

"Mama believes they can save me," I said quietly. "But I don't think you do."

Patrick hesitated. "It's complicated. I don't want to talk about it here. Let me make our apologies to Mrs. Nolan and tell my mother we're leaving. I'll send the carriage back for them."

"We'll be unchaperoned."

"Do you care?"

I looked around at those people who would not even meet my eye because they'd rather believe gossip and rumors than the truth. "No."

"Then I'll be right back."

The music ended. People swarmed from the floor, avoiding me. It hurt more than I wanted to admit. I did care what these people thought of me. They'd known me my entire life; they had been my friends. But then again . . . they were right about one thing: Diarmid *had* changed me, and I did not think I could again be the Grace Knox they had known.

Suddenly I was suffocating.

Patrick returned. "That's done— Grace?"

My protector. I could breathe again. "Are we ready?"

Patrick helped me to my feet. "More than ready."

Once we were inside the carriage, I said, "Tell me why you don't trust the Fomori."

"I saw Miogach lose his temper, and it nearly ended with Aidan being dead. Miogach has apologized for it, but at the time, I thought they *wanted* Aidan's death, even though I'd asked them not to hurt him."

"But that's not all, is it?"

Patrick shook his head. "Bres tells me there's no spell to save you. They've come up with another plan."

"Which is what?"

"A bargain with the Otherworld. Lot plans to trade with them to keep your soul after you die, the same way Aengus Og did with Diarmid—do you remember the legend? Did he ever tell you if it was true?"

"It was true, but he didn't like it. And I don't think I would like it either." I felt deeply cold at the thought.

"It would be only temporary, until they could discover a way to bring you back permanently."

"But there are no guarantees."

"Lot's convinced it will work. But I don't know if *I'm* convinced, and . . ." Patrick paused.

I waited. I felt how much he didn't want to say what came next.

"And they believe you have goddess power. They're not fools. They see what that would bring us. To me, no power is worth losing you, but—"

"You think the Fomori won't be able to resist it."

"The Fianna too. Aidan's just as nervous. They might just be telling us what we want to hear. When it comes to your life, I trust only Aidan."

The name he didn't mention was as loud as a shout.

Patrick's eyes gleamed in the glow of a passing streetlamp. "Grace, I know everything's different now—"

I felt a surge of panic. "Patrick—"

"I want you to know that for me nothing has changed. I still love you. I know that perhaps you no longer love me. But if you think you could again . . . if we survive this . . ."

I'd known this was coming. The hope in his eyes made it hard to say what I must. "You're right, nothing's the same. There are things I can't undo."

"If you mean with . . . with him . . . I know. I don't care."

I shouldn't be surprised. Patrick had known about the lovespot; he must have suspected the rest. I knitted my fingers in my lap. "It's not only that. The ritual and . . . how can we make promises if we don't know that we can keep them? I mean, I may not even be around to keep them."

"Don't say that."

"It's true. And everything's so confusing." I wanted to tell him about the split so badly. *"In silence is your only safety."* I thought I could trust Patrick, but could I really? Iobhar had made no exceptions. "I have to make a choice, and I can't let anything blind me. Not love for him, or you, or . . . or anything else."

"All right," he said, and I saw how I'd hurt him. "But it would be best if everyone thought we're still engaged. You'll be safer if they think I have a claim to you."

"You do have a claim," I whispered. "You know you do. You're my protector."

"But I want so much more than that, Grace."

What could I say? We sat in uncomfortable silence the rest of the way to his house. I wanted nothing more than to go to bed, to not have to think or feel anything. The ball, the snubs, Rose's slight, Patrick's confession . . .

We stepped out of the carriage into a night grown colder; I shivered beneath my thin shawl.

"Grace." Aidan's voice came from the darkness. He stepped into the light.

Patrick glanced toward the porch and the guard, and whispered, "Are you mad, showing up this way?"

"I didn't have a choice." Aidan turned to me in apology. "We can't wait, I'm afraid."

I heard another sound in the darkness. Finn stepped forward. I hadn't seen him since the night of the battle in my backyard, and I'd forgotten how overwhelming he was. He seemed to fill up the night, though he was no bigger than an ordinary man.

And then Diarmid came from behind him.

This could not be good, no matter that everything in me leaped to see him. "Hello, lass," he said.

Patrick took my arm. "What is it? Why are you here?"

"It's Battle Annie," Aidan said. "She came looking for Grace."

"The river pirate?" Patrick asked.

"The *veleda* made a bargain with her," Finn said.

"But . . . but that was to be after," I said. "After Samhain. If I was still alive."

"Did she say that, Grace?" Diarmid asked. "Did she say *after Samhain*? In those words exactly?"

Even in the darkness, his gaze seemed to pierce me. "I thought . . . I thought that was what she meant."

Grimly, he looked at Finn.

"I'm not letting her meet with any fairy," Patrick said. "You must be insane to think it."

Finn said, "She has no choice. She made a bargain. We'll see she comes to no harm."

"You?" Patrick laughed. "I'm to trust the Fianna, when this is *his* fault to begin with? *He's* the one who put her into Battle Annie's hands."

"We were being chased by your Fomori," Diarmid snapped. "I didn't know they were *sidhe* until it was too late."

"Enough," Finn barked. "This arguing is pointless. Battle Annie's asked for Grace, and we've promised to deliver her. Come if you like, Devlin. But a *sidhe* queen is no one to deny. If she has to come after Grace herself, she'll be angry. And it won't be just the Fianna who will pay the price."

"Well, Grace?" Aidan asked.

They were all looking at me. I *had* made a bargain, and I would not break my vow. Whatever it was Battle Annie wanted from me, I had to answer.

"Very well," I said. "Take me to her."

TWENTY-NINE

That night
Grace

As I turned to get back into the carriage, Diarmid was at my side, his hand on my elbow, radiating heat. He whispered, "How respectable you look, lass," and his breath stirred the tendrils of hair escaping my pins. It was all I could do not to fall into his arms.

There was not enough room for all of us in the carriage, so Finn rode with the driver while the rest of us crowded inside. I sat beside my brother, Diarmid and Patrick on the opposite seat, so stiff they looked like a pair of perching statues. We were so close, Diarmid's knees brushed my skirt. He pressed his leg to mine, and I couldn't help glancing at him. His smug smile said he knew how affected I was. Obviously, I hadn't fooled him when I'd told him I didn't love him.

There was no room to move away, and so I tried to ignore him. *No future. You cannot trust him.*

I was more afraid of Diarmid than of Battle Annie. I'd dealt with her well enough before, and Patrick and Aidan and

Diarmid and Finn were here to protect me, though I didn't think I would need them. She wasn't as strong as Iobhar, and I'd learned so much. Whatever Battle Annie wanted from me now, I was confident I wouldn't be trapped.

I had no idea where Annie's lair was, but when we arrived at Corlears Hook, I wasn't surprised. She'd easily navigated the crowded river the night she'd brought me here, as if she'd done it often. The carriage even stopped at the same pier, next to the saloon called the Hangman's Noose. Voices came from inside, drunken arguing. I shuddered, half expecting to see river rat boys swarming from beneath the pier, but there was no sign of them tonight.

Finn helped me from the carriage with a smile that warmed his icy-blue eyes. "Not to worry, lass. We'll keep you safe."

"I won't let anything happen to you," Patrick reassured me.

"She can save herself, if she listens well enough," Diarmid said stiffly. "Remember what I told you, Grace."

"I remember," I said.

Aidan caught my eye, mouthing, *I need to talk to you.* He looked worried and a bit ill. Before I could wonder why, Finn opened the door of the Hangman's Noose.

The saloon was dim, lit only with a single oil lamp. There was no furniture at all. The bar was a plank supported on barrels. Men looked up as we came inside, clearly startled at the sight of a girl in a pink ball gown, clutching a paisley shawl.

The bartender, a young man with dark eyes, glowed faintly silver. *Sidhe.*

"Battle Annie is expecting us," Finn said shortly.

The bartender jerked his head toward the corner, to a trapdoor. I remembered Aidan telling me once about riverside saloons with trapdoors that opened over the water to get rid of troublesome drunks.

Patrick said, "Do you think us fools?"

"'Tis where she is," said the bartender. "The only way."

"Aye. The only way to drown us," Diarmid said.

Finn looked at me. "Well, *veleda?*"

I was puzzled until Aidan said, "I've told him what you can do, Grace. Does the bartender tell the truth?"

I listened. The music of the world filled my head, along with Battle Annie's song, strong and clear, very close. "She's there. She's waiting."

Finn lifted the trapdoor. It opened into darkness and the reedy, muddy smell of the river, cold autumn air, and the lapping of water below.

"For God's sake," Patrick whispered in dismay. He looked at me. "Are you certain?"

She was down there, as unlikely as it seemed. I nodded.

Finn glanced at Diarmid. "I'll go first. If I call up, get her out of here quickly."

He stepped to the opening of the trapdoor and jumped.

We should have heard a splash, but there was no sound at all. He just disappeared. It was bewildering. I wondered if we would have heard Finn's call even if there had been one.

Aidan took a deep breath and stepped to the edge. "Well, here goes nothing," and then he jumped. He, too, disappeared.

"You go next," Patrick said to Diarmid, who shook his head.

"And let you whisk her away from here? Back to your Fomori guard? No."

Patrick bristled. "If I leave her with you, what guarantee have I that you won't abduct her again?"

"My captain's below. I won't abandon him. Nor Aidan."

"We'll go together, then. All three of us," Patrick said.

"There's not enough room," I said, sighing. "One of you go—I don't care who. I made a bargain, and I won't disappoint Annie."

"You're her protector, Patrick, aren't you?" Diarmid taunted. "Why don't you see if there's anything to protect her from?"

Patrick looked at me. I said, "I'll be right behind you."

"I'll be waiting." With a final warning glance at Diarmid, Patrick jumped.

Even a few moments alone with Diarmid were too long. I stepped to the edge.

He grabbed my arm, pulling me back. "We'll go together."

"I can go alone."

"I'll catch you. I don't want you to soil your pretty pink gown."

The thought of his arms around me . . . "I don't care about the gown."

His eyes darkened. "But I like it, *mo chroi*. The pink suits you. I knew it would. But your hair"—he flicked one of the slender curls dangling near my ear—"I'm thinking I like it better down."

My stomach flipped. "Please don't, Derry. I told you. It's over."

"It doesn't feel over to me."

"It will be when you kill me on Samhain."

He jerked in surprise, but his fingers gripped my arm harder. "D'you think I'm blind? I know you still love me."

"You're imagining things."

His smile was wistful. I wished it didn't pull at me so. "Maybe. The gods know I love you enough to want you to love me back. But I'm not imagining that you're afraid. You're hiding something. What is it you don't want me to know?"

"I *am* afraid. Of you."

"'Twasn't fear I saw in that storehouse. You knew about the *geis* then."

"But there was *hope* too," I told him. "And now that's gone. Oh, what does it matter? You have to be true to yourself, just as I do. Please, Derry, there's so much you don't understand—"

"Then explain it to me."

"Battle Annie is waiting."

I thought he was going to insist, and I wasn't going to tell him, and the whole thing would just be impossibly painful.

But he said, "As you like. I'll let it go for now. But I won't let you lie to me forever."

"We don't have forever."

He looked stricken. "Don't say that." He took my hand, weaving his fingers tightly through mine. "Now."

We jumped, plunging into darkness. It was a fall without end. Diarmid's hand clutching mine reassured me in a way it should not.

We hit the ground hard—him first. He grunted as I crashed onto him. His arm came around me, holding me close. I looked up into a terrible blinding silver glare, as if we were surrounded by a hundred arc lights. Pain stabbed through my skull. I moaned and raised my arm to shield my eyes.

"She can't see!" Aidan shouted. "Remember who she is."

Immediately, the light eased, along with the pain. We were lying on the highly polished wooden floor of a large room. The walls were covered with tapestries depicting celebrations in crystal halls, the colors gem bright, shining with gold and silver threads. A crowd of fairies watched us. The hum of their magic, their greedy song, filled my head. *Let us touch you, touch you, touch you* . . . Aidan looked queasy and ready to swoon. Finn grabbed his arm, anchoring him. Patrick stared at me. Diarmid and I were still tangled together, me on top of him.

"Let go of me," I whispered.

"You know you don't want me to," he whispered back, but he released me, and I scrambled to Patrick. He pulled me to his side. I pretended not to see Diarmid's glare. The *sidhe*'s song was so heavy in my ears, I could hear almost nothing else. Aidan's knees buckled; only Finn kept him upright.

Patrick said, "Look at Aidan. Make them stop."

I let my voice ring out. "My brother and I were summoned here. Battle Annie would not want us harmed."

The song faded to a low hum. Aidan staggered as if he'd been abruptly released.

I said, "Take me to Battle Annie."

The fairies turned to look at me as one, like puppets on a single string. A tapestry was pushed aside, and Battle Annie entered from a doorway behind it. She looked the same as when I'd last seen her, the loops and coils of her many braids, feathers and beads, the tattoos dark and menacing on her cheek and her shoulder, countless necklaces jangling around her neck.

"Well met, *veleda*." She glanced at the others. "So long as you do not interfere, I'll have no quarrel with you."

"Why have you summoned me?" I asked her.

Her sloe-eyed gaze slid back to me. "Our bargain, *veleda*. I have use of a *brithem*."

Just the brithem. *She knows of the split.* But no, it was only that she knew of my ability to tell truth from lies—she'd been the one to show me I could do it. It was part of the *veleda*'s power; she could not know that, in me, it was the only part.

"Sarnat says you're stronger. You've been trained by that traitor boy."

"Yes."

Battle Annie nodded with satisfaction and turned back to the door. I followed. Aidan fell into step beside me. He did not look any better now that I'd asked the *sidhe* to stop their song. In fact, he looked worse.

"Do you still hear them?" I asked.

"That's not it."

"You look ill."

Patrick said, "She's right, Aidan. Perhaps you should sit down—"

"I'm fine," Aidan snapped. "Let's just get this over with." But he wasn't fine. I felt his worry and fear as if it were mine— that connection again—and woven into it was a *knowing* that puzzled me.

Be very careful, Grace. His voice was in my head. When I looked at him, his lips tightened into a thin line, and he glanced away.

Battle Annie led us through a labyrinthian hallway and into a huge room, its walls also covered with tapestries—these were dark and creepy, greens and blacks and golds, forests full of twisting, writhing branches, with glowing, disembodied eyes peeking from the shadows. They were awful. At one end was a dais set with an elaborately carved table and a chair. There was nothing else.

It was an unsettling room, which I guessed was the point. The rest of the *sidhe* crowded in behind us, their curiosity shimmering, their glow filling the space like moonlight in fog.

Battle Annie pointed to the table. "Your place, *veleda*."

Nervously, I went to it and sat. Close up, the carvings were more than leaves and flowers. Caught within petals and vines were screaming sprites, kelpies drowning their riders, ravens plucking out eyes. My discomfort grew. *What is this place?*

Patrick gave me an encouraging but wavery smile; Diarmid looked wary; Aidan, distracted and sick. Only Finn stood confident and assured, as if hobnobbing with fairies was something he did every day.

"Are you ready, *veleda*?" Battle Annie asked.

Ready for what? Whatever was about to happen, I had a feeling I wasn't going to like it.

"Bring in the offender," she commanded.

The tapestries on one side of the room parted as if by an invisible hand. Two *sidhe* boys came in, each of them holding the end of what looked like a thick green vine. Behind them came two others, flanking something I couldn't quite see. But then the boys parted, and I realized what the vines were connected to—

A girl. The vines wound about her arms and her waist, writhing and pinching, pulling at her shining blond hair. Her startling cornflower-blue eyes were dark with either pain or fear.

Deirdre. The *sidhe* girl who'd told me and Diarmid the clue about the Druid on Coney Island, where we'd found the ogham stick. Diarmid seemed as surprised as I was.

"I know this girl," I said. "What has she done?"

"Nothing," Deirdre gasped before Annie could answer. "I am not bound by the river queen. I do not have to answer to her."

"You became bound to me when you pledged yourself to Turgen," said Battle Annie coldly. "Or do you claim now that you didn't make the vow?"

Deirdre said to me, *"Veleda,* have I not always dealt fairly with you? I gave you what you sought. I did not turn your lover into a stag when you requested that I not." Her eyes sparkled with cunning; I knew she'd read the mood here and used the word *lover* deliberately. She was either blindingly stupid or far cleverer than I ever hoped to be. *No doubt the latter.* I could not look at either Diarmid or Patrick.

"Compliments will not ease your way," Battle Annie interrupted. "We are here to discover the truth of your crime."

The vines twisted and twined, binding tighter. Pain creased Deirdre's mouth. But she did not cry out.

"What did she do?" I asked.

There was a commotion from the hallway, shouting, a scream. Battle Annie spun around; Finn reached for his dagger. A boy ran into the room, gasping, "We tried to keep them out, my liege, but they could not be held!"

Behind him swarmed a group of fairies, and in their midst I saw Daire Donn, Lot—

And my mother.

THIRTY

The next moment
Grace

I leaped to my feet. "Mama?"

She was dressed as if she'd just come from the ball—they all were—and her eyes were wide with distress as she hurried toward me. "Grace!"

Battle Annie's *sidhe* stepped between us.

"Don't touch her!" Aidan rushed to Mama, Patrick right behind.

Lot glared at Battle Annie. "We heard you had the *veleda*. We could not leave her in the hands of the *sidhe*."

"She was safe with us," Finn said, not sheathing the dagger he'd drawn.

Daire Donn laughed. "You must think us fools."

"You will release the *veleda* to us now," said Lot, sounding exactly like the Fomorian goddess she was.

"The *veleda* made a bargain with the *sidhe* queen," said Finn. "We are her guards. You're intruding where you don't belong."

"Grace, you must come with us." Mama pulled away from Aidan. To Battle Annie, she said, "I want to take my daughter home."

"She is not my prisoner," Annie replied.

Mama looked at me. "Grace, please. You mustn't be here with the fairies. They are so very dangerous—"

"What are you doing here, Mama?" I asked.

"You're my daughter. I want to protect you."

Too late. But I didn't say that; it would only hurt her, which I didn't want to do.

Aidan said, "Grace made a bargain with Battle Annie, Mama. She promised."

"Such a thing is easily remedied," said Daire Donn with a dismissive wave. "Release the *veleda* to us, River Queen, or bear the consequences."

"What consequence would that be, King of the World?" Finn sneered. "Your humiliation when we beat you again?"

Lot's purple eyes narrowed. "You have offered the *veleda* nothing but abductions and fairy spells. We have never lied to her."

"Lies are in your every word," Finn said. "Truth is not in your nature."

"The time of the Fianna is over now, Finn MacCumhail." Lot looked at me. "Thanks to the *veleda*, there will be a new world. Please, my dear, come away with us now." She held out her hands to me beseechingly.

Diarmid stepped before her, brandishing both of his daggers. "You won't get near her without going through me first."

Lot's eyes flashed. "Do not make the mistake of thinking that my past affections will make me merciful now."

"Your affection is poisonous," Diarmid spat.

"The *veleda* does not belong to you, Diarmid Ua Duibhne. Have you forgotten her fiancé?"

Finn laughed. "Have you forgotten the *ball seirce*? Do you really think she still belongs to Devlin?"

It was too much. I banged the table. "I don't *belong* to anyone."

They all looked at me as if I'd burst into flame before them.

Lot's gaze was uncomfortably searching. "Your fiancé tells us you are still betrothed. Does he lie?"

Diarmid went very still. I remembered what Patrick had asked of me in the carriage.

"We're still engaged. Nothing's changed."

I felt Diarmid's pain. Lot smiled in satisfaction. Finn frowned. My mother sighed.

Battle Annie said, "None of this has anything to do with our bargain, *veleda*."

"No, it doesn't," I said. "I'm not going anywhere until we're done here."

As if by silent command, Battle Annie's fairies formed a barrier between me and my rescuers. Mama began to push through, but Aidan put his hand on her arm and shook his head. Daire Donn and Lot looked forbidding. Finn's hand remained on the hilt of his dagger. Diarmid did not put his away. He also would not look at me, and that was the worst thing of all.

"What is Deirdre's crime?" I asked. In the commotion, Deirdre's guards had gathered close about her. Now, they parted to show me that the fairy had fallen to her knees. The vines pinched cruelly into her arms and throat.

"She pledged her oath to my courtier, Turgen." Battle Annie gestured, and a boy with copper hair stumbled forward as if someone had pushed him. His head was bowed, his wrists bound with vines that licked and wriggled like little snakes. "The two of them conspired to mutiny. Turgen has already been punished for his treachery."

At this, the boy raised his head. I saw with shock that his eyes were white and ghostly. Blinded.

Battle Annie went on, "But the girl denies she was part of his plan. She claims that he enthralled her, and she had no will of her own."

"Is that possible?" I asked. "Are there spells to make one a slave?"

Battle Annie lifted a brow. "You seem surprised, *veleda*. I think you know the answer already. You've felt such enslavement yourself, have you not? The *ball seirce* was a fairy's gift."

I knew everyone must have noted my flaming cheeks.

"Turgen claims he cast no spells. And so, a *brithem* must decide."

Deirdre pleaded, "He *did* enthrall me. I would never have joined with him otherwise. Please, *veleda*. You must believe me."

I felt sorry for her. I knew what it was to feel helpless against love, to be foolish and blind. I wanted to help her, and I knew it was in my power to do so. A word from me, and Battle Annie would set her free.

But what kind of *brithem* would I be if I did not seek the truth? I closed my eyes and listened, so many songs, all playing together, and there, woven within them, was Deirdre's. I'd heard it before, the music that had once told me to trust her. She was telling the truth.

But then I heard the false note—only one, but it was enough. Just as I'd been able to hear the complicated truth of how Iobhar had drained Roddy, I understood what had happened between the fairies. Deirdre *had* been in love with Turgen, but he had not compelled her. Because she loved him, Deirdre had helped Turgen with the mutiny. Because she loved him, she had done what he wanted.

The truth, as always, was not black or white, but gray.

I knew what I must say would condemn her, because no one cared *why* someone had done something, only that they had. I felt sick. *This* was what it meant to be a judge, to know your words dealt life or death, punishment or reprieve.

How could I do this? It was so overwhelming—not just this decision now, but the knowledge of what I must do, who I must be. The choice I had to make on Samhain had always been more about dying than anything else. But now, I realized how much bigger it was, what it really meant. It was tied to everything I loved. How could I choose against Diarmid? Or

Patrick? Against Aidan or Mama? How could I possibly condemn any of them?

Reluctantly I opened my eyes and said, "Deirdre *was*
in love with Turgen. It was why she followed him. She was
enslaved by love, but it was no spell."

Deirdre sagged; Battle Annie smiled, showing those
wicked, filed teeth. "Thank you, *veleda*. We bow to your
punishment."

"What punishment?"

"'Tis your power and your duty. 'The *veleda* sees, she
weighs, she chooses.' Do so."

They all looked at me expectantly, waiting for me to
unleash Deirdre's punishment, which I could not do. Not
because I didn't want to, but because I didn't have the power.
I was only the *brithem*; only the *vater* could punish or redeem.
My grandmother, not me. I felt the danger of the truth, the
music of peril all around me. Iobhar was right—to reveal this
would be folly. But what else could I do? Snap my fingers and
say, *I think she's been punished enough, don't you?* They would
only see weakness. They would *know*. Deirdre whimpered.

Battle Annie said, "To delay is no kindness."

Frantically, I tried to remember one of the spells for the
vater. My mind was blank. I stared helplessly at Deirdre.

Aidan's music crescendoed; I felt the tightening of the
web, a fierce buzzing.

Aidan *knew*.

I shouted, "No, Aidan!" Too late. A bolt shot from
his fingertips, dazzling purple. It hit Deirdre and

then—shockingly—bounced off the vines binding her and dissipated into smoke.

The *sidhe* grabbed my brother. Our connection wavered; I gasped as he sank to his knees, weakened by their draw on his power. Patrick rushed to him. "Let him go! For God's sake, let him go!"

"He has taken away the *veleda*'s right to deliver justice," Battle Annie said. "For that, he must pay the price."

"No," I protested. "No! He was only trying to help me."

"What *veleda* has need of help from a stormcaster?" she asked acidly.

Aidan writhed in the fairies' grasp, and I felt the *sidhe*'s pull as he did. Desire and repulsion, *surrender* . . .

Mama screamed. The sound echoed in my head, so loud I put my hands to my ears. She swayed; Daire Donn caught her. Her eyes shone with fear.

"To me!" Finn shouted, but before Diarmid could join him, the *sidhe* swarmed to keep them apart.

One of the *sidhe* jerked back Aidan's head, while another set a shining, ancient knife to his throat.

I screamed, "No! You can't kill him! He's the *veleda* too!"

The world seemed to crack. Everyone halted.

Aidan gasped, "Grace, what have you done?" He was breathing hard, his eyes rolling back into his head.

"What is the meaning of this?" Battle Annie demanded.

"The *veleda*'s been split," I confessed, feeling everything fall apart and helpless to stop it. There was no way to call it back or undo it. "There was a curse. The *veleda* is now three.

Me, Aidan, and my grandmother. *Eubages*, *brithem*, and *vater.* I'm only the *brithem*."

"The *veleda*'s split?" Patrick whispered in relief, as if a tormenting mystery had at last been solved. "How long have you known this?"

"A few weeks. Iobhar discovered it."

"You knew this and you said nothing?" Diarmid asked, looking at me as if I'd betrayed him, but how could that be, when he was more dangerous to me than anything?

"Release them," Battle Annie said. "Take our prisoner back to the dungeon. I'll decide her punishment myself. I am no fool to interfere with prophecies. But *veleda*"—she took in both Aidan and me with her gaze—"there are others who *would* dare."

The fairies drew back. Aidan collapsed on the floor.

Deirdre called out, "Turgen!" as they took her away, and he strained to follow. Those who held him tightened their grips, and he bowed his head in heartbreaking surrender.

I wanted only to leave. I hurried from the dais. Patrick helped my brother to his feet and came to me. When he touched my hand, my fear fell away. I stumbled gratefully into Patrick's arms.

"We should go," he said. "And quickly, before Annie changes her mind."

My mother was there, Lot and Daire Donn behind her. Mama was trembling.

"These cursed *sidhe*," said Daire Donn. "'Tis best to have nothing to do with them. We were lucky today. Next time, my dear, you should heed our warnings."

"Patrick, Aidan must come back to the house with us," Mama said.

Finn came up to us just in time to hear her. He said tersely, "Aidan belongs to the Fianna now." Then he looked at me. "Might I speak with you, lass?"

Mama touched my arm, a shake of her head, and Patrick looked thunderous. But I was surrounded by people determined to protect me, and so I nodded, and Finn and I stepped away from the others.

He stood close, too close, just as he had that day he'd asked me questions in their tenement room. He was just as stunning as he had been then. Anxiously, I remembered the way he'd fingered my hair, the longing I'd seen in his eyes, because I'd reminded him of Neasa, whom he'd once loved.

"We've only a moment before the others will protest," he said. "So I'll be blunt, *veleda*, and ask if you will come with us. You are bound to the Fianna. The Fomori have no claim to you. We will protect you with our lives if we must. I think you know this."

The words were simple, but his plea was not. I felt his longing again, and with it his hope and fear. The way he looked at me—Finn was wise and gifted and canny, and I saw that he understood me in a way even Diarmid did not. He saw all the ways I was tangled. He understood why I struggled. This was why men flocked to follow him. It wasn't just his charisma; it was his perception. The two things together made me want to do whatever he asked. I wanted him to be the hero he'd been in the tales I'd grown up with. I wanted to believe him.

But Iobhar's lessons had taught me to be wary. *Neither, nor.* I'd heard other tales, too, and I knew that truth was not absolute.

And so I said only, "Not today."

Finn pursed his lips thoughtfully. He reached out before I knew what he was doing; his finger swept my jaw, a warm and tender touch, as if he meant to reassure himself that I was real. The warmth of him lingered. "I know better than to argue with a *veleda*. Therefore, we will wait. But a word from you, and we will hasten to your side. Remember this."

I had no time to answer before Aidan was there. He looked as troubled as he had all day. He said nothing to me, instead leaning to whisper something to Finn; but I heard my brother's voice in my head: *We have to talk, Grace. I'll come to you soon. Don't do anything until then. Promise me.*

Mama hurried over. She pulled me away from Finn and Aidan, saying, "Come now, Grace. The carriage waits."

And then . . . I couldn't help myself. I looked for Diarmid. He stood at the door, waiting for me.

"Is that him? Diarmid?" Mama gripped my hand. "Don't speak to him."

"She certainly will not," Lot agreed, taking my other arm.

They rushed me past him. He didn't try to stop me, but the accusation and anger in his eyes were unbearable.

We stepped out into the world just before dawn, into a chill breeze coming off the water that felt as if it settled in my heart.

THIRTY-ONE

October 28
Patrick

Patrick rubbed his eyes in exhaustion. A pink and gold sunrise streaked a slate-colored sky beyond the parlor windows. The fire was burning, but he was so cold, he felt he might never be warm again.

The *veleda* was split. It explained everything: his concern and worry for Aidan as well as Grace, and also for their grandmother. He was the protector of the *veleda*, so of course he was bound to watch over all three. The ogham stick's riddles made sense at last. *Great stones crack and split. All things will only be known in pieces.*

But what exactly did the split mean for the prophecy? For the ritual?

"If we knew what caused the curse, we could know how to mend it," Lot mused. She and Daire Donn and Patrick had been talking since they'd returned. Mrs. Knox had gone to bed, looking more fragile than ever. Grace had followed.

Lot warmed her hands by the fire, her hair deeply golden in the light. "With the power so fractured, the sacrifice may release only that which belongs to the *vater*. It may not be enough to help us, as we'd hoped."

"The power will want to mend itself," Daire Donn offered. "The sacrifice may kill all three."

Patrick made a sound of despair.

Lot said gently, "We don't know, my darling. None of us have seen this before. We're only guessing."

"What would this mean for your bargain with the Otherworld?" Patrick asked. "Is it likely we can barter for the release of *three* souls?"

He saw the answer in Lot's eyes before she turned away.

Daire Donn sighed. "Bres and the others will have to be told that the triune isn't goddess power, but splintered. It won't be good news. Ah, Druid divination. We should have learned by now not to trust it."

"The Fianna believed it too," Patrick said.

"Did they?" Daire Donn's brow furrowed. "They told you this? Tonight when you went to the river queen's lair? Which reminds me: how did you come to be with them there?"

Patrick heard the suspicion in Daire Donn's voice, but he was too tired and confused to care. "The Fianna were waiting when Grace and I returned from the ball. They brought Battle Annie's message. She had gone to them to find Grace. My only hope of keeping her out of Fianna hands was to go with them."

"Of course." Lot sat beside him in a rustle of silk and a cloud of water lily perfume. "Any one of us would have done the same."

"I was surprised when you showed up. How did you find us?" Patrick asked.

"Mrs. Knox was concerned when you and her daughter left the ball," Lot explained. "The guard gave us a description of who you'd gone away with, and Mrs. Knox felt very strongly that Battle Annie was involved. We were lucky she was right. Mothers and daughters have a curious bond. I have often been in awe of it." Her hand came to Patrick's arm. "You have done so well, my darling. Did you see Finn's face when she confessed that she still loved you?"

Grace hadn't confessed that, but Patrick didn't bother to correct Lot. Grace had only been doing what he'd asked her to do—pretend nothing had changed between them. But he'd seen her face when Diarmid had stepped from the shadows last night, and he feared that Grace had lied when she'd said the lovespell had faded.

"Yes, but it might not be enough," Daire Donn said, pushing back his dark hair that had come loose from its queue as he paced to the window. "We came near to losing everything last night. If the pirate queen had killed the lad . . . 'twould have been disaster. We'll need the whole of the *veleda* for the ritual. Even so, the power might be weakened. We're sore pressed as it is. The Fianna's militia grows more skilled. Our spies tell us they've sent men into factories to organize strikes."

Lot said, "The evictions will help, but—"

"Evictions?" Patrick asked.

"We've been evicting strike organizers." Daire Donn turned from the window. "They've followed the Fianna blindly, but we'll see how much they still feel like rebelling when they've nowhere to go home to each night."

"You're putting families on the streets?"

Daire Donn's gaze softened with compassion. "None of us likes such tactics, my friend. But you know as well as I that war requires it. We can't have them organizing for the Fianna."

Daire Donn was right. The Fianna had captured the minds of the poor; they could shut down the city with strikes and riots and protests. Patrick couldn't let himself forget what was important. Beating the Fianna, so they could move on to Ireland, to the real fight.

But none of this was what he'd anticipated when he'd called the Fianna so long ago. It was not what he'd wanted. And now the *veleda* was fractured, and his own loyalties hopelessly divided.

"We're with you to the end in this, my friend," Daire Donn assured him.

It was all Patrick had hoped for. The loyalty of the Fomori. Winning freedom for Ireland, for his people.

He wondered when that thought had become such a cold comfort.

THIRTY-TWO

That morning
Diarmid

Diarmid followed Finn and Aidan back to the tenement as dawn broke over the world. The air was heavy with the mineral stink of coal smoke, streets filling with ragged drovers and peddlers, newspaper boys climbing from their sleeping alcoves near steam vents, and homeless men and women looking dazed and uncertain.

He wanted to be a hero, but a hero wouldn't be so torn. A hero would sacrifice love for his people. A hero would make the choice his brothers expected of him.

And it should be easier now, shouldn't it? It wasn't Grace he had to kill. But it wasn't easier, because he had to kill someone she loved. If Grace lived through it, she would never forgive him. He wouldn't expect her to.

When they reached the flat, Diarmid lay on his pallet, staring sleeplessly at the ceiling, haunted by the desperate fear on Grace's face when she'd revealed that the *veleda* was split. In spite of everything between them, she still didn't trust him.

Almost as disturbing were those moments she'd spent with Finn before they'd left Battle Annie's. What had he said to her? How closely they'd stood, how warmly Finn had caressed her. The start of Finn's seduction, no doubt. . . . Well, Diarmid had known to expect it. He shouldn't care—she didn't trust him, and she'd told him to leave her alone, and he knew he should. But he *did* care.

Finally, he gave up the pretense of sleep. He sat spinning one of his daggers between his fingers, watching as the others went to drill with the militia, and wondered what Finn expected of him now.

He got the answer quickly.

"Go and train," Finn told him.

"What, no hunting down Grace?" Diarmid asked bitterly. "No wresting her from Fomori hands? Or were you planning to do that yourself?"

"I've no intention of pursuing her. I trust that heartens you. We'll leave it to Aidan. If anyone can persuade her to choose us, 'twill be him."

Diarmid let the dagger fall, point first, into the hard-packed dirt of the floor, where it stuck and vibrated.

Finn squatted beside him. His eyes were . . . *sad*, Diarmid thought. *How strange.* He hadn't seen that expression on Finn's face for a very long time.

Finn said, "I know the *geis* torments you, lad. But you seem worse today, even though 'tis not your beloved you must kill, but an old woman who's already seen her best days."

"The *veleda*'s split. Perhaps Grace and Aidan will die with her. Or perhaps the spell won't work at all."

"Perhaps," Finn agreed, his gaze gentle with affection. "There's no way of knowing. All we can do is train our men, fight the best we can, and hope she chooses us. You feel too much, sometimes, Diarmid. 'Tis your worst fault as well as your greatest strength. But we value it. We trust you to make the right decision. You know this?"

"Aye."

"Now go on and train. 'Twill do you good not to think."

The little bit of compassion nearly undid him. Diarmid rose, shoving his dagger back into his belt, going up the stairs, into an overcast day that promised rain.

Aidan joined him. "I want to know what you think will happen. Tell me exactly. Don't try to ease it."

Diarmid kept walking. "You already knew the *veleda* was split, didn't you? Don't bother to lie to me. I know you did."

"Don't act so annoyed. I tried to tell you."

"When?"

"It's what I was trying to say when Battle Annie showed up."

Diarmid vaguely remembered Aidan saying there was something Grace didn't want him to know. "When did Grace tell you?"

"She didn't. We're connected, remember? We're each part of a whole. It explains everything. Something's felt wrong to me about the *veleda* from the beginning. My grandmother's words, the prophecy . . . nothing made sense. Then Grace stepped out of that pawnshop, and everything she knew flooded into my head. But Finn won't tell me what he thinks this means."

"Because no one knows what it means. No one's ever heard of such a thing. A *veleda* split . . . it should be impossible."

"Iobhar says it was a curse to punish a lie."

"Iobhar?"

"The *sidhe* archdruid. The *veleda* is Cormac's Cup made human. A lie broke it into three. Iobhar told Grace the most powerful kind of lie is a broken promise. That's what he thinks caused it."

It made sense. Dishonor. A bad vow. Going against one's most sacred duty: being true to oneself. It was powerful magic. "Who does Iobhar say was responsible?"

Aidan shrugged. "He doesn't know. An ancestor. Does it matter?"

"You're asking me questions that no one can answer. All I know is that Nature tries to heal herself. Things want to be whole."

"So you think we'll all die during the ritual? Grace and me as well as our grandmother?"

Diarmid couldn't look at him. "That's my fear, aye. When your *morai* offers herself for the sacrifice—"

"Offers herself? How?"

The militia gathered in the alley. Oscar called out instructions; the others divided up the troops into training units. Diarmid said, "She has to show that she isn't forced to offer her power, that it's her own free will. In the old times, it was an honor to be so chosen. She would even want to die. Things are different now, but still . . . she could choose *not* to sacrifice herself, though I'm thinking that wouldn't end well. Such magic doesn't like to be thwarted."

"It needs free will?" Aidan's eyes sparked with that vibrant, electric energy.

"Aye. I've got to go train—"

Aidan grabbed his arm. "No. Come with me."

"They're waiting—"

"We have to see Grace."

Her name stopped Diarmid in his tracks. "She doesn't want to see me, Aidan, in case you haven't noticed."

"I want you to tell her what you just told me."

"What I just told you? All I've said is that I don't know what will happen."

"About free will. You have to tell Grace that."

"Tell her yourself."

"Derry, don't be an ass," Aidan said urgently. "My grandmother's comatose. Before that, she was mad. She didn't know what she was saying or doing half the time. How exactly is she supposed to offer herself to the spell? She's the *vater*, but she can't *choose* whether or not to sacrifice herself. She has no free will."

It was too fine a point. It wouldn't matter. But Diarmid's hope flickered. *No free will.* Brigid Knox was the *vater*, but she couldn't offer herself to his knife. And if she couldn't offer herself . . .

Perhaps the *geis* would be forfeit.

Aidan said, "Just tell Grace what you told me. Then we'll think of what must be done."

That hope was more than a flicker now. Diarmid had looked so long for *something.* Barely a straw to grasp, but maybe . . .

"Come on," he said.

THIRTY-THREE

That afternoon
Grace

I slept late, and woke with a headache that made me want to lie in bed all day. *Coward.* Yes, I was, but I could no longer avoid the danger Iobhar had predicted. I had to face it.

I wore the blue watered-silk gown that Iobhar had given me, which only made me look as pale and sick as I felt. Then I went to see my grandmother.

The room was dim, the curtains drawn. The air smelled of gaslight and beef tea. I knew when I saw her that Grandma would soon be gone, and not just because it was only days until Samhain. I wondered if waiting for the ritual was the only thing that kept her alive.

I went to her bedside and took her cold fingers in mine. I closed my eyes and tried to find her music—that of the Prophet, and the grandmother I loved—pushing aside all others, one by one, to hear. First, there was only an unnerving silence, and then a single note. And then another, and another. They flew away and struck one another, notes that had once

harmonized, now distorted so they couldn't fit together anymore, though they wanted to. I'd heard this music once before,
but I hadn't understood it then. Her madness was all through
it. But there must be the *vater*'s music, too, tangled within it.
There had to be——

Instead, I heard another song, sweet and touched with a
frenzied, vibrant fire. It pushed in, insistent, and Grandma's
music fled as if her notes were caught in a cyclone wind,
ripped away. The other music stayed. It, too, held some distorted notes, that touch of madness.

Aidan.

Waiting for me in the park's gazebo. I opened my eyes.
"I'll be back, Grandma," I whispered, though I knew she
heard nothing now. I ran downstairs, right into Patrick.

"There you are," he said with a tired smile. "I've been
waiting for you. There are things we should talk about, Grace."

"I know." Aidan in my head, urgent. *Now, Grace.* "But
perhaps later? I was hoping to go for a walk——"

"I'll come with you," he said.

"Oh. Oh no, I don't want to keep you . . ."

Understanding leaped into Patrick's eyes. "It's Aidan, isn't
it? I need to talk to him too. Is he in the gazebo?"

Patrick was also Aidan's protector. I nodded.

"You never would have got past the guard without me."

I'd forgotten completely about the guards. I followed
Patrick outside. It was cold and looked like rain. I kept forgetting it was no longer summer. Patrick told the guard we
were going for a walk, and we went into the nearly empty

park. When we reached the gazebo, Aidan wasn't the only one waiting.

"Diarmid," Patrick said. "Again? This is starting to be a bad habit."

"I could say the same of you," Diarmid replied, his dark-blue gaze intense. "'Twas only Grace who was summoned."

"I'm the *veleda*'s protector, or have you forgotten? It's my job to protect Grace. And Aidan."

"And that means she's not to take a step without you?"

"If that's how to keep her safe."

"This has nothing to do with you."

"Everything about the *veleda* has to do with me."

"You protectors are always stepping in where you don't belong—"

"Derry, stop," Aidan commanded. "And you, too, Patrick. We've more important things to discuss than who has the right to protect whom."

I asked, "Why are you here, Derry? There are guards everywhere. It's too dangerous."

"'Tis good to know you still worry over what happens to me, lass. And here I'd thought you past all that."

I tried to pretend my heart wasn't in my throat. Patrick stood very close. I saw the quick tensing of Diarmid's jaw, the flexing of his fingers, and deliberately, I stepped away from Patrick, not wanting to make things worse. "Nothing has changed. You shouldn't have come."

"Aye, you're right. I shouldn't have. And I wouldn't have if Aidan hadn't insisted. The gods know I've no liking for having my heart ripped out over and over again."

My brother interrupted. "Listen to what he has to say. Tell them, Derry."

"The prophecy needs free will," Diarmid said bluntly.

Aidan shot me a triumphant look.

I frowned. "I don't understand."

"Neither do I," Patrick said.

"Don't you see?" My brother's voice was high with excitement. "'The *veleda* sees, she weighs, she chooses.' She has to *choose* to offer her power."

"I already know that," I said. "But it's not as if there's really a choice. No sacrifice at all could mean the end of everything."

"But Grace, Grandma can't *choose* anything," Aidan said.

Patrick grasped it more quickly than I did. "If she *can't* offer herself, the ritual can't be completed, through no one's fault."

"Exactly," Aidan said.

I could not keep the strain of hope from my voice. "And the *geis*?"

"I don't know," Diarmid admitted.

Aidan said, "How can the *geis* matter if the *vater* has no free will? This could be the way out for all of us."

I wanted to believe. I wanted it so badly. But I knew too much now. Iobhar had made certain of it. "I thought this kind of magic wanted punishment and sacrifice."

Diarmid nodded. "Aye. If the *vater refused* to sacrifice herself, there would be retribution. The magic would find a way to work and punish as well. But now . . . It seems an opening."

"You believe that? You truly do?"

"I want to believe it," he said quietly.

"Could it really be so easy?" Patrick asked.

"Iobhar would know," I said.

"No. For God's sake, Grace, no. He's too dangerous," Patrick told me.

"If there *is* an answer, he'll have it."

"I agree with Patrick for a change," Diarmid said. "You can't go back there. Nor Aidan."

Aidan said, "Samhain's only in a few days. We need answers now. Grace is right, if anyone knows, it would be Iobhar. I'll go with her."

"And have him drain the both of you?" Diarmid said incredulously.

"I'll go with them," said Patrick. "I'm the protector, after all."

"You might be the protector, but you know next to nothing about the *sidhe* and their tricks," Diarmid protested.

"And you can't see them through a glamour," Patrick pointed out. "But I can. I'm the one who rescued Grace. Not you."

"Enough," Aidan broke in, rolling his eyes. "Both of you go, or neither; it doesn't matter to me. But decide it now, so we can get this over with."

"I'm going," Diarmid said.

"And so am I," said Patrick.

I had to admit I was glad. Between Diarmid's understanding of the *sidhe*, Patrick's ability to see through glamours, Aidan's stormcasting, and my training, I thought we might actually discover something.

We told no one we were going. Who knew if anything would come of it? Patrick told his mother we were going for a drive and ordered the carriage. I felt a growing excitement as we started for Corlears Hook, a hope I hadn't felt since I'd found Iobhar. If there could be no sacrifice, there could be no *geis* . . . It felt as if a tight little knot inside me was beginning to loosen. Perhaps there could be a future for me and Diarmid. *Perhaps* . . .

I told myself not to want so much, but it was like a drop of water in a puddle, circles spreading and multiplying. *No ritual. No geis. Alive. Together.*

It meant that I could love him.

He met my gaze as if he knew what I was thinking. Yearning leaped between us, so strong, I caught my breath and had to look away—right into Patrick's eyes. I saw his flash of pain and knew that he'd seen.

"We don't know what it means yet, Grace," Aidan said, a soft admonishment, my brother feeling my emotions through the web woven between us. He was right. I couldn't afford to think these things, or to want them. Not yet.

It wasn't long before we were in Corlears Hook, and Roddy's Grotto.

I was nervous as we approached. Diarmid's hand brushed the small of my back, making me shiver. He said, "You're stronger now. And we're with you. There's no need to be afraid."

"He's right," Patrick said brusquely. "We'll make sure no harm comes to either of you."

I reached for Aidan's hand and squeezed it tight, and he smiled thinly, then I pushed open the door and stepped inside.

So familiar, the smell of mildew and must, Iobhar's scent. Roddy looked up from the counter, where he was polishing a broach I knew he'd polished six hundred times already. A smile lit his face, then died quickly.

"I want to see him," I said.

Roddy glanced at Aidan. "He should not be here. You should tell him to flee. Run! Run!"

"Iobhar won't hurt him."

"And just how do you know that, *brithem*? You are no *eubages* to see the future."

The voice was Iobhar's, coming from a dark corner that led to a darker hallway and floors upon floors of glamoured stairs. He wore the gold-and-scarlet-edged tunic and the supple leather boots. The bells around his neck tinkled. A feathered headdress fanned from his long curls like a peacock's tail.

His golden gaze swept us. "I see you've brought guests. Or perhaps . . . an offering?"

"My brother, Aidan," I said by way of introduction.

"We've met, though he doesn't know it." Iobhar sauntered over. My brother wavered, leaning toward him. I knew what he was imagining. Putting a necklace of bells around his neck, dancing and dancing . . .

"We've questions to ask of you," I said. "My brother is not your prize."

Iobhar's smile broadened. "As you wish, *brithem.*" His music ceased. Aidan jerked upright, stumbling. Iobhar glanced at Patrick and Diarmid. "Did you not trust me, *milis*? How you wound me."

"She has plenty of reason," Patrick said.

"Sometimes even I get lonely. I have no liking for my own kind, and she at least is clever." Iobhar's fingers brushed my hair.

Diarmid's knife was in his hand so quickly, I had not seen him reach for it. "Don't touch her."

"I could incinerate you where you stand, Ua Duibhne, so do not try me."

"No one wants a fight." Patrick touched Diarmid's arm. Reluctantly, Diarmid lowered the knife.

"We have questions about the split *veleda*," Aidan said. "And the ritual."

Iobhar crossed his arms over his chest. The necklaces jangled at the movement; the feathers in his hair fanned open and closed as if they were alive. "I've already told the *brithem* what I know."

"Not everything, I think," I said. "What happens if the *vater* can't offer her power?"

Iobhar eyed me. "*Can't*? Or *won't*?"

"My grandmother is comatose. Diarmid says she must offer herself to the sacrifice freely. She can't do that. Does it change anything?"

One dark brow rose. "'Tis an interesting question."

"Does it cancel the *geis*?" I rushed to get the words out.

Iobhar glanced at Diarmid, who watched tensely, his knife still in his hand. "You ask me to be certain about uncertainties. The *geis* has bound this warrior for centuries. The *veleda*'s duty has passed through blood and time. It has strength and power."

"But the *geis* was meant for a *veleda* whose power was whole. Who could act," I said.

"Aye. And the ritual requires that the *veleda* see and weigh as well. Your brother is still a Seer. You can tell truth from lies. Together you will know which side is worthy."

"But she can't *choose*. Are you saying that Diarmid is still bound?"

The feathers in Iobhar's hair fanned out again. "I did not say that. I have no idea what will happen with the *vater*. But you and your brother must perform your parts of the ritual. He must see, and you must weigh. As for the rest . . . if the *vater* cannot act, the *geis* cannot be fulfilled. Perhaps the powers that be will leave it at that."

"But you don't know for certain," I said.

"No," he agreed. "Perhaps you and your brother will be enough to satisfy the prophecy, and you will be allowed to live. Perhaps not. Perhaps the inability to fulfil the *geis* will be seen as a refusal, and Ua Duibhne and the others will die."

"Those aren't answers."

"They are the only ones I have. The world is uncertain. The only advice I can give you is this, *brithem*: prepare to die and hope you will live. The ritual cannot be completed—'tis no fault of yours or your brother's, nor even of your warrior. *Intention* matters. 'Twill be accepted or not. There is no way of reading such ancient power, and no way of predicting it. But know this too: fate can be changed by those willing to risk everything to change it."

"Faith or fear," I whispered.

Diarmid gave me a quick look, and I knew he recognized the words he'd once said to me.

Iobhar shrugged. "Life is cruel and unfair. You can only control who you will be. If you act bravely in the world, perhaps it will reward you. If not . . . you deserve the fate it assigns."

Diarmid sighed and put his knife back into his belt.

"And what about the power the sacrifice is supposed to release?" Patrick asked. "If there *is* no power, what happens?"

"Who knows? Death—or worse: perhaps the Fomori and the Fianna will be forced to find a way to live with each other."

"Live with chaos and evil?" Diarmid snorted.

"Or arrogance and abuse of power?" Patrick countered.

"How is that different from anyone's life?" Iobhar asked.

Aidan raked his hand through his hair, electrifying it. "So that's all you can tell us? That we have to be brave? That we have to just *hope*?"

"'Tis the truest answer, *eubages*."

Patrick said, "As I see it, unless your grandmother unexpectedly wakes, we've two options: go through with the ritual up to the sacrifice and hope for the best, or ignore Samhain altogether and face certain disaster."

"Neither's a good choice," Diarmid said.

"But at least one of them gives us better odds."

"'Tis easy for you to say it. What are you risking?"

Patrick glanced at me. "Everything I've ever wanted."

I felt myself blush, and I knew Diarmid noticed it.

"My vote is that we go ahead with the ritual," Aidan said.

"Grace?" Patrick asked.

I didn't see any other way. "Yes. We go ahead."

Patrick looked at Diarmid. "What about you?"

"Aye," Diarmid agreed.

Patrick turned to Iobhar. "We thank you for your help. I trust we'll have no more need of you."

"Oh, you have need of me. You've no *vater.* Someone must forge the connection with the Otherworld. Without me, you've no hope of appeasing the old magic." Iobhar's gaze was both threatening and seductive as always. "You are far from done with me."

"Good news," Diarmid said cheerlessly.

From the counter, Roddy proclaimed, "'Tis disaster."

I could not help shuddering. "Pay him no mind. He's mad."

"Quite mad," Iobhar said. "Or perhaps he tells the truth. Who can say?"

We went back to the carriage in silence. When we were inside, Patrick said, "I think it would be best if we didn't speak of this to the others. I don't want them to take matters into their own hands."

"Are you saying you don't trust your precious Fomori?" Diarmid asked.

"Do you trust Finn to do what's best for Grace and Aidan, whatever it costs the Fianna?" Patrick replied.

Diarmid glanced away.

"We keep it secret." Patrick's voice was firm. "Agreed?"

We all nodded. The weight of that decision filled the carriage. *Prepare to die and hope you will live.* The ritual had to be started. I still had to make the choice between the Fianna and the Fomori, between Diarmid and Patrick. And perhaps none of it would matter.

Once we were back at the stables, Aidan kissed my forehead and said, "We're together in this, Grace."

I hugged him. "I know."

Patrick held out his arm for me. Diarmid said, "A moment, lass. Alone. Please."

Patrick and Aidan said "No," at the same time.

"It's not up to either of you, is it?" I said, though the thought of being alone with Diarmid troubled me as much as I wanted it.

Aidan looked annoyed. "Grace . . ."

"Yes," I said to Diarmid.

He jerked his head toward the stable. "In there."

"We'll be only steps away," Aidan warned. "And you've only a moment, Derry, I mean it."

I was tense with anxiety and longing as we went inside. Out of sight of my brother and Patrick, Diarmid turned, cupping my face before I knew his intention, fingers gentle against my cheekbones, holding me still. His gaze sent a shiver deep inside me.

"I'm asking you again, *mo chroi*," he said, his voice deep and husky. "Come away with me."

I grabbed his wrists to pull his hands away, but instead, I held onto him as if I might fall were I to let go. "I can't. You know I can't."

"We don't know what will happen. Be with me until then. Please."

It was all I could do to say, "I left you because I didn't want how I feel to influence my choice. That hasn't changed."

"Grace, please." His thumb brushed my mouth, a flutter-like touch. "I'm not afraid of dying, but to think of not holding you again . . . that terrifies me. You keep my heart in your hands. If you won't come away, at least spend the night with me. It may be the last time we have together."

Lying with him again, touching him the way I yearned to. Just a night . . . Oh, how I wanted it. What could it harm?

But then I thought of Patrick outside, and everything he wished for. The Fomori and the Fianna, and everything at stake. I already loved Diarmid too much. If I had to choose against him, how would I bear this?

"You're not giving me the same chance you give Patrick," Diarmid went on, his fingers tightening. "He's your protector. You live with him. You haven't broken your engagement, in spite of what I know you feel for me. What is it you're think-ing, Grace? That if we survive this, you'll need him? He's rich, and I've got nothing to offer you, I know, but——"

"That's not the reason," I insisted.

"Then prove it. Come with me. Give me an hour, if noth-ing else. Just an hour."

"You're not being fair. I can't. Derry, I *can't*. You have your honor; I have mine too. You're asking me to be selfish, the way the Fianna once were. The *veleda* exists so that doesn't happen again. How can I be true to myself and my duty if I go with you, no matter how I want to?" I gripped his wrists harder. "We have to trust that this will work. No one's going to die. Not you. Not me."

It was as if we were in that storehouse again, and he was telling me his stories as I searched for truth in his eyes. But now I saw his soul in a new way. I saw how my words spoke to him, and the anguish they wrought, his own struggle between honor and love. I'd already known he loved me, but this . . . the force of his feeling stole my breath.

His fingers trembled. He pressed his forehead to mine and whispered, "You'll do what must be done, I know. And I won't keep you from it. But whatever fate has in store for us, what-ever happens . . . what I said before is true. I love you. I always will. Nothing can change that."

His words settled into me like a familiar, precious song. I could have stood there forever, my fingers circling his wrists, his breathing, his heartbeat, echoing mine.

"Derry? That's long enough. We have to get going. Finn will wonder where we are." My brother's voice was far too loud.

Diarmid lifted his head. Aidan and Patrick stood in the doorway, frowning.

"Aye." Very deliberately, Diarmid kissed me—and this was not like our other kisses had been. It was chaste and sweet, but so powerful it rocked me. He pulled lightly from my hold. He smiled regretfully, that long dimple creasing his cheek. "Until Samhain, *mo chroi.*"

He strode over to Aidan. My brother blew me a kiss, and then the two of them walked away.

THIRTY-FOUR

Patrick said nothing as he and Grace walked back to the house. Her hand was tucked under his arm; he felt her warmth at his side. She was safe, and she was with him, and all he could think about was the way Diarmid had kissed her.

It shouldn't matter to him. What mattered was Samhain and the ritual. It seemed a century ago that Patrick had put these things in motion. So much had seemed possible then. And now . . . everything would come down to one night. One night, and all he'd ever wanted would either be realized or destroyed.

It was impossible.

At the house, the servants bustled about, readying for dinner. In the parlor, his mother argued with Lucy. Grace drew her hand away. "I think I'll go to my room for a bit."

He said, "Might I have a moment?"

An echo of Diarmid's words, he realized when she winced. "I'm sorry, Patrick. Truly. He should not have—"

"You told me the lovespell had faded. Was that a lie?"

Her gaze was frank and honest, and he knew before she spoke that he wouldn't like what she had to say. "I was in love with him before I saw the *ball seirce*."

It was a blow; he didn't pretend it wasn't.

She glanced away as if she felt his pain. "Would it help if I told you that I love you too?"

His heart leaped, but fell just as quickly. "Not in the same way, I think."

"Your dreams are as important to me as his are. I can't bear the thought of destroying either one of you."

"Perhaps you won't have to. You heard Iobhar. Perhaps no one will die, and there will be no power to bestow, and the Fianna and the Fomori will just have to learn to get along."

"Do you think they could?"

"I can't speak for the Fomori. But as for me . . . I called the Fianna first, remember. I'd like them on my side. Diarmid too."

"And you think Ireland is worth all this?"

"If you could see it as I have, you would want to help too."

"But there are Irish here, Patrick, and they're suffering," she said. "There's no work. Their children play in sewage. They need heroes too. You could be that for them."

"We mean to be. They left Ireland because they were oppressed, but once we win independence, there will be jobs for them there, and money. They can return."

"What if they don't want to go back?"

"Why wouldn't they?" he asked. "It's their home. It's where they belong."

She was silent and thoughtful for a long moment. He felt she saw something that eluded him. "You're a good person, Patrick. One of the best I know."

She started up the stairs, and he let her go. He didn't know why her words bothered him. He should be happy she thought of him that way.

He went to the parlor, stopping just before the door. He didn't feel like being with his family tonight. Instead, he went back outside. He was halfway to the Fenian Brotherhood clubhouse before he realized where he was going and why. He wanted back his faith, which had been shaken lately, not just by Grace's words today, but by the Fomori themselves. By Aidan. Even by Diarmid. Ireland *was* the right fight. He knew it in his soul.

Still . . .

At the club, the doorman told him, "There are several members upstairs, sir."

Bres and Miogach and Tethra, along with Simon MacRonan, Jonathan Olwen, and Rory Nolan. At the sight of them, Patrick felt a burst of relief.

Bres smiled in greeting. "We've just been speaking of you."

"We've discovered the Fianna plan," Miogach explained.

"'Twill begin with the longshoremen," Tethra said, smoothing the ends of his huge and curling mustache. "The Fianna will call for a strike the day before Samhain. With that, the battle will begin. The city will see it as worker unrest, another riot. Which will nicely disguise both the ritual and the opening of the veil between worlds. It will end with the *veleda*'s choice, and the unleashing of her power to us, and victory."

Patrick looked down at his hands. "Do you think the ritual will work, even with the split?"

Bres said, "We believe so, if the three parts—*eubages*, *brithem*, and *vater*—are there."

The protector in Patrick roused violently. "All three? But Grace's grandmother is sick."

"You will have to transport her carefully."

"Transport her? To where?"

"The ritual must take place at the edge of worlds," Bres said patiently. "The warehouse where the strike will begin is on the waterfront. The perfect place."

"The prophecy will seek to be whole," Miogach put in. "If 'twas broken into three by a lie, it can be mended by the truth, just as Cormac's Cup was mended. When she chooses us, the truth of our worthiness will bind their power together again."

It was what Iobhar had said in different words. The magic might take all three lives, or none. But to think the truth could mend it—that was something new, and Patrick felt a tug of misgiving. If the truth was all powerful, did that mean the *vater*'s lack of free will didn't matter? He asked Simon, "Have you done a divination?"

"There are many things in play, of course, but I think we will prevail," Simon answered him.

"You should congratulate yourself, Devlin. Thanks to you, there will be the rise of a new dawn, where the Irish will be triumphant." Bres's smile was wide and self-assured.

Patrick smiled back, hoping the Fomori king didn't see how strained his was. Iobhar had told them the sacrifice couldn't be made without free will. Was it possible the arch-druid was wrong, and the Fomori were right?

He started when Tethra pressed a glass into his hand.

"To success!" Tethra toasted.

Patrick raised his glass with the others. "To success."

But his voice sounded hollow in his ears, and when Patrick thought of victory, he no longer saw the green hills of Ireland and British flags flung down.

He saw the honest admiration in Grace's eyes.

THIRTY-FIVE

October 29
Diarmid

Today 'twill be the final day of training," Finn told them. "Then it begins."

Diarmid knew his leader was not as confident as he pretended. None of the others knew of the *veleda* split, and Finn meant to keep it that way. *"They need faith more than worry,"* he'd told Diarmid that morning. *"The fates will play as they will. All we can do is be ready."*

Even Finn didn't realize how uncertain it really was.

"We have to trust that this will work. No one's going to die. Not you. Not me."

Diarmid knew better than to believe it. He knew this kind of magic too well. But to be released from the burden of the *geis*, to have hope . . . it was hard to ignore how much lighter he felt. That morning in training, he laughed with Oscar as he hadn't laughed in a good while, so that his best friend wrapped an arm around his neck and tousled his hair and said, "'Twill feel good to be in the midst of a real battle again."

Diarmid grinned. "And even better when 'tis over."

"That too." Oscar lowered his arm. "You've come to terms with it, Derry?"

"You'll have no cause to worry. Just mind yourself, will you? I don't want to have to be rescuing you every five minutes."

Oscar laughed, his green eyes bright.

Diarmid strode to the back door where Finn stood with an anxious-looking Aidan. Diarmid drank a dipperful of water from the bucket just as Finn said to Aidan,

"She'll be there? And she's prepared?"

"She'll be there. But as for prepared . . . how does one prepare for the unknown?"

"By preparing for what's *known*," Finn said tightly. "And you, Diarmid. Are you ready as well?"

Diarmid did his best not to meet Aidan's eyes. "I am."

"Good." Finn clapped them both on the shoulder before he walked off.

"You've said nothing?" Aidan asked.

"I promised I wouldn't, didn't I?"

"One never knows where your loyalty lies."

"You do know," Diarmid told him irritably. "You'd just rather question it."

Aidan sighed. "Yes, that's the problem, isn't it? I *do* know where your loyalty lies—with the Fianna. It's actually what I admire most about you. But it's also what makes me most afraid for Grace."

"If the *geis* becomes forfeit—"

Aidan silenced him with a shake of his head. "It's not just that. It's also because of the life you'll ask her to lead if we survive this. Even if we win, it won't bring us riches or fine homes, and that's what she should have. I know it's stupid to be talking about this, but if I don't now, and we live through this, it will be too late."

Diarmid tensed. "I don't understand you."

"If this all works out as we hope, promise me you'll leave her alone. She needs someone who can take care of her."

"That's fine talk, coming from you," Diarmid said. "She's the one who's been taking care of your family—without your help."

"Things are different. I'm not as I was."

"Neither is she."

Aidan's eyes glowed vibrant blue, the stormcaster within rising with his temper. "And that's thanks to you, I know. She needed you once, but she doesn't need you anymore."

"How do you know?"

"I'm asking you to do what's best for her, Derry. Leave her to Patrick."

Diarmid felt everything he'd hoped for crumble. He clung to the one thing he knew was true, the way Grace looked at him, the way she kissed him. "What if that's not what she wants?"

Aidan said firmly, "She will, if you walk away. Grace does love Patrick. She would have married him if not for you—she wanted to."

"If Grace tells me to go, I will," Diarmid said. "But I won't make the decision for her."

"Well, that's a safe bet, isn't it? You showed her the *ball seirce*. What are the chances she'll say no? But how can you be sure that she really loves you?"

Another truth. Diarmid hated that Aidan had seen it, that he couldn't just say: *she loves me as I love her.* She claimed she'd loved him before the *ball seirce*, and he wanted to believe it. *But you don't really, do you?* It looked so real. It felt so real. But it had looked and felt that way before. Other girls—Grainne, for whom he'd destroyed everything. All because of a spell that didn't hold. That couldn't. In the end, she'd gone back to Finn and there was nothing. *Nothing.*

Aidan went on relentlessly, "How can you know if her feelings are real? Why would you hold on to her knowing it? What kind of love is that?"

Diarmid heard himself say, "The only kind I've ever known."

"And when she wakes up from it only to find herself living *this* life? A pauper in a slum? Is that what you want for her, Derry? Let her go. Let her find something real with Patrick. If you love her as you say, you'll want what's best for her."

Diarmid couldn't breathe through the pain in his chest. "'Tis a pointless conversation. None of us might be alive."

"That's true. But in case we are . . . think about it. You and I are allies now, but if you keep pursuing my sister, we won't be. I'd rather we not be enemies, Derry, but I'll do what I must to keep the two of you apart."

Diarmid struggled to find his voice. "I understand."

Aidan left him.

Diarmid stared down at the mud beneath his feet. He felt as he had when he'd gone off with the first Grainne so long ago, as if everything conspired against him. What he wanted was the least important thing of all.

Fate is ever-changing, he told himself.

Change mine.

THIRTY-SIX

That night
Grace

We will be with you every moment." Lot took my hand between her velvety white ones. "'Twill be frightening, I warn you. Such things as come into the world when the door is opened . . . you should not listen to them. They can be terrible liars. Trust what I say and know we are with you. And when 'tis over, I will come to you in the Otherworld and bring you home."

Across the room, Lucy's fingers stumbled over the pianoforte keys, and she laughed with Miogach as he turned the pages of sheet music. Flirting, as I hadn't seen since . . . well, since Diarmid had shown her the lovespot. It was a relief to think that I no longer had to feel guilty, that maybe we could be friends again—

It was so hard to live as if there might not be a future. As if what I felt didn't matter.

"You mother worries so for you," Lot said gently, nodding to where Mama stood gazing out the French doors. "I have told her that she should be proud."

"Tell me why you think I should choose you," I said. "Why shouldn't I believe the old stories?"

Lot sighed. "We ruled Ireland long before the old gods came and wrested it away. And even after, we learned to live with them. We had children together. Many of those children served Ireland well. We have never been the monsters the Fianna claim."

"Then why do they hate you so?"

"'Twas a way to hold onto their power. Victors must reassure their subjects that they are ruled by the best and strongest and most just. People must believe their kings are good. I know you have a fondness for Diarmid, but he is Fianna, and in the end, their own people turned against them. Now we have the chance to make Ireland a sanctuary, one where want and worry are unknown." Again, her glance slid past me, to my mother.

"And what of the plan you have to save the *veleda*? You really think you can bring all three of us back?"

Lot's purple eyes glowed. "I can be very convincing, and I have grown very fond of you and your mother."

"What of my brother? And my grandmother? You don't even know them."

"I wish only to bring you happiness." Lot's smile was sweet and sincere. "If their lives are your condition for choosing us, I will see it done."

"What are you two whispering about?"

I turned to see my mother. She met Lot's gaze as if she and the goddess shared a private joke.

"I'm telling your lovely daughter how little she has to fear," said Lot.

Mama nodded as if she were comforted, but I knew she dreaded Samhain as much as I did. I hadn't told her what Iobhar had said. I didn't like to be cruel, but neither did I want to give her false hope. And I'd promised Patrick to say nothing.

The room was bright and warm. Lucy flushed beneath Miogach's gaze, and Bres laughed low as he talked with Daire Donn and Patrick. The world felt safe and easy, but I was overwhelmed. I rose. "If you'll excuse me just a moment . . ." My tears were falling before I was halfway up the stairs. It wasn't until I stood at my bedroom door that I realized why I was crying.

How could I choose against them? What if Lot *could* do what she'd promised? The Fomori believed in Patrick's fight. What if the old stories were lies? Worse, how could I choose against Mama, or Patrick and his family?

I couldn't. And yet . . . The Fianna. Diarmid. *Aidan.* How could I choose against *them*?

I thought of Iobhar's test, the visions in the cave. Irish dying in Ireland. Irish dying here. Iobhar said I would see the truth once the ritual began. But what if the truth was as messy and complicated as I suspected? No matter what choice I made, I would destroy someone I loved. The burden was unbearable. If I lived, my choice would change everything for me. If I died, it would change everything for those I left behind. How could I do this? How could I possibly do this?

Take this from me, I prayed. *I don't want it. Give it to someone else, anyone else—*

"Grace?"

Quickly, I wiped the tears from my eyes and turned to Mama, trying to smile.

She saw through me. She held out her arms. "Oh, my darling."

My tears turned to sobs. She held me tightly, and I breathed deeply of her lilac scent, which I hadn't smelled for more than a year. Instead, she'd smelled only of cheap lye soap. And now here was the perfume again, a reminder of everything Patrick had given us.

It only made me cry harder. Mama soothed me until I was done.

Finally, she drew away. "I've been afraid, and because of that, I've let you take on far too much. But I won't let you take this on alone, Grace. You will make the right choice, and you and Aidan will survive. The curse is not your fault. The world would not be so cruel as to punish you."

"Diarmid says this kind of magic is *meant* to be cruel. That it *wants* punishment."

"But not yours," Mama whispered. "I suppose I always knew the *veleda* was split. Or at least, I suspected it when your grandmother began to fade and Aidan fell away. And there were . . . other things too."

"What other things?"

"Well, I knew about the curse, if not what it truly meant."

"You knew?"

Mama sighed. "I told you about Grandma following that boy to America? Her leaving was what brought the curse upon us. The *veleda* is bound to the Fianna, to Finn's grave. She is not to leave Ireland. But Mother did. She might have gone back, but then she met Father, and I was born. Even then, she spoke of returning. But the Irish were coming here to escape poverty. Nearly all of the Knoxes emigrated, and Father had no wish to return to a life of struggle. When I fell in love with his cousin—your Papa—and Aidan was born, Mother abandoned any idea of Ireland. It was the past. Her family was here. She would not leave us."

"The broken vow," I said.

"Mother knew her duty, but she denied it. She couldn't foresee what it would cost. How could she? It didn't matter unless the Fianna were called, and why should that happen? It was only a legend. Who might have imagined it was real?"

"Do you think she'll die during the ritual?" I whispered.

Mama looked sad. "I don't know what will happen, Grace. But you aren't like my mother. You won't throw away your future, or your family's, for a hollow love."

"What if it's not hollow?" I asked hoarsely.

She tucked a tendril of hair behind my ear, but she wouldn't meet my gaze. "Be true to yourself, my darling, and you will have nothing to regret. That's all I ask. Now . . . should we go back downstairs? Before the others worry?"

"Yes." I grabbed her hand, squeezing it. "I love you, Mama."

"I love you too. Perhaps more than you will ever know."

THIRTY-SEVEN

October 31—Samhain
Grace

The night before Samhain, I lay awake listening to the music of the world, all the different melodies clanging and blending, weaving and cresting, and it was comforting to hear it, to know that there would always be that music, no matter what I did, no matter what choice I made.

Dawn came with a burning red sun, half-hidden beneath dark-blue clouds, striating the sky with orange and rose. The old rhyme came to mind: *Red sky at morning, sailors take warning. Red sky at night, sailor's delight.*

Take warning.

It's hard to know what to wear on your last day alive. In the end, I decided on the watered blue silk Iobhar had glamoured for me. A gift from an archdruid seemed appropriate. Beyond that, I could hardly think. *"You and Aidan will survive."* Mama had sounded so certain, as if it was the one thing she knew above all to be true, and I hoped she was right.

But then again, what was the point of surviving, if what I loved was gone?

Perhaps Iobhar's guess would come to pass, and the worst thing to happen would be the Fianna and the Fomori learning to live together. There had been more unlikely miracles, hadn't there? I remembered the battle in my backyard, swords drawn, lightning blasting, anger thick in the air. *Perhaps not.*

Patrick and Mama sat at the dining table. The newspaper was folded before Patrick. He said, "The longshoreman's strike started."

"What has that to do with anything?" I wasn't the least bit hungry, but still I spread gooseberry jam on a piece of toast. After all, it might be the last time I tasted it. The last time I sat at this table and said good morning to my mother. The last time I saw the red of sunrise fade into an overcast blue or smelled eggs and oatmeal or noted the fine dust from coal ash on the hearth—

Stop.

"It's meant to divert attention from what's really happening during the ritual." Patrick's voice broke into my thoughts. "The strikers are Fianna soldiers. Our own set out this morning to meet them. This is the battle, Grace. The winner will be the one you choose."

I put down the toast, no longer caring if I never tasted gooseberry jam again.

Mama took a careful sip of her tea. Her hand was trembling. "You must watch over Grace and Aidan, Patrick. I want no harm to come to them."

"It's my only goal, to keep them safe."

"You won't be fighting?" I asked.

"If I have to fight to protect you, I will," he said gruffly. "You need only worry about your part in the ritual. I'll worry about you and Aidan."

I wished . . . well, how much easier life had been when the most I'd had to worry about was bill collectors and losing the house and Aidan's drunkenness and Mama's distraction and wondering if Patrick would propose . . .

Not small things, but they seemed small now. I could not even remember who I'd been then, and even stranger, I didn't think I wanted to be that person again. But if I was no longer that Grace, who was I?

I spent the rest of the day near Mama, leaning into her constant touch, taking comfort from her as if I were a child. When Lucy asked me to help her untangle ribbons, I told her I'd love to, and I meant it.

"Is something troubling you, Grace?" she asked suspiciously.

"Nothing," I said, taking the knot of ribbons from her. "I'm surprised you want my help."

"I've decided to forgive you. I see he's abandoned you too. What fools he made of us."

I took an embroidered length of satin and unwound it.

"And I've decided perhaps I might like gray eyes better," Lucy went on.

Gray eyes. Miogach. Those gray eyes had disconcerted me at first, but then they'd become gentle, shining with good humor. I thought of Diarmid saying that Miogach was the worst of them, the greatest liar, and Grandma telling me that Finn had been too arrogant in his kindness to understand Miogach's grief and hatred over the death of his father, the King of Lochlann, at the Fianna's hands.

Neither black nor white. I let my hands and the ribbons fall listlessly in my lap. Mama touched my arm, and when I looked at her, I heard her words again: *"You will make the right choice, and you and Aidan will survive."*

The hours slid by far too quickly. I spent the last of them with my grandmother. "I don't know what's going to happen tonight, Grandma. But I love you. And I forgive you, too, for the curse. I understand."

I closed my eyes, listening to my grandmother's music, that awful, jangled sound, and for the first time, I heard the notes I'd searched for, the *vater's* music, there at last. The notes were delicate and yet insistent. I heard the strength in them, and I felt reassured. Not just madness. The Prophet was in her too. Whatever happened would happen. I had done everything I could.

Patrick and Mama waited outside the door. I heard her tap. It was time.

I left my grandmother and flung myself into my mother's arms. "You'll live, Grace," she whispered. "And when you do, I hope you can forgive me."

"Forgive you for what?" I asked.

"For letting you take on so many burdens."

I hugged her. "I love you, Mama. If I don't come back—"

"Sssh. You will."

"We'd best hurry," Patrick said.

I gave my mother a final hug and kiss good-bye.

"Patrick, keep her safe," Mama said, and I saw a desperation in her eyes that made me want to turn back again. But Patrick had my arm, propelling me forward, downstairs, out to the carriage. Waiting with it were Daire Donn and Lot.

I looked at Patrick.

"They insisted," he said. "They wanted to be certain you got there safely."

"Safely? But *you're* my protector."

"I've told them nothing of that. It might worry them because of Aidan."

As we approached the carriage, my stomach dropped, my mouth went dry. There was no turning back.

"We'll bring the *vater* separately," Patrick said to them. "She can't be moved in the carriage. I've hired a wagon and a driver I trust."

How well he lied. I hadn't known he had the talent. What would the Fomori do—or the Fianna—once they realized that my grandmother would be nowhere near the ritual, but safe in her bed at Patrick's house?

If this worked, it would be worth their fury. It would be worth every lie I'd ever told.

Lot said, "You've hired a guard as well, I hope."

"It's taken care of," Patrick assured her.

We got into the carriage. As we drove toward the waterfront, I looked out the window, taking it all in, every passing scene, every building and person and horse and carriage. *It won't be the last time you see it,* I told myself. *This has to work. It has to.*

The carriage jerked to a stop. "Can't go no farther, sir," called down the driver, Leonard. "There's a mob ahead."

"This is it, then. We walk from here." Daire Donn's eyes danced with excitement. "Are you ready?" he asked me.

"I am," I said, but who could ever be ready for this?

Ahead of us was a jam of stopped carriages, delivery wagons, and drays. I heard shouting and gunshots.

Patrick's face was sharp with tension as we got out of the carriage. "Stay close, Grace," he whispered.

I hadn't thought my dread could get any worse, but it did. A band of threatening clouds gathered, darkening the last hours of the day. "What time is it?"

Patrick didn't even take his watch from his pocket. "Two hours until sunset. No more than that."

I gripped his hand, and he squeezed back, and we followed Daire Donn and Lot, weaving through the stopped traffic to a swarming mob of people.

All I saw was a swirling, moving riot. Men and women, gang boys and policemen pitched in battle already. Fists cracking and clubs thudding. Screaming and shouting. Police cursing as they dodged rocks and struggled to keep back the crowd. I didn't see any of the Fianna—or the other Fomori.

"Quickly now," said Daire Donn, pushing through. The world smelled of blood and smoke, garbage and sewage and the river. I saw a boy stabbed, dead before he hit the ground;

a policeman battered with his own club; blood running from gashed foreheads and noses and cheeks. We were pushed and shoved about; Patrick's grip on my arm was so tight it bruised.

Diarmid had said that no one loved battle once they were within it, and I understood that now. This was terrifying and horrible. Cries of pain and anger filled my ears, along with the caws of ravens, though when I looked up at the sky, I saw none. Purple-tinged clouds boiled in a building storm. *Aidan.*

Daire Donn led us out of the mob and behind a warehouse fronting the river. My boots slid in the mud of the riverbank; only Patrick kept me from falling into the water. Lot skirted to the foot of the pier beyond, reaching out to help me climb onto the rickety wharf.

She glanced at the sky. Blue lightning ricocheted across the purple clouds. Tethra. "'Tis nearly the hour."

There was another warehouse on the other side of the pier, its great doors open, and beyond them, the fight raged. Now I saw Balor towering above the others, brandishing a long-bladed knife. The riot flooded into the street. There was Finn, screaming orders, his golden-red hair streaming.

The river rushed a murky, muddy green littered with flotsam—boards and twigs, more garbage. Lot gave me a little push, forcing me to take a step. When I looked down, I realized why. I now stood with one foot on the riverbank, the other foot on the pier over the river. The borderland. Neither, nor. Both.

"Keep her here!" Daire Donn shouted. "I'll light the pyres."

"The pyres?" I glanced nervously at Patrick, who gave me a nervous look in return. My stomach was in knots. The world went dark, the sun behind the purple-black clouds, streaks of blue lightning. "Where's Aidan? He should be here with me. What's he waiting for?"

"Sunset," Lot said. "Do not forget, we need Diarmid too."

And Iobhar. I tried not to look as terrified as I was. I didn't see any of them.

Then, a terrible scream. Furious, unending, circling and circling until there was nothing else to hear. I covered my ears, cowering as ravens filled the sky, a cloud of shivering, glittering black, screaming frenzy and hatred and fear, raising panic. There was Ossian in the midst of it, his pale-blond hair swirling around his head, as he fought Miogach. Beyond them a mass of ravens swirled up through the crowd, feathers ruffling and jerking as they preened, shining feathers—

No, not ravens. The crowd parted, and Iobhar stepped through, his feathered cape moving and shifting, his black hair gleaming, haloed with a silver *sidhe* glow.

He was here. *It is time.*

He glanced at me, at Lot, at Patrick. His mouth curled in that familiar cruel smile. "Where is the rest of the *veleda?*"

"Aidan's here," I said. "This is his storm."

"And the *vater* will be here shortly," Lot said from beside me. Her hand gripped her skirt—the only evidence of her tension. "She'd best hurry."

Iobhar lifted a brow, and I shook my head slightly.

He looked toward the horizon. I followed his gaze to see the fiery ball of the sun just touching the line between earth and sky. My heart pounded so hard, it was all I could hear, above even the screaming and the shouting. Iobhar raised his arm, sending a huge bolt of red lightning whipping and stabbing through the clouds.

There were more screams; the crowd parted as if compelled, and my brother staggered from it, looking dazed. When he saw me, his gaze cleared. He came to me, hugging me hard before he let me go again, taking my hand firmly in his.

"We need the *vater*." Lot sounded almost desperate. "Where is the *vater*?"

Again, Iobhar raised his arm. Again, the lightning struck, and this time it blossomed, turning the clouds red, spreading fire in the sky.

And then . . . Diarmid stalked from the mob with an already bloodied knife in his hand. His expression was forbidding, his cheek bruised, and there was a cut across his jaw, another at his eyebrow. He looked filthy and bloody and frightening, but his gaze on me was tender as a caress. I saw in it the hope I shared. I felt Patrick stiffen beside me.

Diarmid's gaze swept over Lot and Aidan and Patrick before it came back to me, and then he said to Iobhar, "Let it begin."

"There's no *vater*," Lot said. "What is delaying her?"

"She'll be here," Patrick said brusquely. "Diarmid's right. *Begin*."

Aidan squeezed my hand. My ears filled with a music like raindrops, the tinkling of tiny chimes, a melody that shifted into a hushed eerie darkness. I recognized it—the sun going down. The silence before the storm. I turned slowly, looking west.

Iobhar sang, "In darkness met, blood calls to blood. Let worlds collide."

His arms were raised, his eyes closed, his face lifted to the heavens.

An explosion rocked the ground. The warehouse where Balor and Finn had been fighting exploded into fire, one that burned but didn't consume. Square windows of billowing, black, oily smoke formed mysteriously within the flames. I'd seen it before, in a vision. An Irish plain, the sea churning and foaming just beyond. The pyres of Samhain.

The air shivered and wavered. Before me was a transparent curtain, a veil over the world, and in its translucent ripples I saw movement, spirits, ancient things. I was struck with terror.

Lot murmured, "Do not listen to them, *veleda*. Remember, they lie."

There was a *whoosh*, a burst of wind. The pyre stretched and pulsed.

"Now!" Iobhar shouted.

The veil rolled back. Spirits rushed through, a Pandora's box of appetites, some angry and some confused; some looking for vengeance, others wanting only blood.

"Here they come!" Lot's purple eyes glowed.

My head filled with a deadly music, clanging notes and broken harmonies, and then beneath it rose a thunderous, dominating song, and another melody of gnashing, slashing chords. Two songs calling to restlessness and chaos. The spirits swept over me, twining around me, curling around my arms and my throat. The hair on the back of my neck rose. Aidan's hand tightened on mine; his eyes grew wide. Together we felt them pulling, jerking, pleading. Diarmid stood motionless and tense, watching, waiting.

Patrick shouted, "Stop them!"

Iobhar said sternly, "There will be no interference, protector."

"*Protector?*" Lot asked.

. The heat of the warehouse fire raged, scalding me where I stood. Bits of burning timber, flakes of soot, and embers fell in a dense rain, casting us all in a reddish glow. Tethra's blue lightning split the sky. The music of the Otherworld clanged in my ears, its call to chaos and terror. Those dominant notes, the gnashing teeth of sound, swelling and swelling.

Iobhar put out his arms, fingers splayed, toward Aidan and me. His hands glowed red; his eyes burned like the hellhounds of Slieve Lougher. "Choose!" he cried.

I shook my head against it, but I could not stop it. At his command, my body felt pried open from the inside out, an impossible pain. I screamed, and Aidan did, too, sharing it, doubling it. Above it all, I heard Patrick's shouts of protest, and Diarmid's anguished, "Grace!"

But my skin was peeling away, my head splitting apart, and the words meant nothing. There were only spirits. Only Aidan. My brother's fingers gripped mine in a death lock, the connection between us, forging and burning and snapping into place, melding so I couldn't tell where I ended and he began. His visions and his music forced their way into me, along with those demented notes. I heard Grandma. *"Don't forget the stories,* mo chroi.*"*

The world opened beneath me, around me. There was only a bottomless chasm, images bombarding without stopping, my brother's vision of the future: Irish men and boys collapsing on a ground red with blood, British soldiers charging with swords and bayonets. Women huddling next to their crofts with their starving children, their faces stark with hope and fear.

I saw Irish flags rising and British banners trampled in mud. Victory and triumph. Then bloated bodies in an Irish gutter, and land stripped fallow, dust covering everything, and men stumbling drunk from taverns while babies cried and mothers buried their dead.

And then the vision changed—no longer Ireland, but the bloodstained cobblestones of New York City streets. Children screaming and glass breaking as rioters broke storefront windows, calling for bread and work. Death and chaos and anger, and then a parade with banners flying, banners bearing harps, shamrocks, and horns, and gang boys in a militia, smiling proudly as they marched with precision down a city street. The cheers of those watching.

Through the vision, that thunderous, dominating music again. Now it took on other colors: tones of betrayal and vengeance and greed. It called to the Otherworld spirits. *Fight for us, and we will let you stay. We will rule the world.*

No, that couldn't be right. No one had talked of this. No one had suggested that the Otherworld spirits might stay. I opened my eyes to see Daire Donn standing at the edge of the crowd. The music belonged to him. Beside him stood Finn, his pale eyes lit with a steady fire, and I heard his song—bold and brave horns trumpeting—arrogant and boastful, yes, but I heard something else beneath them too: a sad and hopeful song.

The truth wasn't black or white, because truth never was. I saw the strength of the Fomori and their power. They would bring independence to Ireland, but then their power would corrupt.

I saw the willfulness of the Fianna, the bloody and relentless conflict that would come with them before it brought new life to the immigrants. I understood now why the *dord fiann* had brought the Fianna to New York City instead of to Ireland, why it had landed them in a tenement room. Ireland's heroes, to be called in her time of direst need. And Ireland's direst need was *not* in Ireland.

It was here, in New York, with her people, and their blinding, blistering hope for a new life and a new world.

The truth whispered my name, commanding me to listen, not to fail. And it was so beautiful, I drew it close; and in my head, it grew and grew into something golden and fine. I could finally choose—

"No!" my brother cried.

He jerked from me. The connection between us shattered. Everything—his visions and the music—fell away.

A bolt of purple lightning electrified the darkening sky, fingers blasting in every direction, dipping into the terrible red flames of the fire. It illuminated the crowd before us, Finn and Daire Donn. Ossian and Tethra. Balor and Oscar and Bres.

And a woman stepping from the crowd. A woman with blue eyes and red hair.

"The *vater*, at last," said Lot with satisfaction. She held out her hands to the woman, who smiled and took them.

Mama.

THIRTY-EIGHT

The next moment
Grace

No," I whispered, and then screamed, "Mama!"

I lunged toward her. Patrick pulled me back with an iron grip. "No, Grace."

Diarmid paled; he looked from me to my mother. "The *vater*? But I thought—"

"I am the *vater*." With a trembling smile, Mama held Lot's hands. "And it's time I took my rightful place."

"No, Mama, no," I babbled desperately. "It's Grandma. It's Grandma, and she can't make a choice. She can't . . . She's not supposed to. There's not supposed to be a *geis*—"

"Sssh, my darling," Mama said. "I've faced the truth. You must do so as well."

Helplessly, I turned to Aidan, who looked as stunned as I was, and then to Iobhar. "She can't be the *vater*, she can't be!"

Iobhar regarded me with those impassive eyes, and I *knew*. Everything we'd planned and wished for fell into darkness. No, it couldn't be happening. This was all wrong, so wrong. . . .

The spell of the ritual shivered, urging us on.

Mama's voice was quiet, so quiet it was a moment before I realized what she was saying. "The Erne shall rise in rude torrents, hills shall be rent . . ."

The same incantation Iobhar had tried to teach me, spoken in Gaelic, a language I hadn't thought she knew. Diarmid stood in stricken silence. Again, I tried to break from Patrick's grip. "No! No, Mama, stop! You can't! It can't be this way."

"I must be what I am, Grace. I love both you and Aidan, but I must do this. Trust me."

The Otherworld spirits spun around us, a torrent, a cyclone, pushing and shoving. I felt them gain a hold in the world with every moment that passed.

"You must close the door, Grace." Mama's voice was a lullaby, good-night instead of good-bye. "You must make your choice. Do your duty. Choose what's right." She turned to Lot, smiling with this terrible confidence.

And I whispered rawly, "It isn't the Fomori, Mama."

Mama gave me a confused look. "Not the Fomori? But it must be."

Lot's expression curdled. Into those purple eyes came a fury. She wrenched at the collar of her gown, ripping it to expose a breast, deformed and gruesome, with bloated black lips and needlelike fangs chomping and slavering, so hideous it distracted from the knife in her hand that she'd hidden in her bodice. Daire Donn dashed onto the pier, and Miogach jumped Aidan. And I realized that they had always planned to kill all three of us, that they meant to take no chances. Their promises of bringing us back from the Otherworld were lies.

Everything moved around me as if in a dream. Diarmid threw himself at Daire Donn; Aidan's purple lightning struck Miogach. I saw a flash of movement at my side, and Patrick surged past me, barreling into Lot, the two of them falling onto the pier. She screamed, "You traitor!" and raised her knife.

I shouted, "No!" just as she drove it into Patrick's shoulder. As he cried out in agony, purple and red lightning clashed and joined, striking Lot, raising her in the air and flinging her into the river below. Daire Donn writhed where he lay, white-faced, clutching his chest, which was blooming red with blood as Diarmid stood victoriously above him; and Miogach was still and unseeing, killed by my brother's lightning.

I fell to my knees beside Patrick.

"I'm all right," he gasped, but his shoulder was soaked with blood.

Diarmid said, "'Tisn't as bad as it looks, Grace—"

"Every mountain glen and bog shall quake." The words intoned over my head. I looked up. Mama continued the spell as if nothing had happened.

"No," I whispered. "No, no, no."

Diarmid's gaze was a heavy weight. I felt something leave him, the leeching of our last hope. I watched him turn away, to Iobhar. I felt the loss of him deeply and purely, a piece of me torn away.

Iobhar held out his hand. Diarmid stepped forward, gave Iobhar his knife.

My mother's hair tumbled about her shoulders. She had hold of Aidan's hand, and my brother staggered as if only her touch kept him standing.

"You're her protector too," I said to Patrick. "Can't you stop her?" But I knew already what his answer would be.

Patrick's eyes were black with pain. "Free will, Grace. She's chosen. It's what she was meant for. You must let her be what she is."

Iobhar held Diarmid's knife to my mother's wrist. Diarmid stood like a statue, watching.

Iobhar said, "Make the choice, *brithem*. Finish it."

My vision blurred. No, I wouldn't do it, whatever it cost me. If I didn't choose, she wouldn't die, no one would die—

But the music pushed its way in, not allowing me to deny it. It grew louder and louder and louder, taking on harmonies until the song was so poignant and strong and real that I felt I might burst with it.

"It is as it must be, Grace." My mother's whisper was in my head, too, and I recognized her—the hovering, silent presence that had been with Aidan and me the whole time. I saw how she'd discovered the truth of what she was at Battle Annie's, when her power had surged in response to my judgment. *In truth, I think I have always known.* I saw the conversations she'd had with Lot, her decision not to tell me or Aidan, her fear that we would keep her from this. *I am willing to make this sacrifice. I believe it will save you both.* And through it all, her acceptance and relief. "It's all right, my darling."

The music surged at her words. My choice—the Fianna—pushed out the voices of the Otherworld, the brutal symphony of the Fomori. I heard its leaping joy as it settled and stayed. I couldn't hold it back. The Fianna's music seeped into the web, threads vibrating as it spread to Aidan, to Mama.

"This is my choice," Mama said loudly now, the voice I hadn't heard since I was a child, that I'd almost forgotten. Powerful. Every word pulsing. "I deem it worthy and just. I deem it mine."

No.

Patrick grasped my hand, keeping me anchored.

"I am the *veleda* chosen," my mother intoned. "Long the journey I have made from yesterday to today. The Erne I passed by leaping, though wide the flood."

Beyond us were the sounds of battle, the roaring of the fire, shouting. But those who watched were silent and still, Mama's words a solemn prayer, a vow that filled me with reverence even in my misery. The connection strengthened between us. The *veleda* fused, the power of the whole vibrating through me, unassailable. I felt her love for us and her pride, her determination and sorrow, and I knew she would not allow me to stop this. I had made a choice, and so had she.

She took the knife from Iobhar, running it along the vein in her arm, cutting, her blood dripping over her pale skin. She painted it in a circle around her wrist and the knife hilt, knowing the spell as I had not, ancient rituals remembered in blood. She sang, "I have seen and weighed. Great stones crack and split. Storms will tell and the world is changed. I release my power to the chosen." She held the blade out to Diarmid. He hesitated, but he took it.

Lightning crackled and burst. Flames from the warehouse leaped as if trying to reach heaven. The air shuddered, as if gathering for a great explosion. Hovering, waiting, expectant.

"This is the word that is spoken. This is complete."

A slip in time. A pause like the world held its breath. Everything went silent.

My mother looked at Diarmid. I felt the power of the *geis* tremble and take hold.

And I could do nothing but wait for my world to end.

THIRTY-NINE

A moment later
Diarmid

Maeve Knox had the bluest eyes, like water on a clear spring day. Like Grainne's eyes, the day Diarmid had gone to his death. He felt the power of her gaze burrow into him, hold him. He felt—as he had once before—the grip of a *geis* twist and bind.

He saw Manannan smiling. *"'Tis by your hand the veleda must die. Else all fails, no matter the choice."*

All his hopes . . . how futile they'd been. He should have known. He *had* known. The future he'd wished for faded to a barely remembered dream.

He saw Finn, whom he'd already betrayed once. Oscar and Ossian. The weight of what he owed them staggered him. His friends—no, more than friends—his family. He alone held their lives and their hopes. It should be an easy choice. The only choice.

But there was Grace.

He couldn't bring himself to look at her. Deliberately, he turned back to her mother. Maeve's eyes met his unflinchingly.

The *geis* knotted. He felt his strength fading and knew what it meant. *Kill her or die. Kill her, or sacrifice those who love and trust you.*

Kill her, and destroy any hope of his own future.

Maeve wrapped her slender white fingers around his wrist, bringing the point of his knife to her breast. Her fingers were slippery with the blood streaming from her wrist. It dripped, warm and wet, on his skin.

She pulled him close, her lips against his cheek as she whispered, "You know what you must do, Diarmid. I am not afraid, and she loves you. She would not forgive you for being less than you are."

The *geis* had its hooks in him; he gasped at the pain of it. *'Tis all right. It is not more than I can bear.*

But then—it was as if his whole life rose to meet him. Riding in battle with Finn and Oscar beside him, the banners of the Fianna flying, the red spear in his hand. His regret as he lay dying on the plain of Ben Bulben, and the promise he'd made himself, never to do anything to hurt the Fianna again. Grace, saying, *"This is what we were meant to be to each other. . . . I will never regret this. . . ."*

He was Fianna. He was part of something that mattered. His honor was more than just a word. It was who he was. Without it, how could he be anything at all?

Whatever Maeve saw in his eyes made her smile. "Be who you must be. And love her well. That's all I ask."

He plunged his knife into her heart, unerring, wanting to cause her as little pain as he could, and she grasped his hand and the hilt as if she welcomed it and crumpled into him with a hush of breath. He caught her before she could fall.

Then Grace screamed, and the whole world went mad.

FORTY

I watched in horror as Diarmid killed my mother.

Aidan's agonized cry rent the air. It could not be true. No, it was a dream, and soon, I would wake up and—

And the world went dark. Absolutely and profoundly. We had died after all. All of us together, but Diarmid had said there would be no pain, that there would be peace. This was not peace. My heart was breaking, just crumbling to pieces, and it hurt so I couldn't breathe.

The silence gathered, a thunderous voice, a terrific crack, the world splitting. My mother's music rose into crescendo and shattered, her power reverberating, a roaring, rumbling thunderclap that knocked back the Fianna even as it flowed into them. Finn and Ossian, Conan and Keenan, Oscar and Goll. They were illuminated, as bright as if they were the sun, the glow I'd first seen within them blinding. Diarmid staggered, my mother still in his arms, and it lit him, too, until I was looking at seven stars, seven suns. Patrick gasped beside me. It was so powerfully bright, I had to close my eyes.

The music of the Fomori and the spirits shrieked, tearing apart, rushing back through the veil, which unfurled like a heavy drape, shuddering closed. The ground trembled; the river slapped the shore. When I opened my eyes again, the glow of the Fianna had faded. Bres turned and ran into the crowd; I knew he would not last the night. Balor and Tethra dissipated into smoke, their spirits joining those in the Otherworld. Daire Donn and Miogach lay with dead eyes. The Fomori warriors scattered.

I pushed away from Patrick and ran to my mother's side just as Diarmid lowered her to the pier. Her bodice was soaked with blood, her arms ribboned with it.

"Get away from her!" I screamed at him. "I'll never forgive you for this!"

He jerked back as if I'd hit him, and then Aidan fell to his knees beside me, and I forgot everything but Mama. She was still alive but barely breathing.

"We need a doctor," I called. "Someone find a doctor!"

"Grace, no." Aidan's electric blue eyes shone with grief. "This is what she wanted. You can't take it back. None of us can."

Her eyes flickered, her lips moved.

"Mama, don't talk," I said. "We can save you. I know we can."

She lifted her hand weakly. I held it against my cheek, her warm, soft skin already growing cold. "It was my job to save

you," she whispered. "It's a new world, *a leanbh.* Remember
. . . be true . . ."

She gasped. Her hand went limp in mine. Everything
faded, the fire and the mob, magic and power. I heard only
her *vater*'s music, wavering in a final note before it silenced,
and I was just a girl kneeling at the edge of worlds while my
mother died in my arms.

FORTY-ONE

After
Diarmid

The *vater*'s power gave them victory before the night was
out. By dawn, the fight had become a celebration, the
neighborhood one giant party even in the freezing cold of a
November morning.

But the vision of Grace's mother haunted Diarmid. Those
fierce blue eyes, those slender fingers wrapped around the
hilt he'd thrust into her heart, her blood on his hands. And
Grace . . . Grace . . . He felt a despair so deep he knew he would
never be free of it.

And yet, he was a hero. The Fianna were alive, and worthy again, honorable again. They had a future, and Diarmid
had been the one to give it to them. Kegs of beer and whiskey
flowed. He couldn't turn around without someone shaking his
hand or hugging him.

"I'm proud of you, Diarmid." Finn's smile was bright as
sunlight.

Any other time, those words would have been reward enough, but now they only made Diarmid feel empty. He wanted to crawl into some dark corner and sleep—and if he didn't wake again, so much the better. Then he wouldn't have to think about what he'd done.

"I'll never forgive you for this!"

He slipped away to the empty flat, curling beneath the blanket on his pallet. But Grace's words, her tears, accused him when he closed his eyes. Finally, he gave up and sat staring into darkness, listening to the shouts and laughter outside.

"Be who you must be," Grace's mother had said, and he'd been that. He'd made the choice he'd had to make.

So why did he feel that it had been the wrong one?

He heard the creak of the door, a loud, brief blast of the party, and then footsteps on the stairs. There was flickering candlelight, and with it came Oscar, looking tousled and a little drunk.

"There you are. The others are asking for you."

"I've had enough celebration."

Oscar squatted beside him. "We're *alive*, Derry. The Fomori are gone, and because of you, we've a chance to change this city for the better. The Fenian Brotherhood wish to meet. They want to discuss a partnership to make things right."

"No doubt 'tis Patrick's doing."

"Can he be trusted?"

"Aye. He's loyal to Aidan and Grace, and Aidan will help him see what needs doing. Grace, too, once they're married."

Oscar frowned. "Married? But . . . she loves you."

Diarmid laughed shortly. "I killed her mother, Oscar, or weren't you paying attention?"

"Her mother was the *vater.*"

"Does that mean Grace loved her any less?"

"No, but . . . but her mother offered herself freely. She knew what was to happen. She chose it."

"Grace didn't know her mother was the *vater* until that moment," Diarmid said. "None of us did."

"I see." Oscar sat back on his heels. "She'll need time to grieve then. But she'll come to accept what was meant to be."

"When did you become an expert in how women think?"

"'Tisn't about men or women, Derry. It's about war and loss. I've seen enough of it to know, and so have you. Men do things they didn't think they could do, that they can't answer for. You learn to live with it. 'Tis easier when you know the sacrifice wasn't meaningless. Grace's mother bought a future for the Irish in this city. Grace will see that in time."

All Diarmid heard was, *"I'll never forgive you for this!"*

But Oscar was watching him carefully, so Diarmid said, "Aye, you're right, I know."

"Then you'll come out?"

"In a bit," Diarmid said.

Oscar rose. "Don't be too long."

"No, I won't."

Oscar paused, looking uncertain. "I'll come looking for you again in a quarter hour."

Diarmid watched Oscar leave and told himself his friend was right. Grace would accept her mother's fate and forgive him, and he would come to terms with what he'd done. And—

No. No, he didn't believe that. Grace's love for her family was too strong. She *shouldn't* forgive him. He would never forgive himself.

He rose, going upstairs, slipping into the narrow yard. The morning was overcast, gray and cold, and he shivered. Everywhere gang boys were quaffing beer as if there were no tomorrow. He'd thought he was looking for Oscar and the others, but suddenly he was walking to the alley, escaping a celebration that pained with every smile and every raised glass, trying to escape her accusing eyes. He didn't realize he was sneaking out until he was two blocks away, and the laughter and talk were behind him.

He didn't realize he was leaving until he was already gone.

FORTY-TWO

*After
Grace*

We arrived home that night to discover it wasn't only my mother who had died, but my grandmother as well.

"In the middle of that terrible thunder," Mrs. Devlin said, tears in her eyes. "But her suffering is over at last, my dear."

I wasn't surprised. I'd suspected that she was only waiting for Samhain. I'd already said good-bye. But it didn't ease my grief, and there was no comfort to be found.

The next days passed in a blur. I knew of the celebrating in the streets, and Patrick told me that the Fenian Brotherhood and the Fianna had agreed on a new course for the city. It was a new world.

I tried to be glad, but not everyone had paid the cost I had. All of my family was gone—but for Aidan, who stayed with the Fianna, where he said he belonged. I relived that night over and over again in my dreams, waking with a scream caught in my throat and tears streaming down my cheeks and thunder exploding in my ears.

The world did not seem quite real—or at least, it seemed a pale imitation of what it had been. I grieved as I was supposed to. I dyed my gowns black and bore condolences with numb thanks, and I felt nothing and everything. When the funerals were over, I moved out of Patrick's house, despite his pleas, and back into my own. Aidan stayed there sometimes. Patrick hired a maid to look after me, and I let him. But I had trouble caring about anything. The future stretched bleak and empty before me.

"You have to start thinking of what you will do, Grace," Aidan told me. "You can't go on this way."

I ignored him. Fall turned to winter, and the first snow fell, powdering the roofs and icing the streets and deadening the stink of the city. My dreams began to change; now I no longer relived that horrible night. Instead, I dreamed of Diarmid beside a river or a rocky beach. I dreamed that he loved me. Each morning I woke, expecting to find him with me. And then I would remember, and fall into despair. I hated him. I loved him. I missed him. I never wanted to see him again.

I felt I was going mad, and in a way, it was even what I wanted.

Then my power began to hum within me, hovering, waiting, impatient. *You are done with grieving,* it said. *Use me.* It tempted me with memories of the pawnshop and Roddy's endless polishing. Training with Sarnat, and the pride in Iobhar's eyes when I'd done something well. How much I'd loved learning. How powerful and confident I'd felt.

No. I'd had enough of magic and ancient power. I wanted no part of it.

But what else was I made for? The only other thing I was trained to be was a wife, and Patrick waited for me. He'd put aside his dream of a free Ireland to work with the Fianna and the immigrants here. He'd done it at least partly for me and Aidan. He had given us everything, and I knew he would do more if I gave him the chance.

Mama had wanted me to have the life Patrick offered, and any other possibility only brought me pain. Being a wife was something I could do for my mother, and for Patrick. A way to make up for everything, a small absolution. Eventually people would forget my past. Rose had sent a letter asking forgiveness, saying, *"I won't let Mama influence me so again. I promise you I'll make all of society miserable until they accept you back. You know I can do it. They'll be begging for you at dinners before the spring."* I thought I was ready to let Rose try.

With relief and determination, I made up my mind to do it. When Aidan came the next day to help me reply to letters of sympathy, I said, "I know what I'm going to do."

My brother had taken to watching me as if he thought I might explode at any moment. He scrawled his signature across the bottom of the note I handed him, and said carefully, "I can't support you, Grace. You know that. I'd do it gladly if I could, but there isn't any money—"

"I'm going to marry Patrick."

"What?"

"Isn't that what you wanted me to do?"

"Well, yes. But what about . . ."

Diarmid was a ghost between us, a pain powerful and sharp and unbearable.

Aidan put his hand to his temple and groaned as the connection between us flared.

"You're feeling my thoughts again," I accused. "I can block you out, you know, when I don't want you there."

"It's harder for me. Grandma's still there, like cobwebs. It makes it hard to concentrate."

Grandma's death had cleared his head somewhat, though we both suspected bits of her insanity would always remain, crippling his ability as a Seer. Because I could hear the world's music, and because I was the *brithem*, I could discern the lies caused by her madness. But sight was the sense most easily fooled, and Aidan had a much harder time.

Aidan said, "It's what's best, Grace. Patrick loves you. He knows what you've been through. You'd never have to pretend with him."

Except it would all be pretending.

I pushed the thought away. I'd made a decision. No going back. *"There's only going forward."*

Diarmid's voice was so loud in my head that I started. I looked down at the letter in my hand: *"Aidan and I appreciate your thoughts at this sad time . . ."*

Because of him. Remember what he did.

My fingertips tingled as if in protest. I heard the faint strain of music—the world, my life, and within it, a discord I refused to hear. "You're right, I know."

"You don't sound happy."

"Is happiness even possible anymore?" I asked bitterly. "Anyway, I mean to go over there today to tell him. Would you walk with me?"

Aidan frowned, but he said, "Of course."

I got my cloak, and together we went out. A thin layer of snow crunched beneath our boots. The freezing air burned my lungs. "After I've moved to Patrick's, there will be no one in the house. You should live there. It belongs to you. It's better than the tenement."

"We've moved to a new place off the Bowery. At the corner of Rivington and Eldridge. Finn thinks we should be near those we mean to help. He says it reminds him to be thankful of"—Aidan swallowed hard—"sacrifice."

"I'm glad he doesn't take it lightly."

"He never would. None of them do."

When we reached Patrick's, Aidan said, "Patrick's a good man, Grace."

My smile was more forced than I wished. "I know."

He was off, both hands shoved in his pockets, breath fogging the air. If there had been one miracle to come from this, it was my brother returned to me.

I turned back to Patrick's house, the empty stoop, the frosty yew, and suddenly it was a hot summer day, and a glowing boy swooped to catch me as I fell.

I closed my eyes, pushing the memory and the pain away. *No more of that. A new life now.*

The butler took my shawl. On the table in the foyer was a huge bouquet of flowers—pink roses and carnations. Beside it was an open book of Irish poetry that I recognized as Patrick's. The butler led me to Patrick's study. "Miss Knox to see you, sir."

"Grace!" Patrick's smile was as warm and welcoming as the cozy fire crackling in the hearth. "What a pleasant surprise."

He appeared thin, and he looked as if he hadn't been sleeping well. The sling he'd worn for weeks was gone, his shoulder mostly healed, though I knew he didn't yet have his full strength back.

"I see someone's been sending you flowers," I said.

"They're for Lucy. Rory Nolan's son Ian returned from Dublin two weeks ago. You know how quickly she falls in love, but this time, he's at least a decent match." Patrick laughed. "She's suddenly become fascinated by the Irish cause. She's even borrowing my books. It's too early to say, but I have hopes we may turn her into a woman of substance yet."

"I'm glad." I ran my hand over the brass rivets of the leather chair, unable to look at him. "I wanted to talk to you. I thought it was time we discussed the future. Our future."

"Our future?"

"I know . . . I know I've made you wait a long time, Patrick. You've been so patient, and I . . . well, I want you to know that, if you still want me, I'll—" The words stuck in my throat. I forced them out. "I'll marry you."

I expected to feel relief. I expected the heaviness that lived inside me to ease now.

But it just felt heavier.

Patrick said, "Is this really what you want, Grace?"

"Yes. I know you love me, and I've been wrong to make you wait so long, and—"

"Do you love me?" he asked gently.

"Yes. Yes, of course. You've been so good to us, Patrick. To me and Aidan. We—I—owe you so much."

He only looked at me. Perhaps he'd changed his mind. Perhaps he didn't want me. I couldn't blame him—

"What about your Druid training?"

Again, I heard the whisper of power, faint music. "I think it's time I gave that up, don't you? I'm done with it."

"Are you?" His gray-green eyes glowed in the firelight. "You know what I think? You're not done with it at all. You're suffocating, Grace. You have been for months. Before that even, I think. You've a great power. You could help the cause so much. Tell me you wouldn't rather be studying and training. Tell me a *brithem* isn't what you're meant to be."

I stared at him.

He stepped closer, whispering, "I'd marry you in a moment, Grace, you must know that. You would try to be the wife I need. You'd try to love me. But we both know you don't. And . . . and I'd have to watch you die a little every day. Don't ask me to do that. It would destroy us both."

"Patrick, I—"

"You're not who you were six months ago. I won't let you turn yourself into some society matron. I watched you just . . . fade in that ballroom at the Nolans'."

The tightness inside me loosened and floated away. The faint music in my head swelled, notes falling into place, one after another, harmonizing.

Patrick went on, "Choose for yourself, Grace, not because it's what I want or what your mother wanted or what Aidan wants. What do *you* want?"

Faced with the honesty in his eyes, I wanted to be honest in return. "I want to train." The truth of *me* was in those words. The music took on depth and focus. "I want to learn. I can manage Iobhar now. I'm safe because of you. You would know if I were in danger."

"I see you've thought about this," Patrick said with a small smile.

"No, actually. I haven't thought about it at all—or, I don't think I have. Patrick, I love you. I do, but—"

"I know." And then, in a very, very quiet voice, "What about Diarmid?"

"What about him?"

"You've been avoiding the mention of him. Isn't it time you faced what you feel?"

"How could I possibly feel anything for him? He killed my mother."

"She was the *vater*, and she sacrificed herself willingly. What other choice did he have? It wasn't just about him. It was the *geis*. It was Finn and Ossian and Oscar—"

"You're *defending* him?"

"If you'd been forced to choose between him and your family, what would you have done?"

"I can't believe you're saying these things to me."

"I'm your protector," he said. "And sometimes that means I have to tell you things you don't want to hear. If you decide your future without considering his place in it, that will be because you're running away. I meant what I said once before. Run *to* something instead."

Faith or fear.

"Forgive him, Grace," Patrick said tenderly. "Until you do, you won't forgive yourself."

I whispered, "Maybe I don't want to forgive myself."

"Then everything your mother did was in vain." Patrick raised my chin, forcing me to look into his eyes. "'If you act bravely in the world, perhaps it will reward you'—isn't that what Iobhar said? You're the bravest girl I've ever known. Don't dishonor the sacrifice she made by being afraid now."

I heard again my mother's last words, the ones I'd refused to listen to until this moment. *"It's a new world*, a leanbh. *Remember . . . be true . . ."*

To yourself.

When Mama had told me that Grandma's madness and regret came from not being true to herself, I'd thought she was telling me to choose duty.

But she hadn't been saying that at all. She had only wanted me to do what was right for *me*.

Act bravely in the world.

To be brave meant never flinching from the truth, no matter how hard it was, or what it told you about yourself. And the truth was that I was grieving not just because of what Diarmid had done, but because he was gone. In spite of everything, I still loved him. I did not want to be without him.

And now—at last—I knew what I was meant to do.

FORTY-THREE

Later that afternoon
Grace

It was already late, moving into evening, and Patrick insisted I take his carriage. When Leonard heard where I wanted to go, he reached into his pocket and took out a gun, laying it on the seat beside him. "Are you certain about this, miss?"

"I am. I'll be safe enough," I answered.

Once we arrived, I knew why he was worried. It was a terrible part of town, and the building was almost worse than the tenement they'd lived in before. People were everywhere, shivering in the cold, huddling on fire escapes and around fires leaping from ashcans.

I saw the curious, almost threatening stares, but I wasn't afraid. I felt Aidan's question and concern almost the moment we stopped, and so I knew they were there. I asked Leonard to wait, went past two scowling women on the stoop, and up the dark and narrow stairs to the top floor. When I reached it,

Aidan was already hurrying toward me from an open door at the far end. "What's wrong? What happened?"

"Nothing happened. Well, something did, but . . . I'm here to see Derry."

Aidan froze. "Derry? Why? What about Patrick?"

The others emerged. Finn leaned against the doorway, watching; Oscar cocked a brow. I tried to look past them for Diarmid.

I lowered my voice. "I have to see him, Aidan."

"What about Patrick?" My brother asked again. "Why would he let you come here?"

"I'm not going to marry him."

"I thought we'd agreed—"

"I've decided to continue my training instead."

"You're not going back to Iobhar's! He's too dangerous."

I glanced at the others, who were unabashedly listening. "I am going to do this, Aidan. Patrick's agreed that it's best. And I'd like you to see that. But if you don't"—I lifted my chin— "if you don't, it doesn't matter. I'm a *brithem*. I'm not meant to be a wife. I think you know it too."

"Patrick loves you."

"But I don't love *him*, Aidan. Not the same way I love—"

"He can't support you." My brother looked agonized. "He has *nothing*. He killed Mama, for God's sake!"

"Because he had to," I said calmly. "She accepted that, and I know you have as well, or you wouldn't be here."

"Grace—"

"It's my right to choose the life I want. I'm the one who has to live it. I've tried to stop loving him, but I can't. I just want to see him before I go to Iobhar in the morning."

"The lass knows her own mind," Finn put in. "No use arguing with a *brithem*, lad. 'Twill only bring you sorrow."

"I'm your legal guardian. I can stop you," Aidan said.

"But you won't."

He sighed. "No, I won't. I'd be lying if I said this surprised me. But Grace . . . I want you to come home every week or so. I can't hear you in that pawnshop. I want to know you're safe. Otherwise, I'll send Patrick and half our militia after you."

"Agreed." Again, I tried to look past him into the room, but Diarmid was nowhere to be seen.

"Derry's not here, lass," Oscar said.

"Then I'll wait."

"Grace . . . he hasn't been here since Samhain," Aidan said.

I was startled. "Not since Samhain? You didn't tell me."

"I thought it was better not to mention it." Aidan raked his hand through his hair, looking weary and miserable. "You didn't want to talk about him anyway."

Which was true. "Where is he?"

Finn said, "We don't know. But I'd like to have him back. We need him. If you find him, will you tell him that for me?"

"You don't know where he is? How could that be?"

"We've been looking for him," Aidan said. "But he obviously doesn't want to be found."

Diarmid was gone. He'd been gone for months. Even through my grief and anger, I should have known.

The music would have told me if I'd listened, but I had banished it. I felt stunned as I let Aidan walk me back to the carriage. "Don't leave for Iobhar tomorrow without me. I'll take you there. Promise me you'll wait."

I was hardly aware of agreeing. When Aidan left me, I looked unseeingly at Leonard, who held open the carriage door for me, and I had an idea.

"I want to ride up with you."

"Miss, it's too cold and too dangerous—"

"I want you to take me somewhere. But I don't know where yet. I'll have to tell you as we go." I climbed up to the driver's seat, my skirts tangling about my legs. He looked displeased, but he climbed up beside me and took the reins.

I said, "Just go anywhere to start."

I closed my eyes and listened. The city's music descended upon me in a tidal wave, a thousand melodies, a hundred thousand, the heartbeat of the river, and the pulse of the lowering sun. I felt as if a part of me had been gone, and now it slipped so easily back into place, I could not imagine how I'd lived without it. I searched for the song I wanted, the song I knew as well as my own, focusing until, one by one, the others fell away.

There it was. Faint but true. "North," I breathed. "Hurry."

We went into an even worse part of town and then out again. The music grew stronger. I bade Leonard turn *here* and then again *there*. When we reached it, I understood why Diarmid had stayed hidden so long. No one would have expected him to be in a place that catered to society—a livery in Central Park. I wanted to laugh, because when I'd first met him, he'd been Patrick's stableboy. *The end is the beginning.*

I flew into the building, nearly bursting with nerves and excitement and fear. The floors were scattered with straw. A chalkboard listing names and dates and times hung on the wall. Just beyond, a man waited impatiently while a tall stableboy, his back to me, saddled a big bay horse.

Diarmid.

The waiting man looked at me and tipped his hat. "Afternoon, miss."

"I'll be with you in a moment," Diarmid said without turning around, his deep voice caressing my skin.

"I'll wait as long as you need," I said softly.

He froze. Then, slowly, he looked over his shoulder. That dark-blue gaze had seared me the first time I'd seen it, and it was no different now. His jaw tensed. He finished saddling with abrupt, tight movements. "She's ready," he said to the man, and the whole world stopped until Diarmid and I stood alone in that vast barn.

This was not how I'd imagined it. I wanted to be in his arms. I wanted to see joy in his eyes, not that bleak expression.

He called to an older, sandy-haired boy near the stalls. "D'you mind covering for me a bit? I need a break."

The boy looked at me and winked. "I'll say you do. Oh, won't Susie be mad!"

My courage wavered in the wake of jealousy and dismay. I'd waited too long. He'd found someone else. I followed him past the wide-open door. I saw him note Patrick's carriage. He led me into the tack room and turned to face me, crossing his arms over his chest. It was obvious that I was the last person in the world he wanted to see. "Why did Patrick bring you here?"

"Who's Susie?"

"The owner's daughter. She's twelve."

"A little young for you, isn't she?"

He regarded me steadily. "Is he waiting for you?"

"He only lent me the carriage to come to you."

His surprise would have been comical if I hadn't been so tense and afraid. "To come to *me*?"

"I thought you were with the others. I didn't know you'd gone. No one told me."

"Would you have cared if they did?"

My pulse was racing. "Aidan said they didn't know where you were, so I listened for you. For your music."

"You still have your power?" He looked astonished.

What we weren't saying was so loud I couldn't hear above it. "Yes. So does Aidan."

"Did you tell Finn where I was?"

"I've only just found you this minute. I haven't had time to tell them. But they want you back. Finn says they need you."

It hurt to see the stark pain in his eyes. He glanced away. "I'm not returning. You can tell them that. Now you've done what they asked, so you can go home."

So hard, so controlled. So . . . angry. He didn't want me or the Fianna, and the knowledge was so awful, so unendurable—but no, a jarring note, one that didn't belong, and I realized that what I heard in his voice wasn't anger but sorrow.

It gave me hope. "I didn't come here for Finn. They didn't send me. I came for myself."

A flash of longing, ruthlessly snuffed. "Why? D'you mean only to torment me?"

"Why would I do that?"

"Because you hate me. I understand, believe me I do."

"I don't hate you."

He frowned.

"I've been angry with you. And afraid. But I'm not anymore."

"Maybe you should be."

"Diarmid—" I stepped toward him, and he backed up hard, sending a halter swaying. I stopped. "My mother was a *vater*. She knew what she was doing. She wouldn't want you to feel guilty or to turn from everything you—" *love*. I couldn't say it.

"My hands were covered with her blood, Grace. Your *mother's* blood. How could I even touch you now?"

"You couldn't have acted otherwise, not without betraying yourself. I understand that. Truthfully, I always knew it."

Something flickered in his eyes. Hope perhaps? I was almost afraid to believe in it, but I took advantage, moving closer still. He was already against the wall; there was nowhere for him to go.

"I saw Mama say something to you before . . . What was it?"

"She said she knew what I had to do." He wouldn't look at me. "And she asked me to love you well."

She'd known how I felt about him in the end and accepted it. The evidence of her love for me erased the last of my fear. "So when were you planning to start doing that?"

He made a sound of despair. "Sweet Danu, Grace, how can you ask me? You come here in Patrick's carriage, and I know you're meant for him—"

"Patrick and I broke off our engagement."

His fingers flexed as if he struggled to keep still. "Why?"

"Because I'm in love with *you*."

He blinked. "The lovespot will wear off in time. When it does, he'll take you back."

"I'm not going back to him, and it's not going to wear off. I forgive you, and I love you. That's not going to change, and I don't want it to."

He flinched.

"Don't tell me it's too late," I whispered. "Don't tell me you don't love me anymore."

A desperate, short laugh. I felt his misery as my own. "Why would you want me to love you? 'Twould be best if you just . . . forgot I existed. 'Twas what I meant for you to do, and—"

I leaned forward and stopped his words with a kiss. He went motionless, and I thought he wouldn't kiss me back. But then he moaned and pulled me closer, and I felt the quick burn of him and knew he was as helpless as I against what was between us.

The kiss lasted forever. It didn't last long enough. He drew away, pushing a loose strand of my hair behind my ear. "Aidan told me to leave you alone. I've nothing to offer you. In the eyes of this world, I'm only a gang boy, a stableboy. Who knows if I'll ever have more?"

"I don't want anything. Just you."

"I can't ask you to live in poverty with me."

"Then don't. I'm not ready to be a wife. Not Patrick's and not yours. I've so much to do first. In the morning, I'm going back to Iobhar to take up my training. I think my power can help the Fianna and the Fenian Brotherhood. It's what I was meant to do."

Diarmid brushed his thumb against my mouth. "You'll be a good *brithem*, lass."

"Iobhar says it may be fifteen years before I'm done. Maybe then, if you'll still have me, we can talk about a wedding. But for now . . . I only want to be with you. I don't know what will happen in the future and neither do you. I'm not asking for anything. Just that you love me."

His eyes blazed with a love and desire that thrilled me. "I can do that. But I'm warning you, I won't be able to stop. Not even when the lovespell wears off, and you don't want me anymore."

I smiled at him, because I knew that how I felt had nothing to do with the lovespot. Someday, he would believe it too. "I suppose I'll just have to live with that."

Wonderingly, he touched my face. "I never thought to hold you again."

He leaned to kiss me, but a noise at the tack room door made us spring apart.

"Oh, sorry, Derry. But I need that bridle, if you don't mind." The sandy-haired boy grabbed a bridle hanging near the door. He gave me another wink before he left again. I went hot with embarrassment.

Diarmid said wryly, "'Twill be a miracle if we ever have a moment alone."

I put my arms around his neck, tangling my hands in his hair, my face growing hotter as I said, "I might be able to manage something. I mean, I do have an empty house. And a bedroom with a door."

He smiled so that long dimple creased his cheek. His hand went to my upswept hair. He drew out a pin, and then another, dropping them to the ground. *Click click click.*

"What are you doing?"

"Making you mine. So no one can mistake it."

I could have stayed there, kissing him for an eternity, but he led me from the tack room, calling to the other stableboy, "Taking the night off, Johnny."

The boy laughed. "Aye, no doubt. 'Tis slow enough; I can cover it. Have a good time, eh?"

Diarmid drew me close, his arm around my shoulders. The sun was setting, gold and red and purple layering the sky. It was like every romantic dream I'd ever had, everything I'd ever wanted in those days when I'd spent my hours reading

Tennyson. Except the reality was better, because then I'd yearned for a white knight to save me, and now I knew that I could save myself. I *was* the white knight that Diarmid had once told me I could be. It had been hard won, but I owned it. The power to determine my life was mine. I was never letting it go.

Music spun in my head, a hundred melodies, some wrong notes, an unfinished symphony waiting for my hand, and the one I loved was beside me, and the whole world smelled fresh and clean and new.

We walked into it, together.

ACKNOWLEDGMENTS

It's always so difficult to say good-bye to a book, but this time it is more difficult than usual. Over the three novels of The Fianna Trilogy, I have worked with some wonderful people. My editor, Robin Benjamin, has been a joy, and I have appreciated her insight more than I can say. Thanks also must go to my team at Skyscape, who have made this journey a very smooth one: Miriam Juskowicz, Timoney Korbar, Erick Pullen, Andrew Keyser, Vivian Lee, and Courtney Miller. Thank you to art director Katrina Damkoehler, artist Don Sipley, and designer Regina Flath, who together created such beautiful covers. As always, I am hugely appreciative of Kim Witherspoon and Allison Hunter and everyone at Inkwell Management. I could not have done this without Kristin Hannah, who brainstormed, critiqued, and generally listened to all my tales of woe with a compassionate ear, or without Elizabeth DeMatteo, Jena MacPherson, Melinda McRae, Liz Osborne, and Sharon Thomas, who enthusiastically helped with early drafts. And lastly, I owe all of it to Maggie and

Cleo, who were my inspiration, and to Kany, for his continuing and patient love and support.

ABOUT THE AUTHOR

Photo © 2012 C.M.C. Levine

Megan Chance is the award-winning author of several adult novels, including *Inamorata*, and The Fianna Trilogy for young adults: *The Shadows*, *The Web*, and *The Veil*. A former television news photographer with a BA from Western Washington University, Megan lives in the Pacific Northwest with her husband and two daughters. Visit her at www.meganchance.com.